# BUSY BEING BORN

## Laurence Seidler

The Book Guild Ltd

First published in Great Britain in 2024 by
The Book Guild Ltd
Unit E2 Airfield Business Park,
Harrison Road, Market Harborough,
Leicestershire. LE16 7UL
Tel: 0116 2792299
www.bookguild.co.uk
Email: info@bookguild.co.uk
X: @bookguild

Copyright © 2024 Laurence Seidler

The right of Laurence Seidler to be identified as the author of this
work has been asserted by them in accordance with the
Copyright, Design and Patents Act 1988.

All rights reserved. No part of this publication may be
reproduced, transmitted, or stored in a retrieval system, in any form or by any means,
without permission in writing from the publisher, nor be otherwise circulated in
any form of binding or cover other than that in which it is published and without
a similar condition being imposed on the subsequent purchaser.

This book reflects the author's present recollections of experiences over time. Some names
and characteristics have been changed, some events have been compressed, and some
dialogue has been recreated.

Typeset in 11pt Minion Pro

Printed on FSC accredited paper
Printed and bound in Great Britain by 4edge Limited

ISBN 978 1835740 323

British Library Cataloguing in Publication Data.
A catalogue record for this book is available from the British Library.

To Alistair and Peter
Both guides, both gone

# ENTRIES

| | |
|---|---:|
| *Fore letter Word* | 1 |
| The Intimacy of Species | 5 |
| Lady Trocknell | 22 |
| The Soldier's Wife | 46 |
| Cockenomics | 71 |
| Whatever Gets You through the Night | 97 |
| Dipping the Woodwork | 124 |
| Sweet and Sour Porking | 154 |
| Chitty Chitty Gang-Bang | 190 |
| Away Game | 226 |
| Blue Eyes | 256 |
| Ella | 279 |
| Pillow Talk | 296 |

# FORE letter WORD

*Warning! This book is explicitly sexual. A book whose main character is a call boy without sex would be absurd: an old crone by a well that never granted wishes; a cat without malice.*

*But don't look for 'honeypots' or 'love wands'. No 'rubbing against thin fabric', or 'feeling his swollen manhood'. Neither are there any 'love grottos', 'pork swords' or 'fun bags'. We'll leave all that to seaside postcard humour.*

*'Love wands', maybe I can understand. "Here, shake my wand and I'll magically turn into a loving person." But what on earth is a 'pork sword?' Something to kill a Jewish vampire with? The alternative, the killing of a pig to forge a weapon from flesh, would irretrievably tarnish the armour of any knight.*

*And 'fun bags'? Do breasts have zips that I've never noticed? Are they filled with Kinder toys and stamped out crêpe sheet hats? All too ridiculous and demeaning. Euphemisms don't sanitise; they pervert. Like Victorians putting pantalettes on the piano legs. It doesn't make the daughter of the house less sexy, just makes the piano look ridiculous.*

*A group of Afghan Taliban were asked who they had preferred to fight, the Russians or the Americans. The Russians, hands down, they all agreed. They killed them man-to-man, face-to-face, offering some dignity, whilst the Americans terminated them, downsized the enemy's assets by clicking on a mouse between swigs of Coca-Cola. So I'll go Russian in this book and renounce the antiseptic chill of euphemisms. I'll give it to you face-to-face. I'll give my characters some dignity.*

*Warning! This book doesn't have much sex in it. The trouble is, sex stands out: you can show a rainbow to a bull, but all he'll see is red. So am I taking a risk by including sex? Will it eclipse the other stuff, or worse, suck it in like a black hole, until nothing else in the book escapes the page? I hope not. If it does, then the fault is mine, or you've cheated and skipped chapters.*

*I mean it; I worry. I had a literary agent reject this book, saying it was 'far too rude'. Too rude for what? As a manifesto for the Amish, sure. As a recreation of the psychedelic rollercoaster that was me and mine, I think not. Rude times require rude telling. Anyway, the sex is all, though real and true, something to be smelt and tasted, also all analogy. A way of viscerally recounting other excesses, like Thatcher's disbanding of communities or the rise of money to godlike status.*

*When writing, I rummage in my head for memories: yesterday's leftovers. Some I've kept chilled, crisp and clear. Others are a little dry and need some sauce, whilst some are too rotten, even for this book.*

*I empty all the cupboards of my mind, dice and sieve, mixing and balancing experiences to be tasted. Some dishes*

*I will slow cook so as not to lose the delicate aroma. Others are so vital, so perfectly self-contained, that I'll serve them cold, al dente.*

*But mainly I'll be throwing stuff together: an ad hoc stir-fry. No menu, I'm afraid, just the recommendations of the chef. The food is a little spicy, a trifle hot. Can you take a little chilli with your meat? You can? Then take a seat and tuck your napkin in. There will be spillages and this book stains.*

*I've also tinkered with the truth, to make it all more truthful. I was once with a friend, Big Dave, in the Berggruen Museum in Berlin, to see the Picassos. We stopped in front of a nude, all abstract curves and body parts, shuffled on the canvas.*

*"Doesn't look like any woman I know," said Dave. That's the point. Picasso didn't capture any woman, he captured all women: the essence of the female. He tore up and reconfigured reality to let us see the truth. I am no Picasso but have tried to do the same. To say it as it really is, you sometimes have to lie. So please, no indignant letters, pointing out a mentioned bus route not compliant with London Transport's planning. To get to places off the map, even sometimes off the wall, I've had to customise the vehicle and the route.*

*Where permissible, I have used real names. I say permissible not from a legal standpoint, but rather from a moral one. I have chosen to lay bare my body and bits of soul and mind (anyway, you bought the book, so I'm not the flasher, you're the voyeur). I don't, however, have the right to expose the intimacies of others to prying eyes. So some details and names have been changed where their inclusion would cause undue distress. After all, I gained so much from the people in this book that I owe them, at the very least, their privacy.*

*That leaves the acknowledgements. Annette Green, my literary agent; Mark Booth from Coronet for coming up with the title; and Andrew Trimbee, a friend, for unwavering encouragement. Thanks also to Maria Elena Blanco for editing my anarchistic spelling and taming my punctuation. Also to Isabel, my partner, for putting up with me spending four months writing about the past instead of being with her in the present. Thanks, Natty, good dog, for showing me which were the best trees to bark up. And most of all, thanks to all the people in this book for making my life more interesting. Good luck and safe passage to you all.*

# The Intimacy of Species

I spent the back end of 1980 having sex with women for money. I was twenty-four.

Sex for cash isn't a vocation. At twelve, asked by my teacher what I wanted to be when I grew up, I think I said the usual 'fireman' or 'astronaut'. I'm certain I didn't say 'call boy'.

Some people see life as a series of moments. Others as a journey. As always with points of view, the truth is both. Freeze the frame to get the moment; run the film to see the journey. To understand why we end up doing something, being somewhere, we need to wind back and see the frame in context. Here's mine.

I had gone to a 'decent' public school where teachers imparted Truth. All questions had a correct answer. Knowledge was not a collection of opinions but rather an iron-bound tome of fact and we were drilled in conformity. We sang soldiers' dirty ditties on the bus to rugby games, swore allegiance to Queen and Country, and lived in a white and English world apparently comprising only middle- and upper-class families.

Sure, there was the local town which we could visit

on Saturday afternoons. But in our self-congratulatory reverie, the people who lived there were merely spear carriers in our play, there to make up the numbers, whilst we held centre stage.

We were, I suppose, as grubs, boring our way through an onion. We lived in our tunnel, passing cut edges, oblivious that each was a layer, encompassing and unique, worlds within worlds.

Cambridge next and with it, diversity of opinion. Where school was built on the certainty of knowledge, university thrived on doubt. To agree was to capitulate. We questioned everything. We signed up for the lot: existentialism, communism, feminism… Intellectually, I was beginning to break through the walls of the tunnel.

India followed, where I did my required stint with a shaven head, bag of ganja and lungi. I borrowed a Royal Enfield single cylinder bike and drove without apparent purpose for months on end. I lived naked with a tribe in the protected territories, I washed and burnt the dead, meditated in ashrams and drank from the Ganges.

When my money and intestinal flora ran out, I returned to London. For months, I couldn't sleep on a bed or wear shoes and had difficulty communicating. My old life just didn't cut it, as I had become addicted to the journey, to going always farther. I was also homeless.

So when two friends proposed that I squatted a building with them, I jumped at the opportunity.

Glading Terrace, London N16, was objectively a dump. Abandoned by council tenants as unfit for habitation, it had been thrown up in 1912 to house factory workers migrating from the countryside in search of a pay cheque. Comprising thirty flats in five blocks, the place was semi-derelict.

Each flat had three rooms. Unlike these days, the rooms had no pre-assigned function. Lay down a mattress to make a bedroom. Set a tin bath by the fire and there was your bathroom. Smoke a cigarette and read the newspaper and hey presto, you were in a living room.

The old boys in the pub remembered when the place was heaving with life. Families of six and more would live in those three rooms, birthing and dying, feeding from allotments by the canal and drowning out the noise of factory shifts with a good sing-song and a pint come Saturday.

I loved the place. It was a blank canvas and my home.

I vividly remember my first night there. The floorboards had been ripped up for firewood and the power turned off. I bought candles and a pack of Red Stripe beer. I found some wood in a skip to lay over the joists and scavenged three fruit boxes from Mr Guzman's store on the High Street. The boxes became a table, the candles and a roll-up were lit. I snapped open a beer and felt deliriously happy.

Glading Terrace was like India; a place which thrived on diversity, on the edge of madness, unfathomable, heartbreaking, mesmeric. My school and university mottos, translated from the Latin, are respectively:

*The heaven from the East* and, *From this place we gain light and precious knowledge.*

Had Glading Terrace had a motto, it might have been: *There are no limits.*

Just as Cambridge had shown me diversity of opinion and India diversity of belief and ritual, Glading Terrace brought me face-to-face with the diversity of people. Let's visit some of them.

Flat One: Anne Dee, a transvestite neo-Nazi whose real name was Andy. He would open the door in a negligee and storm trooper's helmet. He was a social worker who helped juvenile boy offenders. Helped them with what, I never dared to ask.

Opposite him was Trilvin, a physics professor at North London Poly whose recent divorce had left him penniless. Poverty suited him, rebranding the vice of a miser as virtuous necessity. He would scavenge discarded fruit and veg from the gutters of Ridley Road market and grew a beard to save on razor blades.

Flat Three was Shoda's. She had emigrated to planet Zog sometime in the '60s and had one answer for everything: "Yeah." Opinions were divided in the community as to whether this reply was final proof of her transcendence to a state of enlightenment or that industrial quantities of acid had melted her brain. She grew carrots on the windowsill and drew maps of imaginary lands by candlelight, maybe in a vain attempt to locate her memories.

Across the landing was the door that never opened. Rumour had it that a Rasta the police were interested in talking to lived there. The only sign of life was the thud boom thud of base speakers, which had been set to

Jamaican time. One night I woke up disorientated. Some detail of the celestial heavens that was Glading Galaxy was out of alignment. An unfamiliar silence. The thud boom thud had stopped. After three days and still no music, a posse of us broke the door down. We found twenty-seven empty Marmite jars, eleven beheaded Barbie dolls and a pair of socks, which I kept.

The top floor was ours. Two flats shared by the three of us: Sue Stiles, Nina Newington and I. Sue and Nina were lesbians and I the honorary male.

Sue and I tried to get it on at a festival in Devon. She still had one foot in the wardrobe and, I guess, wanted one last look inside. A predictable disaster, the sex a flop, but an intimacy shared all the same. Sue's body was lesbian. It just took a while for her brain to catch up.

Nina was the opposite. Uniquely cerebral, her speciality something about gender stereotyping in nineteenth-century American literature. It was almost as though she had reached the conclusion, through intellectual argument and research, that she was gay and passed the order to her body to follow suit.

I loved them both as one might exotic sisters.

Thirty flats, some forty different lives, but all explorers. A band of pioneers staking their claim to the right to be unique.

Glading Terrace was demolished sometime in the '90s. Life is so ephemeral. We were indeed poor players, our stage so much rubble buried in a landfill site, somewhere in the Lee Valley.

The dump has now been grassed and planted out. Swings and slides have been installed. Children play and parents take their ease, unaware that under their feet lies a building that was our home.

In 2007 I went and found the park, sat on a bench and watched the children play. Was it the beer and sun? Perhaps the hypnotic pendulum of the swings; the rhythmic see-saws? I don't know what took me back, but one by one, that band of pioneers emerged out of the earth.

Colin the Artist, dressed as always in his skinhead uniform: Doc Martin boots, straight jeans held up by braces – red, of course – the Ben Sherman shirt and number one cut hair. In one hand he held a paintbrush, in the other a spliff. One for canvases, the other for his brain, just another kind of brush.

"Oy, Laurence, you cunt. Wan a toke?"

"Not now, Colin. Too early in the day."

Buster Blood Vessel, a giant of a man who sang with Bad Manners, a band that made it for a while. He had the biggest tongue I've ever seen and used to get teen groupies naked in large numbers. He would lay them on the floor and, stripping off, roll over them shouting the lyrics from his songs. Is he rolling still?

"All right, Buster?"

"Hanging loud, Laurence."

Here comes Trevor, Sergeant Pepper jacket and goatee. Off the chart of madness, that one. He used to collect cat tins from around the world and shag a girl called Trace. He was certain of nothing.

"So, Trevor, good to see you well. The cat tin collection must be monumental."

"Hmm... ah, yes. Perhaps. Mon-u-men-tal. Could well be. Hard to say. Tricky beasts... cats."

That day they all came back: a reunion of ghosts. Don't get me wrong, a couple may be dead but most, I'm sure, are still alive. It's not their bodies that have gone but how they were back then.

For a start, we had yet to have replaced experiences with things, 'stuff' as Kevin Spacey calls them in *American Beauty*. Remember the scene? Kevin is feeling horny and pulls Annette Benning onto the sofa. She kills the moment with her concern that the fabric might get soiled, putting the inanimate before the intimate. Our sofas were from skips or jumble sales and came pre-stained; our prized possessions were what we did, not what we owned.

All generations do the same. I have a teenage son who leaves his room a mess. He has a wardrobe but prefers to leave his clothes spread out on the floor. I find myself frustrated, tense. Why can't he hang them up? But then I realise it's only jealousy. He's too busy living life to bother with such foresight.

Another thing. We still had time ahead to rectify mistakes. Let's fall in love. So what if it doesn't work and ends in tears? There's time to wipe your eyes and find another lover. Let's drink all night, we have our lives to sober up. I'll be a vegetarian; the meat will still be there when I return. Let's try everything. Later on there won't be time, or rather, we will choose not to find it.

Add a lack of conscience: the accumulation of shame has yet to fill the moral cistern and flush us out. My baby son shits in his pants and laughs. I lay paper down so no one can hear the splash. We don't learn, selecting from the many rooms of life to find the one that's right, we simply abandon the others as too littered with our shame and pick the one least compromised.

But there was more. What holds true for every generation was especially true of us, our place, our time. In Glading Terrace, in 1980s London, living in the moment wasn't just condoned, it was required.

Same old story: the needed peer group approval, to be endorsed, to fit in. Same old story but with a different ending. For the only way to fit in was to be a misfit. Only those outside the envelope got posted with a first-class stamp. Is it any wonder, when excess spelt success, that we did the things we did? We conformed to expectation, but fucking hell, what fun conforming was!

Today I wake up and, looking out the window of my Andalusian mountain home, find comfort in the continuity of life. The cat on the windowsill, the peaks of the sierras, the pines of the forest, all just where I left them the day before. My life map has no blanks, no cartographer's note of *Uncharted*. Back then, looking out, I saw an ever-shifting landscape, a magical topology of wardrobes to Narnia, where buses are all signed *Destination Unknown*.

I had my little rituals, islands of certainty in a sea of 'what the fuck is going to happen next?' I played tennis in the park with Jamie McKenrick, a brilliant poet even then, and used my father's wooden racket. I learnt the congas with a Ghanaian from Dalston and how to juggle balls somewhere in Covent Garden. I took up carpentry, the thinking man's dabble of choice with manual work: a kind of self-imposed cultural revolution; a meaningless pretence of solidarity with our working-class brothers. Ironically, I ended up doing bits and bobs for the rich. They preferred a chap who knew his wines working in their kitchen.

But my favourite ritual of them all was my weekly visit to Bethnal Green bath and steam house. This was no emporium of middle-class self-love, no oasis of hot stones, fluffy white towels, mud packs and tonics, juice bar and aromatherapy. It was a place with baths and steam. Somewhere to go when you were dirty.

Hot water was rationed and an old boy with a faucet key would come along and release the allotted minute of open tap.

Towels were provided, but any fluff they might once have had had been ground away on the buttocks and hairy backs of bathers, leaving the thickness and finish of a tea-towel. The bath was a necessity and the steam rooms my little luxury.

The jewel in the crown of this working-class leisure centre was the Reposing Room. A cross between the sun deck of a cruise ship and a retirement home lounge, the room comprised some twenty day beds, a bloke at a desk and a dumb waiter. Having bathed and steamed, I would retire there, swaddled in my tea-towel and, well, repose.

The attendant, once he saw you settled, would wander over and take your order. Beans on toast, egg on toast,

toast. Tea or Ribena. That was the menu. I always had the same: beans on toast and tea. He would call out, "B and T," down a tube, like a captain barking orders to the chief engineer. Presently a bell would ring, and he would saunter to the collection hatch and retrieve the food and tea. I adored the place.

A conservative minister was later to notoriously comment: "The problem with public transport is that you have to sit next to someone you don't know." Something like that. Bethnal Green bath and steam house celebrated the tribal, naked men at their watering hole taking their ease and toast together. Rivals when dressed, we were levelled by nudity. We didn't sit next to people we didn't know. We sat next to well-met fellow men. We had a communality of purpose, of situation. The men would massage each other and take turns swirling the towels to whip the steam to scalding heights. Humans pruning each other, we shared the intimacy of species.

One particular Saturday, a guy I had never seen before parked himself on the bed next to mine. He was thin as a wire coat hanger, void of body hair and very tall. I ordered my usual and he asked for the same. We struck up a conversation. His name was Peter, and he was to become my pimp.

Had I come an hour earlier, laid on another bed or fallen asleep, I would never have met him, never have fucked women for money, never have written this book. We see ourselves as masterful, steering the ship that is us on studied course, bound by charts and instruments of precision. Maybe for some the journey of life is like that.

Mine was not. I was too busy being born to think about who steered my course. Had I done so, I would have come to the conclusion that I was blindfolded, accompanied by someone tossing a coin. Heads go that way, tails the other.

Now I know that neither wilful purpose nor random leaps of faith guided my decisions. We are all the same. Opportunities arise and we can choose to accept them or not. Some are simply a chink of light from an unmarked door and others full-blown proposals, but if not taken up they all recede, never to return.

People sometimes remark that unusual things happen to others. That some lives are full of adventures that they are denied, as though singled out to live in interesting times. Not true. We are all offered the opportunity of adventure, of pushing and transcending the boundaries of the everyday. The difference is that some of us recognise them, and others don't. And of those that recognise opportunity, some take it, and others pull away. At twenty-four, I never said no.

My Cambridge friends thought of themselves as weird because they dressed in a kaftan and leg warmers or kept a pet snake in a suitcase. These are not the hallmarks of the weird but rather affectations, or at best idiosyncrasies. Peter, on the other hand, was truly weird.

He had been born to deaf and dumb parents and thus grew up in a silent world where their intimacy was absolute. It is said that 'in the kingdom of the blind, the one-eyed man is king'. Not so. In that kingdom, the one-eyed man sees nothing of the darkness and is shut away in light. So it was with Peter, shut out, unable to share, left to wander alone in a world of sound. Sure, he signed, and they lip read. But he was an outsider, an immigrant to their country of two.

He was also the most promiscuous homosexual and never passed a day without being sodomised. It was as though he was compensating for a childhood bereft of intimacy by seeking intimacy with one and all. He was ostensibly a masseuse and had a table set up in the spare room. His parents retired at nine, cuddled up in bed whilst he sucked cock and was buggered in the room next door.

Peter was also the kindest man I ever met and sought the company of the broken, the down and out: migrant workers, cripples, the emotionally damaged and the damned.

"If you've no need for your second sugar, could you pass it over? If it's not too much trouble. I like my teaspoon to stand up," said the coat hanger.

I did and we began to talk. He spoke quietly, slowly, careful to not give offence. Most of my friends talked about ideas: politics, philosophy and literature. We dissected society with surgical gloves, emotions subordinated by intellect. Peter's domain was people. He gossiped and shared intimacies about strangers until I knew them as friends. Where we saw the big picture and diminished it to trivia, he took the trivial and built the big picture. He never criticised, only observed. I felt the comfort and ease which come from being with someone who you know instinctively will accept you for who you are. He talked, I listened; an hour passed, and seconds of toast were ordered.

The bath house was a rendezvous for men who had sex with other men. I have chosen not to say 'homosexual' or 'gay' as most of them would not have recognised these labels as appropriate. They mainly fell into two categories.

The first, old working-class men, married all their lives, who were impotent and could no longer satisfy a woman. Nature is cruel and the need to be sexually appreciated outlives potency. So they took their teeth out and sucked cock. Giving another human an orgasm reinstated their macho pride. The fact that the human was a man was secondary.

Then there were the young studs. They would fuck guys to show that, compared to them, even men were as women. They adored women so much that their lust literally spilled over into men. Gender isn't defined by what genitals you have but by complex inter-relationships.

I guess the gender extenders, as I came to call them, made up around half of the bath house regulars. The rest of us were straight. I never saw friction between the two groups, nor even approbation. We were just a motley crew of men, thin and fat, old and young, black and white. Different sexual proclivities went as unnoticed as your choice of toast.

Anyway, given the reputation of the place and I a pretty boy, I suppose it's not surprising that Peter came on to me. The details of his verbal seduction are irrelevant, and I pick up the story from my rejection.

"Thanks for the offer but I'm into women."

I have no sympathy with straight men who get annoyed when another man tries to proposition them. It's bad enough being rejected without being insulted. Their righteous indignation is misplaced and marks them out as insecure.

"Nothing wrong with that, Laurence. None of us would be here if it wasn't for the straights. You don't mind me asking, I hope? I don't want to offend you. Only hoping, you know. Can't blame a man for that, can you?"

"No, trying is always good, Peter."

We settled back into our personal reveries.

"How much into women?" he asked.

"I'm twenty-four and single. What do you think!"

Another pause. The old boy to my right got up to leave.

"Bye, John. See you, Peter."

"See you, Ron, take care."

Some sips of tea. A man passed his newspaper to another.

"Anything good?"

"Same old bollocks but page three's not bad."

I liked these lazy exchanges. Just friendship maintenance, no striving to impress. Peter's next comment was therefore all the more impactive.

"I saw you naked in the showers. Good body!"

"Come on, Peter! As I said, I'm into women."

"Oh dear. I've upset you, haven't I? I'm a daft bugger, you know. I've gone too far as usual. Sorry, Laurence. Still friends, I hope?"

I've never been fazed by sexual talk. Nothing skin deep should cause embarrassment. It's the stuff inside that needs protecting.

"Still friends, Peter. No problem."

He swung his legs over the side of the day bed and leant forward, all conspiratorial.

"It's just, I might have something for you. Something you might like. A job of sorts." He sipped his tea, weighing me up. "Would it bother you to have sex with women you didn't know?" he asked.

That made me laugh! "Most of the girls I pick up at 4am at a party should be classed as strangers. So, no, I guess not."

"Good. Then that's settled. I knew from the start that you were the sort."

Nothing seemed settled to me except the old boy opposite who was snoring. I told him as much.

"The thing is, Laurence, I get calls from people. They answer my ads or hear about me, you know, through mates and people I've sorted things for. They… ask for guys. Blokes who wouldn't mind a bit of sex. Sometimes a husband wanting to see his wife pleased, or a woman wanting a bit of extra fun. Sometimes it's more complicated. All sorts. You'd be surprised. They pay. I think it makes them feel better. You know, keep it all separate from… well, just separate. You know what I mean. The money isn't good but the work… the work's, sort of, I s'pose you could say… rewarding."

The last time I had heard that phrase was in a careers pavilion at Cambridge, from a guy looking for graduates to do voluntary work in Africa. Well, they do say charity starts at home.

"Let me get this straight, Peter. You are proposing that

I fuck women for money. That I work as a male prostitute. Correct?"

"You make it sound dirty. I've offended you. I'm sorry. Peter the plonker strikes again. I prefer to use other words. It's all about helping out. But I suppose if you want to call it that, then that's up to you."

"Why me?" I asked. "There must be guys queuing up to shag girls and get paid for it. What's the catch?"

"Less than you think. Bothers most. Sometimes there are situations. Bit strong. Not everyone's cup of cha. The women will love you. You're posh, proper manners, and cute. Anyway, by taking you on, we keep in touch and old Pete can live in hope that you'll end up, you know… on the massage table."

I ate the last of my toast and licked my fingers.

"If I don't lie out on your table, do I still get to keep the job?"

"Ooh, you drive a hard bargain, Laurence. Yes, of course. Can't be mixing business with pleasure, as they say."

I was standing in front of a locked, unmarked door; a stranger was holding out the key. I looked him straight in the eyes.

"When do I start?"

That was the frame. A bath house rest room. Two men. A proposition offered and accepted.

We've wound back, stopping here and there to look through windows, eavesdrop, to see enough to understand the frame. Enough, perhaps, to see it as inevitable.

Now, settle in. Got your snacks? Is the glass within hand's reach? Take your shoes off and clear your mind of preconceptions. Dim the lights. Ready? Adult themes ahead. More than bodies are going to be laid bare.

# Lady Trocknell

Peter broke me in gently. A week passed and I had pretty much given up on him when the phone rang.

"Hello, Laurence. Have I caught you at a bad time? Is it OK to talk?"

I was taken off guard. "Who's that? Who's calling?"

"Peter. From the baths. Can we talk? You're probably doing something interesting. I can call back."

"Hello, Peter. Of course. I wondered if you would ring. No, now's fine. I was just getting up, actually. Busy night."

"Being a naughty boy, were you? Lucky girl."

"Cleaning the kitchen. Has someone come up?"

"Yes. I've had a few punters on the blower but none quite right for your first time. This one is, I think."

"I'm all ears."

"She's widowed, poor dear. I've never married. Well, you can guess that. But it must be hard. Losing a loved one. Not just any bloke. An ambassador. Mind you, she's grand as well. A real aristocrat. A proper Lady. Lives in Kensington. Dead posh address. Just wants a bit of fun. Remember what her bits down there are for."

"Sounds great!"

"Speaks like the queen, you know. When she rang up, she said she was – what did she say? – enquiring about the hired help, like she was taking on a new maid. I'm daft, am I. I didn't cotton on and said she had the wrong number. She said she never got the wrong number, that wrong numbers were for the wrong sort of person. That made me laugh, that did. Made matters worse. She said that I was in business and that clients were not to be laughed at. I never thought anyone could embarrass me, but she did. Anyway, her highness said that obviously I was a person who needed to be spoken to clearly and that what she required was a young gentleman to attend to certain personal needs. I remember that bit. Such a way with words, like you. Real educated."

"And that would be me, Peter."

"It would, Laurence, it would. So I go on to ask what those needs might be, and she, all hoity-toity, says that her husband had opened her eyes to stuff – though she wouldn't have used the word 'stuff'. I can't remember. Anyway, she says he'd shown her the satisfaction which could be got from giving boys a proper education. She said that in other places – hang on… no, she said in certain parts of the world – boys knew their place and duty and that – what did she say? – education was never wasted."

"Christ, Peter, sounds like she's wants to whip me."

"Yes, Laurence, that's what I thought. Don't you worry. Peter wouldn't let you come to harm. No one, however posh, is going to whip my Laurence unless you want to be."

"Well, I don't want to be. Anyway, what else did she say?"

"Hang on. Let me remember. Oh yes, she assured me that you would find great satisfaction in the job and that she had never had a complaint."

"Hmm, sounds interesting. Anything else I should know?"

"She wants you there this Sunday, 3pm, and not to be late. She said she couldn't – what was it? – abide people who weren't punctual. When she opens the door, you are to ask if she has any odd jobs that need doing."

Peter proceeded to give me her name, Lady Trocknell, and the address.

"Is that it?" I asked.

"You get a hundred quid. She paid up front. Had someone come round with the cash, all crisp tenners in an envelope."

"That's brilliant!"

"But the cost of the school uniform you need to buy comes out of that. Must rush, Mum's signing me."

He put the phone down before I could reply.

I love aristocrats. Even those that don't have a 'Lord' or 'Baroness' to decorate their names and hide in the rank and file. Aristocratic is a state of mind, a title earned through being it as well as something bestowed, and never to be confused with trust fund babies: parasites who never left the cocoon. They are so vague, so apparently purposeless. I knew my share from Cambridge.

Ivo Hemond-Halting, two doors down from me. He burst in one evening, stripped to the waist, a bottle of Veuve Clicquot in hand. He'd grown a second chest hair, a companion for the first, and was inviting us to the christening.

"Let's toast young Edward's arrival on my tit, a playmate for Randolf."

We were discussing Marx and were dismissive, probably insulting. Come the revolution he'd be gone for sure, chest hair and all.

"All right, my friends, more for us, eh, Randolf?"

Months later we were picnicking by the weir at Grantchester. One of the girls fell in. She couldn't swim. It was Ivo who dived in and brought her back.

The rest of us took everything so seriously but committed to nothing. Ivo saw life for what it was, a joke in bad taste punctuated by moments when you have to stand up and be counted. Of course, there are the abusive ones who should be guillotined, but most are harmless vaudeville, peacocks that brighten up the lawn. Exotic birds by day, they guard the house at night.

By 1980, England was an aspiring meritocracy. What an irresistible idea! Success based on merit. No barriers between your dream and its fulfilment except your own ability. I have in mind a competition of best ideas. The three finalists all line up. Food for all, living to be a hundred, and meritocracy. Meritocracy wins. The judges are unanimous in their decision. Imagine the winner's speech: "I want to let all children have equal opportunity. I will rid the land of vested interest, class and prejudice. All men shall be judged on merit." The applause is resounding, the face of meritocracy front page news.

But as the months and years roll by, the rankings of the winners in the polls begin to slip. Food for all, but at what price? Genetically modified crops controlled by a cartel of multinationals? More to eat but less nutrition – a kind of classical torture, like being left to die of hunger in a supermarket. And this living to a hundred? Fine and dandy, but then we get the bill. No one mentioned, when that winner was announced, that there wouldn't be enough money to pay for all the elderly. Besides, even with the best of parties, there's a time when we all want to go home to sleep. Oh, the crowns are slipping, and meritocracy's handmaidens are looking a little ragged.

What of the Queen herself? Surely merit has no downside? Wrong, I think. Merit on its own has no meaning. It has to be defined, like good or evil. A medieval healer might be classed as evil for using herbs to stay a fever. The torturer set to extract her confession, good for doing God's work. Of course, today the labels would be reversed.

By the 1980s, merit was beginning to be applied to actions and results of dubious value. Robert Maxwell showed merit by revitalising the press, but then he stole the pension fund and lobotomised his readership to do so. Margaret Thatcher, the grocer's daughter, rose to rule the land and in so doing became the pin-up girl of the meritocracy. But do we want a grocer as our ruler? Not everything can be put on a shelf and priced up. Do we want merit to be assigned to policies which fractured society, turned bankers into speculators and had as a chorus line 'show me the money'?

Equal opportunity isn't a statement of moral intent but only half a question. Equal opportunity to do what? Equal opportunity to be different, creative, valued for who you are, to be excellent, rewarding to yourself and others. Bring on the meritocracy. Equal opportunity to charge as much as possible for as little in return, to optimise production by minimising self. Meritocracy? No, thanks. Give me Ivo's chest hairs any day.

I still had my school tie and borrowed some grey trousers from a mate. The jacket I got from the Oxfam shop down the high street. Grey socks and Y-fronts (I thought my boxers inappropriate), courtesy of Woolworths, and I was all set. I did a private dress rehearsal in our squat. To this day I've never told my flatmates what I did for Peter. Nina looked up from sieving a yoghurt culture, saw me from behind, and said that with a cap on I would look like a schoolboy. Of course, the cap. For the rest of the morning, I scoured the second-hand shops. No luck. Desperate times, desperate measures. So I headed off to the local secondary. These were the days before any adult found loitering outside a playground would be arrested as a pervert, and I had no difficulty attracting the attention of a group of schoolboys.

"Here's the deal," I told them. "One of you lends me his cap and gets a quid."

Four caps were held out for inspection, and I picked the one least travelled in.

I arrived at 2:50pm, chained up my bike and stowed my coat in one of the panniers. The Trocknell residence was imposing. Gloss black wrought iron railings spanned out from a central stair which led to the broad, fielded panel front door. The house was Georgian, had high windows with dainty glazing bars, and lead gutters and downpipes. On four floors, smooth rendered and stone painted, it spoke of power and influence. Unconsciously, I found myself polishing my shoes on the back of my trouser and straightening my tie before climbing the seven steps to my first client.

The door was opened by a woman in her mid-forties. Tall and slender, with haughty eyes and a big, bony, curved nose, her clothes echoed her expression: severe. Her hair was pinned close to her head, and she wore no make-up. Her blouse, simple black satin, was buttoned to the neck and tucked in a mid-length pleated skirt. Stocking or tights – time would tell, but I bet they were stockings – covered her lower legs, ending in black, sensible shoes.

"Yes, young man?" she enquired in imperial tone.

"I wondered if you had any jobs that needed doing," I replied as scripted.

She looked me up and down as one might a side of beef, to see how many portions could be obtained.

"You are a lucky schoolboy. It just so happens that I do have a task you could… discharge." And with that she turned and lofted down the hall.

As with most aristocrats, they don't ask, they simply expect compliance. I duly followed.

"Close the door, young man," she called without turning. I had received the first of many orders.

She led me into a large, well-furnished living room and reclined on a chaise-longue, leaving me standing.

"I doubt that we shall meet again, so the matter of exchanging names does not arise. I shall call you 'boy' and you will address me as 'madam'. I have been accustomed to being read to after lunch and as your voice suggests an adequate education, that will be your allotted task. You may sit." At which point she vaguely waved in the direction of a footstool. "There," she said, pointing to a book on the French escritoire. "Commence at chapter seven."

I did as asked. I can't remember the title of the book or who the author was. I do remember that it was bound in leather and dated 1893. I know the year because that's when Gaudi started work on one of my favourite buildings, the Sagrada Familia cathedral in Barcelona. It's important to the chapter to try and recreate this business of reading from the book, so I will invent one. Let's name the author Colonel Earnest Wilkinson and his offering to the corpus of world knowledge, *Observations Regarding the Habits, Costume and Customs of the Goruba, North Benin Territory.*

I had expected the only leather binding to have been round her breasts and the only thing earnest, our coupling. I was nevertheless enjoying our play, had bagged £100 less expenses and was most certainly intrigued.

I opened the book at chapter seven. I warn you, this passage is quite long. But the essence of the old aristocracy is that life is an aside, an amusement. A thousand years of traceable ancestry provides a different scale of time. I want to slow the chapter down, show that the proof of power for the upper classes isn't in achieving more, but by being beyond the need to do so. Enough, let's begin.

*"I beg my reader's indulgence to further impose upon their attention with my humble study of the rather unusual educational practices of these savages, as regarding the boys of their tribe on reaching manhood. The Goruba, sadly lacking in the noble traditions of our British public schools, are ignorant of the value of the classics. Such titans as Plato and Aristotle and the wisdom of the ancients are denied these heathens. So, too, even the most elementary of trigonometric calculation, the motion of the heavenly bodies or the history of our great island nation. Their nudity of body is mirrored in their nudity of mind.*

*"Indeed, these youths, far from being trained to take up the mantle of empire, to serve and further the interests of nation, spend their time spear-throwing, dancing with the abandon of the epileptic and carving gourds to adorn their membri virili. It shall therefore surprise my dear reader to know that in the matter of coitus, of the training of these purposeless youths for procreation, the Goruba show surprising commitment indeed. Though to speculate, that demon enemy of fact, is rightly the whimsical pastime of the fairer sex, were one to do so, one might conclude that if the Goruba ever commit the same consideration to warfare as they do to coitus, her majesty would have a worthy foe indeed.*

*"Having completed my catalogue of the 27 headdresses and 67 nose bones of the southern hill dwellers, I retired to the relative comfort of King Umbungo's mud palace. Any*

*hope of rejoining my regiment was, if I may be permitted the pun, washed away by the impending rains. My staple diet of pre-masticated flies and yam had become palatable, though I confess to the occasional hankering for the Savoy carvery. My mornings continued to be occupied with teaching these chaps the rudiments of cricket and my afternoons with writing up my field notes. Life, though not able to reach the salutary straightness of bat nor unwavering seam of ball of my dear home in Cheshire, took on an acceptable regularity.*

"*Such unaccustomed lack of pressing commitment allowed me to accept King Umbungo's proposal that I represent my county at the forthcoming ritual of manhood to be held for a week commencing with the full moon. I had harboured hopes of holding the first test match in these parts and giving my friend Ripper Hodgekins a run for his money. My attendance at the ceremony would interrupt practice. What to do? My duty was to chronicle these heathens, but my passion, the imparting of the game of Lords. However, the ceremony would come but once a year and practice could be resumed thereafter. I agreed to go.*"

I paused and looked at Lady Trocknell. Her eyes were shut, but any notion that she might be asleep was promptly dispelled.

"I do not recall saying you were to stop. Proceed, boy."

I found my place and continued.

"*The ceremony, known as Kandu Maku, began at dusk. I had in my youth attended two seasons. Oh, the dazzle of swirling silk, the blooming of Cheshire society, Monty Ponsonby and I freshly commissioned and proud in our uniforms and manhood! Indeed, I had found my own wife, Elizabeth, at her coming-out ball, captivated by her charms from the first waltz. I may not be the cleverest of chaps, have not Monty's way with numbers nor Ripper's command of our fair tongue, but nevertheless was under no delusion that Kandu Maku would reach the elevated heights of social decorum of our Cheshire balls. Indeed, I thought my ability to be surprised long gone, lost under memories of witnessed ritualistic self-mutilation, exorcisms and the eating of departed parents. Yet just as the flogging of the rank and file for insubordination does not prepare one for the thrill of battle, so too did my experiences fail to prepare me for what I saw those nights.*

"*The ceremony took place in King Umbungo's great hall, a round mud building with a roof of adze hewn timbers, tiled, if you will, with overlapping palm leaves. The floor had been freshly dressed with dung mixed with straw and river silt, watered until a slurry and stamped to a hard, smooth finish. The torches had been lit. The king sat on his throne carved from a single tree trunk. As custom dictated, he wore his lion skin and was otherwise naked except for his crocodile tooth testicle piercings. His fourteen wives were divided in two groups of equal number. To the left, those who had borne the most children and to the right, the seven younger wives.*

"*The boys who had reached their sixteenth year, bodies daubed with blood from the wild pig and yellow pigment made from the stamen of flowers, stood in a line facing the king. I counted six.*

"*The drumming which had begun perhaps an hour before came to an abrupt halt, whereupon the older wives took up positions on raised thigh-high platforms. Each struck a different pose: on their knees, their back, squatting, on their side... They were all naked.*

*"Two of the younger wives, carrying clay pots, approached the platforms. They proceeded to rub the bodies of their elders with oil mixed by the village shaman with a potent opiate not dissimilar to that used by our own Mr Holmes and other literati of the London scene. Having completed Satan's anointment, they lay down their pots and were joined by the other five. Each then took up a position beside an older wife.*

*"The men of the tribe proceeded to form a circle around the paired-off wives and began to beat in unison, drumming an insistent throbbing beat with sticks that had been carved to clearly represent the male sex organ.*

*"Meanwhile, I noticed that the boys, too, were to have their anointing. Theirs was a concoction of pulped plants and secretions extracted from the anal glands of tigers, the sexual stimulant so eloquently studied in Dr Worthington's seminal work,* The Copulatory Preparation of the Wakiki. *The thick, oleaginous paste was applied to the length of their penises, which promptly elevated as Neptune's trident might from the deep, swollen in girth and majestic in length and rigidity."*

For some time now I had been noticing out of the corner of my eye that Lady Trocknell was no longer reclining and was in fact sitting bolt upright, legs akimbo, her hand loitering over her crotch. I myself had a throbbing erection. I stopped reading and looked straight at her.

"Impertinence is inevitable in the working classes but something I do not expect from my readers. Kindly desist from your gawking. You may not be able to prevent, as is apparent, the swelling of your penis, but that is no excuse for bad manners. Proceed with Colonel Wilkinson's enlightening work."

I obeyed.

"*The village crone, a woman of incalculable age, shrivelled as a Christmas walnut, led the first boy forward.*

"*The beating of the staffs abruptly halted, and the shaman addressed the youth. It shames me to say that after seven months living with these people, I had yet to fully master their tongue. However, the boy's subsequent actions left in little doubt the meaning of the shaman's words: he was to smell the bodies, or rather those parts of a sexual nature, of the older women.*

"*As in any decent society, orders should be carried out to the letter, and I found myself nodding in agreement when the boy received a light crack of the staff as he succumbed to his lust and attempted to mount the particularly splendid buttocks of the king's favourite wife. Even without the stimulation of her labia, the boy had but reached to smell the Venus mound of wife five when his semen burst in a jet worthy of the regiment's spittoon champion. Another crack of the staff in reprimand for his precocity.*"

"Enough," said Lady Trocknell. "Thank you, boy. That will do. I am familiar with this opus. So tell me, have you had the advantages of a proper sexual initiation? Has a more experienced woman taken you in hand?"

In truth, the answer was 'yes', as indeed I had been seduced by a woman more or less her age when I was seventeen. But the situation required an altogether different answer.

"No, madam, that part of my education has been sorely lacking."

"I see. That is an omission which should be corrected. Stand up, boy, and approach me."

I did as I was told, coming to a stop an outstretched arm from her.

"Unzip your fly and extract your penis," she commanded.

My erect cock, imprisoned throughout my reading of the good colonel's study, appeared and stood uncomfortably between us like a gauche guest at a cocktail party.

"I would remind you that our relationship is one of teacher and student. Should the moment arise when I consider it appropriate that you masturbate, I shall make that known to you. In the meantime, you will desist. I require you hard. You will, in the course of the afternoon's lesson, be ejaculating copiously, though I will set the bar at a modest three discharges and not the seven demanded of the Goruba boys. Whereas clement in my demands, I will not tolerate unauthorised ejaculations. I have given my maid the afternoon off and even were she to be here, I doubt that scooping your cum into a gourd, an artefact I do not possess, would fall within the remit of her duties. Mind you, she is French so one cannot be sure. Now, strip naked, get on your knees and remove my undergarment."

I set about taking my clothes off whilst she watched me, legs spread, hand idly moving across the crotch of her black silk knickers.

"My late husband was a potent man, capable of servicing both of our Malay housemaids and I, but age pardons no one and his semen in his later years had taken on the unsatisfactory consistency of mustard water. You, I trust, purvey an altogether thicker sauce?"

"Indeed, I do, madam. More of a school custard."

"Excellent! Now remove my knickers."

So, crouching down, I slid her panties over her bony buttocks and down her legs. Stockings. I was right. The aristocracy rarely, in my experience, wear tights, a terrible invention.

"Give them to me," she ordered. "We shall not be outdone by those savages. I want you to inhale deeply from the crotch. I think you will find the smell to your liking."

I most certainly did and found myself inadvertently stroking my cock again.

"Really, boy, this is too much. I believe I made myself perfectly clear. You were not to touch your member until told. I do not recall countermanding that order? Did I countermand that order?"

"No, madam."

"I see you are not a boy to be trusted. Give me your school tie. Stand up, turn around. Hurry up. Now place your hands together behind your back. Good."

She then proceeded to tie my hands with a speed and professionalism which spoke of years of practice.

"Now you will not be able to play with yourself and perhaps focus your attention on doing what you are here to do, namely, providing me with pleasure. Turn and kneel as you were before."

Back in position, she placed her pants over my head so that the crotch was firmly over my nose.

"Continue to inhale. Deep breaths now! Good. Inhale! Excellent. Again. Yes, just as I thought. With each inhalation your cock swells as surely as in a whore's mouth. Why, I do believe you could come simply from the smell of my cunt. Still, we have the afternoon, and I am sure that by your second ejaculation you will have the stamina necessary to sodomise me for at least the half of an hour."

I was going absolutely crazy. To date, and with the exception of the older woman I mentioned earlier, my sexual experiences had mainly been limited to clumsy and unimaginative encounters with girls of my age. Kensington, in that moment, could have been washed away in a flood and I would have just stood there, rhythmically breathing and pulsating. She proceeded to lower her panties till the crotch was in front of my mouth and pushed the fabric between my parted lips, driving them ever deeper with her three middle fingers. Occasionally I could feel something hard against my upper teeth. It was her wedding ring.

"Tongue! Use your tongue, boy," she commanded. "Run it forward and up as though you were scooping ice cream from a cone. Good. Again. Good boy."

My eyes were beginning to water, and I felt a mixture of frustration and relief when she finally removed her fingers and slipped the panties from my head and paraded them to me. They were completely saturated.

"Now, suck me, boy!"

I went about my business with diligence. Her pussy was, well, aristocratic. Long and understated with pursed lips, close cropped pubic hair and a hooked, aquiline clitoris. I worked steadily, running my tongue from her perineum to her hood, slowly and methodically. I heard the snap of a lighter's lid and the spin of the wheel and, judging from the smell, she had lit a cigar. With her other hand she absent-mindedly stroked my hair as one might a lapdog.

Any thoughts I might have had that this token of affection was the beginning of a more tender and egalitarian phase in our play were soon dispelled.

"Heavens above, boy! You are not licking stamps for some pathetic philatelic collection. I have seen servants dust the Ming porcelain with more vigour than you exhibit. God has not given you a tongue just to praise the Lord at morning prayer!"

She firmly grabbed the back of my head and, raising her haunches clear of the chaise, ground her cunt into my face. Skilled women learn early on to breathe through their noses when sucking cock. As Lady Trocknell was bent on using my nose as a stimulator for her clitoris, I had no such recourse. Perhaps, had I taken that course in tantric yoga instead of juggling at the Covent Garden Adult Education Centre, I might have learnt to breathe through my ears. Instead, I came up for air. Madam was not amused.

"Why, you barely lasted a quarter of a cigar! I have had boys go a full round of cucumber sandwiches and one endured a Pimm's. Now do as I say. Breathe in, slowly and with your diaphragm, not just your chest. Hold it. Hold it. Now slowly breath out, push back from your stomach until voided. Good. Again. Good. Again. Now take half a dozen short sharp breaths. Now one last big one and down to business."

Whether I was simply determined to impress or her lesson in hyperventilation had worked, I managed to go twice as long between coming up for air. She was lubricating freely by now and those pursed lips had swelled and folded out. The upper classes may maintain a stiff upper lip, but when they commit to debauchery there is no stopping them. She had me work my tongue in her arsehole, as clean as saddle-soaped leather, suck her clitoris until I thought I could taste her bone marrow and delve so deep into her pussy crack that I felt my jaw would dislocate.

She came violently, almost crushing my head with her bony thighs. Red faced, nose and mouth slick with her juice, I sunk back on my haunches like a discarded rag doll. I had been well and truly face-fucked and had loved it.

She soon recovered her composure. That's another hallmark of the upper classes. The ability to snap back to form, to never forget who they perceive themselves as being. She was like some hussar who drinks all night in the company of whores, kills a man for breakfast and then accompanies his mother and sister to church. The agonies of conscience which paralyse the rest of us, the melding together of all the parts of our lives into a confusing whole, never seem to bother the aristocracy. Morality is the shackle of the working classes, the aspiration of the middle classes, and simply ignored as rather silly by the toffs.

"Now let's see what that young cock of yours can do." Her challenge delivered, she laid the length of the chaise before getting up on her knees. "Enter me from behind, my boy; concentrate on the cunt for the time being. I don't wish to scandalise Judge Hewitt."

Now, I've heard my share of elliptical comments. Any habitué of temple ball hashish in the late night company of Cambridge undergraduates will not be phased by a non sequitur or two, but this reference to Judge Hewitt beat the lot.

"Who is Judge Hewitt?" I timorously asked.

"A judge, of course."

Well, that explained everything!

"Now, stop asking silly questions and fuck me, boy!"

I manoeuvred as best I could with tied hands until my cock was in the ballpark of her cunt. Actually getting it in was as impossible without hands as pouring tea on a surfboard. Madam became impatient.

"Am I to do everything!" she barked, reaching behind and inserting the head between her lips. "I take it you can push on your own!" I could and was forcefully fucking her when she said, "Time for the call, I think." She reached for the phone.

In my life I have only once fucked a woman whilst she spoke on the phone. It had been a mutually agreed precaution. We were on the top floor of her house and were keen that her husband, who was working downstairs, didn't appear. By keeping him chatting on the internal line we knew that we wouldn't be interrupted. Peter had been clear that Lady Trocknell was a widow, so the good judge – I assumed that was whom she would be calling – was not a husband.

She dialled and put the phone on speaker.

"Crown Courts, how may I help you?"

"Yes, I wish to speak to Judge Hewitt; you may tell him Lady Trocknell is calling."

"May I ask the nature of your call?"

"No."

"Well, Judge Hewitt's court is sitting at present. May I take a message?"

"No, you may not. I assure you that Hewitt will wish to take the call. The matter is of some urgency."

"Well, the best I can do is have an usher place a note on his bench, but I assure you that calling a judge when court is sat is most unusual."

"Yes, well, the usual is rarely of interest. I shall hold."

I came. Bountifully and noisily.

"Sorry, I missed that. What did you say, madam?" This from the receptionist.

"Interference on the line. Now run along and deliver my message."

As euphemisms for orgasms go, 'interference on the line' wasn't bad.

I continued to fuck her. A good ten minutes passed, during which time my teacher untied me so I could reach down, unbutton her blouse, raise her bra and cup her small but surprisingly firm breasts. I remember thinking that her nipples were unusually large. Doubtless the result of interbreeding, like Prince Charles's ears. Eventually the receptionist returned.

"I'll put you through." Clearly, Lady Trocknell was a woman of influence.

"Sabrina! You know this is terribly irregular. I was judging a murder trial. It won't do, you know."

"Now, now, Henry, don't be so boring. I have far more important business to discuss than your stupid trial. Listen."

And with that she swung the phone over her shoulder and placed it close to her cunt.

"I say, Sabrina! You haven't got one of your odd job boys with you?"

"Indeed, I have, Henry. He's flooded my cunt once already and is all set for a second ejaculation."

"Oh, Trockers, you're a frightful woman. Why do you taunt me so? I would convict the innocent just to lick your shoe, yet you scorn me for boys."

"He made me come hard with his tongue. Your maggot of a penis would hardy suffice to clean the spout of my Wedgwood teapot. Now, boy, say hello to Judge Hewitt."

She waved the phone in the general direction of my face. I must say, I was enjoying this. I had once been hauled up in court for trying to sell china in Oxford Street out of a shopping trolley. I wanted to make some money to buy my mum a birthday present. The police nabbed me, and I ended up in front of a judge. He was incredibly condescending, a bully, and fined me £20. This was payback.

"Hello, Judge Hewitt."

"Have mercy, Trockers. Send the boy away. I'll get the Bentley and we can take a room at Claridge's."

"Silly Henry. I believe the boy is ready for another discharge. I can feel his cock swelling. Ah, yes! Excellent! A handsome load, the second of the three I shall be extracting this afternoon. Now go and be a good little judge. Maybe I'll send you my knickers to sniff when the jury is out deliberating. Go now!"

"I beg you, release me from purgatory. Let me see you again! Give me hope! I am your knight, set me your lover's challenge. Require what you will of me!"

"Well, Henry, there is something you can do for me."

"Anything. Anything. Just ask."

"You can tell that fool of a secretary that the next time I ring she is not to keep me waiting on hold!"

With that she put the phone down.

The rest of the afternoon followed in similar vein. True to her word, she extracted my allotted three orgasms. The last was up her arse, a first for me and something she particularly enjoyed. Women who genuinely like anal sex are rare and not to be confused with the cohort who permit their men to sodomise them on special occasions as one might permit a child to watch an extra hour of TV on Sundays.

Lady Trocknell was a genuinely sexual being. Her sexuality was not a sad and borrowed thing, something acquired like a peek-a-boo negligée or this season's lipstick colour. Her sexuality came from within, was an extension of her life and personality. She understood and had mastered her own unique eroticism and required no toys, no instruction manual.

When the time came for me to leave, she escorted me to the door and shook my hand.

"You have proved a good student," she said and turned to go. I started to descend the steps, stopped, and called after her.

"Madam," I said.

"Yes, boy, what is it?"

"My name is Laurence, and I will remember you. Thank you."

She was momentarily lost for words and stood in the doorway, with, dare I say it, a look of uncertainty.

"I… let's not be forgetting ourselves. Run along now."

And with that she was gone.

I was going to leave but something prompted me to ease the letterbox, to look into her world one last time. She was standing still, looking in the mirror. I saw her smile and touch her hair before snapping back to form and departing down the hall.

So that's it. My first assignment. Did it make you… uncomfortable? Were you sickened, grossed out by tribal rites of passage, fem-dom role play, humour conjured from humiliation, my shameless use of dirty words describing dirty deeds? I hope a little, but just enough to feel the way I did: a little scandalised that it had turned me on so much; a bit shook up but addicted now; a photographer used to baptisms and weddings who goes to war, sees what's underneath and can't go back.

**Laurence Seidler**

Nice is nice. Sunlight lights our superficial snaps, the photographs we put in albums, post on walls. But it's the ones shot in the shadows, in the half-light of our primal selves that really tell the story.

# The Soldier's Wife

I was becoming part of the community, my thread of a life weaving itself into the collective fabric. Not enough to be subsumed into the bolt of cloth and not be recognised, but enough to connect, to attach and fix myself in time and space.

Once a week I had lunch at Luigi's. It was the archetypal Italian family restaurant, a comforting cliché like the hot water bottle at Gran's with the worn fleece cover. The pleasure of these encounters is not in being surprised, but quite the opposite, by the beautiful predictability. And so I always ordered the same. Minestrone soup with ground pepper, milled by Luigi himself.

He would say, "Some black pepper for your soup, sir?"

And I would reply, "Yes, thanks."

I knew what he would offer, and he knew I would accept. That's the point. It was a ritual laid down, layer by layer, week on week, until something solid: stamped earth, dependable.

For my main course I would have the fillet of veal in breadcrumbs with a side serving of spaghetti al dente with butter, more black pepper from Luigi's mill and a healthy covering of Parmigiano. He would sprinkle out the first two spoonfuls and then say conspiratorially, "I'll leave the cheese so you can help yourself." This little touch, this leaving of the cheese, made me a regular, someone offered privilege.

For drinks I had a dry white wine. Just one glass. All in all, an island of self-control in a sea of none.

He always brought the bill on a silver-plated tray, folded so that the sum to be paid would not be seen by both of us at once. Thus, the fulcrum balancing us out remained the pepper mill, the largesse of the cheese, and not a settlement in coin.

The net of what is art should be extended to capture Luigi and his like. We gush about a virtuoso performance on the cello. We enthuse over such and such a dance. So why not Luigi? His show was exquisite, and he gave a hundred performances a day.

Each time I ate, I discovered something new; some missed detail of his routine. The way he trained his eyes to look ahead and not at you, but catch your slightest gesture when attention was required. The way he nodded when taking the order, somehow able to imply with a simple tilting of the head that your choice of food was good. His astounding ability to be of service whilst retaining all his dignity.

Ezra Pound, when asked what literature was, famously replied, "News that stays news."

Well, Luigi, at least for me, has been just that.

We tend to focus on the people who do the dramatic stuff. The ones who make the other sort of news. But what impact do they really have on us? No, it's these unsung heroes who quietly enrich our lives.

General Building Supplies was another place that kept the beat, the underlying rhythm of my life. Everything about it was perfect. From the buff brown cotton coats the assistants wore to the little boxes of brass screws counted into squares of newspaper. From the smell of linseed oil, the pen and pencil set in each top pocket, to the room at the back, reserved for exotic hardwoods.

No self-service here. You had to go through the Milken family, purveyors of paints, brass door furniture and imported timbers. They sold so much more than stuff to fix your house. They gave the opportunity to eavesdrop, as customers came with little fragments of their lives in paper bags: a broken cup to glue, a hinge so David Milken could gauge the screws required. They included theatre, wisdom, encyclopaedic knowledge of their trade, comments on the weather and the impact of the high street's one-way system, all thrown in for free with every purchase.

I became friends with the two sons: Michael, so steeped in the disciplines of pipes, spigots, dowel pins and the like that he had an academic's air, and David, a grumpy runt who was their father's whipping post. I will tell you a story about each of them.

Michael beckoned me over one day and led me to an alcove between stacks of mouldings. He pulled out a hundred quid and asked me to buy books for his son.

"Stuff that he should read to be an educated man."

I ransacked Foyles and delivered a hefty package. Two weeks later, he rang me up, delighted. The family had been sitting at home watching *University Challenge*. A question came up about Aldous Huxley's work. His son had known the answer, *Brave New World*, one of the books I had chosen.

Alistair, who you will doubtless meet later, his friend Paul and I were having the mother of all parties. David was put on the invite list on a whim. Picture this scene, if you will.

Lost Jockey, a minimalist orchestra are reaching the climax of their piece. Bonfires are blazing. Four hundred twenty-somethings, all semi naked, daubed in tribal paint, are raving. A naked man with a clothed dog is walking through the throng, passing out magic mushrooms. David is sitting cross-legged on the grass, the party milling about him, he the eye of the storm. I am wearing only a golden rag and headdress, am bathed in sweat and someone has written a poem on my chest. He catches my eye and calls me over.

"So, David, hey, enjoying the party?"

"Yes, but there's something missing."

I rummaged in my mind for what. We had two bars, five bands, a film show, a treasure hunt, more drugs than in a chemist, naked people, a stately home and two impromptu restaurants.

"What?" I asked.

"Can't you guess?"

"No, I really can't."

"Some of those little cocktail sausages on sticks."

Now, why hadn't I thought of that!

There are two types of friends: the kindred spirits who come from your world and share your tastes, values and views; but there are also the others, the ones that living in a community brings you up against. The Luigis, the Michaels and the Davids. I cherished them. The kindred spirits shared my life but they, the others, were the ones that built it.

These days I shop at AKI, a DIY superstore. I know the checkout girl's name because it's printed on her shirt. Oh, and she knows my postal code, all the better to target my consumer preferences. That's it. That's our relationship, a printed plastic name tag and a numerical reference.

"It's stand-in charity work, a three-man job. Twenty quid. 8pm. Mick and Trish. Here's the address."

I'd completed six assignments and never seen Peter so abrupt, so decided. It just wasn't like him. He just dumped the details of the next job on me, pressed twenty quid and a folded paper in my hand and got up to leave. I think he was annoyed with me. Maybe not annoyed, just disappointed. I had told him about Shiaza, whose voluptuous body will be gracing a later chapter, and he'd gone all distant.

"Hey, I'm the new boy. What's charity work?"

I thought he wasn't even going to reply, just walk out the door. But he stopped halfway and came back to the table. He didn't sit down though.

"One of the blokes knows her. She's apparently ugly as sin."

"And stand-in?"

"The husband's impotent and will be watching. You're his dick."

"Sounds like I'm to be one of his three dicks! Christ, Peter, I thought you said this work was rewarding!"

"I told you that it sometimes gets complicated. Not all fun and games. Gotta take the rough with the smooth," said Peter.

"You're annoyed with me, aren't you? About Shiaza. Come on. Tell me what I've done wrong."

"Nothing. Nothing at all. Don't know what you mean."

"Peter, you've hardly said a word since I told you about Shiaza. You've even left your beer. Now, tell me, what's up?"

"You're a clever one, aren't you? A proper Sherlock. Mind you, I suppose I'm pretty obvious, aren't I? Wear my heart on my sleeve. Fuck, yes, you did piss me off a bit."

"Now, sit yourself down, finish your beer and let's get this sorted out."

Peter put his arm on my shoulder. "You're all right, you are. I'm not used to people worrying about me, about what I think. It's nice. You should come round my place for a—"

"Peter! Don't go there!"

"Why are all the best ones straight?"

"Now, let's start again. What did I do wrong?"

Peter finished his pint and wiped his mouth with a handkerchief as always.

"For starters, you saw her again. And not just once. Four bloody times! You mixed things up. Superman is Superman. Clarke Kent, Clarke Kent."

"So who's who?"

"Superman does the shagging, you daft brush!"

"So what's wrong with mixing things up?"

"You'll get hurt."

He wasn't annoyed or disappointed. Just worried for me.

"There's something else, isn't there, Peter?"

"Maybe. Maybe not."

"Come on, mate. Spit it out."

"Well, you don't need me, do you? You found her on your own. Flying the nest."

It's strange. I have no problem listening to gay friends talk about their sex life, but find myself uncomfortable, in uncharted waters, when the talk gets emotional. My problem, not his. He was probably just looking out for me.

"Peter, just stop, OK? This is freaking me out a bit. Don't be so soppy and tell me more about this job. Come on, business as usual."

"Are you sure you don't want to nip back for a quick—"

"Peter! Strictly business!"

"All right. All right. Keep your hair on. Just trying. Let me see. Look at it as a social service, doing your bit for our boys at the front. The guy's a squaddie, what you might call cannon food."

"Fodder."

"Fodder, that's the word. Anyway, they put him to work with radioactive paints and his nuts went black and blew up. He's got no balls, poor sod, and no hair from the chemo. He's going to die. The way I see it, he gave his all for King and Country. So go over there and give your all to his wife."

Momentarily, Peter succeeded in making me feel guilty that I had actually questioned the advantages of the job in hand, but as his tall, skinny frame slipped out the pub, the reality of my forthcoming mission struck home. I was going to fuck an ugly woman along with two other guys whilst her dying husband watched. Not exactly the dazzling prom queen beneath the stars on a punt but – how had he put it? – ah yes, I was to take the rough with the smooth.

There are places where you can leave your bike on the street unlocked and places you can't. That Saturday night I carried my bike up the four flights of stairs, chained it to railings and took the front wheel with me. Anyone who knows Lower Clapton would know that these were minimum precautions if there was to be any hope of not having to walk home, and anyone who doesn't know Lower Clapton is blessed. Imagine being clapped out and with the clap, but lower.

I was once at a dinner party in Hoxton, where some yuppie gave another the dire warning that with only 100k to spend, he would end up living in Stoke Newington (a comment I let pass, as I lived in good old Stokey myself). The opportunity never arose, but I vowed I would frighten some house-hunting client back in my borough with the grim prediction that with their limited money they would end up in Lower Clapton. Beneath Lower Clapton there is nothing except the abyss, so I imagine that the only threat used there is the horrible promise that you will never leave the place.

Of course, like Dante's *Inferno*, Lower Clapton has its circles of hell, and my destination was, more correctly, the Lowest of the Low Clapton.

Imagine my journey, if you will. It's dark, bitterly cold, and raining. Rain is generally associated with cleansing. The rain in Lower Clapton is a family member so distant that all it shares in common with its refreshing relation is a name. Lower Clapton rain, whipped by wind, is actually liquid dirt, a witch's slurry concocted from UB40s, gambler's stubs of never-made-it horses, stale beer, the grime of decades of who-gives-a-fuck, and urine. The witch adds water so everyone can get a splash.

The streets are deserted except for a few drunks and some fat chicks in shell suits who shout, "Show us your knob," and, "Get a car, you wanker," as I cycle past. A bus pulls up beside me at the lights, empty but for a few old folk hunched not against the cold but against life itself. Them, and a boy pissing out the window. The odd truck rumbles past taking goods from places where people still make things to places where people could afford to buy them.

Lower Clapton Road is wide, but few cars circulated. Those that do all seemed to have been doctored in the same chop-shop. Born Ford Fiestas or other boy racers, they had been Frankensteined into base speakers on amphetamines. Tinted windows, spoilers, lowered suspension, custom paint job, shotgun exhausts, they prowled the night hunting pussy and violence, trading drugs and killing enemies or, simply, time.

I knew a guy with one. He was a Cypriot with a lock-up in front of my squat. He spent months on his motor till it glistened and roared. One summer's night it was ready and slid from its lair into the urban hunting grounds. The following morning, a pick-up dragged its broken body home and the rebuild began all over. These cars were like ghetto boxers, trained for the big fight, brought back smashed to be rebuilt for that next night of brief glory.

Wide streets supporting architectural drama and flash commerce have their virtue. The Champs-Élysées ennobles and the Mall empowers, but Lower Clapton Road simply depresses. It's as though a suitably scaled community had been stretched, leaving buildings dimensioned for a local street marooned on the banks of a vast tarmac river, the flotsam from a planner's brainstorm. Most of the shops were boarded up, though, in fairness, it was hard to tell which were still in business and which abandoned. Those that still limped on, selling booze, kebabs and curry through meshed openings, were lit like operating theatres and had a bombed-out look. What remained of their Victorian heritage – the sash windows, the stucco reliefs, the Thames Basin flush point brick – was obscured behind graffiti, bars, lurid neon and plain filth. All in all, my journey seemed a fitting prologue for the night's work ahead.

At 7:45pm, I finally turned into the council estate, a collection of five storey blocks built in the '60s. People today seem amazed that generations past thought the world was flat or that fossils were put here by God to amuse us as we took the country air. In years to come, the same will be thought of these estates but with one difference. Empirical evidence might lead a person to believe the world was flat or, in the absence of evolution, that fossils were *ludens humanis* (playthings for humans). But no evidence exists to support the idea that taking people out of ground level houses, with corner shops and pubs, back gardens and a sense of privacy and ownership, and sticking them in featureless boxes approached via concrete piss-and-shit-smeared stairways was, or ever will be, a good idea. The only things a working class community has going for it are work and community. A sink estate has neither.

I walked the open corridor, counting off the doors: 41… 42… 43… 44… 45. This was it. The gateway to my next experience. I could walk away, go home and read a book, or fuck a dying man's wife. No contest. Life was here to be lived. I pressed the buzzer.

Bolt, security chain and deadlock drawn, and I was standing in front of Mick, Sick Mick, Fuck-my-wife Dying Mick. He was neither tall nor short. A standard issue man but thin as a model's wrist, gaunt and bald, sleeved in tracksuit bottoms and singlet. The army had indeed extracted their pounds and pounds of flesh.

So, how does one greet a chap whose wife you are to fuck? Is there an agreed etiquette that I was too new to the game to know? Does one parody the Spanish '*mi casa es tu casa*' with 'my cock is your cock'? Would a euphemism be safer? Something along the lines of, "I'm here about the blocked drain," or a conspiratorial, "A mutual friend sent me."?

I settled for, "Hi, I'm Laurence. Peter gave me your address."

He looked me over. A cursory inspection of the guy who is going to ejaculate in your wife is to be expected.

"All right, mate? Come in. Find the place all right, then?"

I nodded and must have passed muster.

I followed his shadow into the hall. The place was standard issue council, designed to depress. The media hacks of the middle classes, who were to become my clients, poured over swatches of off-white paint, searching for that elusive hue which would impart sotto voce status. Mick's walls were also off-white, that is to say, white that had gone off. The wizards of Dulux had had no part in this. Time, fags, cheap frying oil was the making of this colour. Some Woolworth's prints in gilt Bakelite frames broke the monotony, but only in the way that a fart could be said to ease the boredom of sitting in traffic.

I was led into the kitchen.

"Trish, this is Lol. Pete's friend."

Now, I hate being called Lol almost as much as Larry, but as my host was graciously going to offer me his wife's cunt, it hardly seemed appropriate to pull him up.

She stood perhaps five feet two, counting her fluffy pink slippers. I was expecting horror, the next stop in my tourism in hell. In fairness, she was simply plain fat. Trussed up in a black girdle and knickers some five sizes too small, she resembled a Chirkey roll.

Now, for those of you who aren't familiar with this icon of British cuisine, a Chirkey roll is a boneless mass of chicken and turkey which has been liquefied and reconstituted into a blob. Pallid and squidgy to the touch, Chirkies are scary.

So there I was, standing in the kitchen, wet and sweaty, with a Chirkey and the ghost of a squaddie.

"Hello, dear," said Trish. "Get here all right? Hungry?"

I said I had and that I wasn't.

"It's no trouble, really, Lol, I've made sandwiches for everyone. Crab paste – Mick's favourite. Since we were stationed in Oman, he's gone all foreign with the food. Me, I won't touch crab. All those legs and beady eyes. I wouldn't sleep. How about you, Lol? Mick says Pete told him you're all educated. I suppose you have crab all the time?"

I had the feeling that turning down the crab sandwiches would have been a social gaffe. I was plagued by the image of Mick having chemo and chatting with the soldier in the next bed.

The other soldier. "So how did the missus's shagging go?"

Mick. "Yeah, good, except for this toff who didn't touch a bit."

The other soldier. "What, the wanker didn't shag her?"

Mick. "Oh, he shagged her all right, but never laid a finger on the crab sarnies Trish took the trouble to prepare."

The other soldier. "What a cunt!"

I ate my sandwiches. The crab turned out to be Shipman's paste, the bread Mother's Pride with a good spread of marge, and the experience, I hope, never to be repeated.

I want to go back to Trish. Apart from the size issue, she was not unattractive and, indeed, had a kind, gentle face. She seemed a simple soul who would accept life as it came. Maternal by instinct, I expected her to perhaps darn my socks whilst I took her from behind. She fretted, in fact, that I was wet and could catch my death of cold, and seemed genuinely concerned that I would be cycling back in the rain. She clearly loved Mick, who in turn would absently touch her shoulder or get her something from a high shelf without being asked. Somehow, in the midst of a scene of total despair, of personal and collective abandon, of imminent death, I saw a beautiful relationship.

And then I had my epiphany. This was no brute wanting to see his wife humiliated by being offered to strangers for sex. This was a man who loved his wife and felt unmanned and grief-stricken that he couldn't fulfil what he saw as his matrimonial duties. And here was a woman who returned that love by helping him believe he could satisfy her, could still be a man, albeit by proxy. And why three of us? Because that way, he could give her more than any healthy husband ever could.

When the Caliph of Chelb, in the Al-Gharb (now Algarve in Portugal), took a wife from the Atlas Mountains, he hadn't bargained on her missing the snow that hung in the fields of her native village. She locked herself in a tower and sickened. The Caliph couldn't give her what came naturally – snow – so he planted thousands of almond trees all around the palace. Come spring they blossomed and carpeted the landscape with tiny white flowers and one sunlit day he entered her chamber, threw open the windows and proclaimed, "I bring you snow, my love."

The princess recovered.

Mick, the Caliph of Lower Clapton, had brought cock to Princess Trish. However, unlike the Moorish princess, I don't think Trish enjoyed his gift at all. She took it because she wanted her man to feel that he wasn't letting her down and to restore something of his manhood. He was trying to love her as he thought right and she in turn agreed to reciprocate that love.

Of all my adventures as a lover for hire, I have never had worse sex, never been so disturbed by the setting of the tryst and never been in the presence of such tenderness. It wasn't the rain that wet my face on the way home, but tears as I pondered the horror and mysterious beauty of it all. At twenty-four, I was beginning to realise that human relationships were far more complex than I had imagined.

Sandwiches and beers set out on a tray, we moved on and into the living room. My fellow fuckers were seated on the sofa watching some game show and smoking. I knew one from the parties Peter arranged. A Nigerian minicab driver with a stumpy cock, a stammer and bad acne. He had a cushy deal going on with Peter, whereby he ferried the single women from their homes to the designated location and got to join in. In essence, a swap of free rides.

The other guy was new to me. The Nigerian said he was Turkish, but as he spoke no English, I never got to know for sure. He formed part of the underground population of London, the people we overground dwellers rarely got to meet unless we went looking. Peter always went looking and knew a vast network of illegal immigrants or 'Undergrounders', as he called them. The name denoted not just their legal status but also the fact that a lot of them literally worked underground. These are the guys who peeled the onions in the basement cold stores of burger bars, who cleaned the subway and sewers at night, and worked in the sweatshops of Dalston.

Peter was their hero. A bridge between two worlds. He took them into the light and found them a pussy or two. In exchange, they brought him pistachios and spicy morsels from the old country and fucked his arse once his parents had gone to bed.

A sordid world? Maybe. At any rate, no more sordid than any other. These guys did what we all do. They made out as best they could. I remember one of them telling me his ploy to get a shag on Sunday afternoons, his only time off work. He would stand in Piccadilly Circus with a sign saying *Fuck me please*. He claimed never to have failed to have been slapped or to get a screw. Bereft of language or the time to form a relationship, he cut to the chase. Was he any different than I and my clever friends who wielded our wit and casual charm to do precisely the same thing?

The team ate their crab sandwiches and drank their beers watching TV. For all the world, we could have been a typical dysfunctional family having a night in round the telly.

There is a general protocol about where to sit in these situations. The lady tends to take the armchair with her man standing or crouched beside her and the sex invitees sit together on the sofa. At some point, the man will move and sit opposite, a signal that his wife is ready. Often the couple will retire for a few moments to another room, usually the bathroom. Here, any last requests and limitations are set out and agreed, and the couple kiss. Meanwhile, the sex recruits tend to sit quietly, men at arms calming themselves before battle. The husband then returns on his own and addresses the assembled men. He passes on the woman's requests, typically that she wants us one at a time or all together or that we can't come in her mouth but can on her tits. That sort of thing. Personally, I hate this phase. It's so mechanical. Like planning a holiday with an agenda for each day. Once the rules of engagement are established, the lady returns or lies waiting in the bedroom, as in this case. Mick appeared in the doorway.

"Trish is waiting, lads."

The Nigerian – who called himself Ben – and I shuffled past him to find Trish lying face down on the bed, looking for all the world like she was ready for a colonoscopy. The room was functional, a bed in a room with a built-in MFI teak-effect wardrobe with sliding doors lining one wall.

Mick promptly stripped and squatted on the only other piece of furniture, a chest of drawers. There he was, a skeleton with a shrivelled dick and no balls, sharing space with their wedding photo. It was a weird and poignant moment. He couldn't have been more than my age, a lad who had married young and signed up for service. The photo depicted a simple registry office ceremony, he in uniform, she in white, a squaddie friend and a girl school pal as witnesses. Did they have hope back then? What were their dreams? Did ambitions spin in their heads or were ambitions the right of others and theirs the duty to accept what came along? Either way, had the wizened crone of fairy tales crossed their path and warned that his balls would shrivel and men from strange lands would have sex with his bride, they would have dismissed her as another Clapton nutter.

Ben was a no-nonsense man with tidy habits. He always came and went first and always neatly folded his clothes. I could see his look of consternation as he searched the room for a chair to set his garments down. Anal sex with a stranger is one thing, but to him, having to put your clothes on the floor was downright gross.

"Put them on the shag pile; Trish vacuums every day," said Mick, pointing to the purple spaghetti carpet.

Shag pile. Very fitting, I thought, though Ben was clearly not at ease with this offer.

"Put them on the bed, dear. I don't move about much," said Trish, voice muffled by the pink quilted bed cover.

Good old Trish, always the thoughtful one. Ben finally set his kit down, and climbing onto the saggy mattress, tried to get his cock in her mouth. Meanwhile, I stripped off and began to run my hands up her legs.

It is a tribute to youth that even this most unerotic of scenes didn't deter my erection. I have on occasion talked to my cock, though never claimed to have had a reply. Should my dick ever find his voice, I imagine our conversations would be brief.

"Hello, my old cock, this is going to be tough."

"Has she got a cunt?"

"Yes."

"So let's do it!"

I continued my ascent up Trish's legs, stroking and gently scratching her inner thighs. Meanwhile, Ben was still trying to get the tip of his cock in her mouth, a clear impossibility. His efforts were rather like watching a three-legged sausage dog try and mount a seated Labrador.

I had by now reached what with other women would be the crotch of their panties. In the case of Trish, all my fingers found were compressed folds of fat. I tried to lever them apart as one might the rubber flaps on a subway door. It was an impossible task, akin to parting suet with chopsticks. I gave up and moved to plan B, the removal of her pants.

Later on in life, I spent a winter skiing wearing Lycra trousers, borrowed from a girl two sizes smaller than me. I remember a freezing afternoon when I struggled for what seemed like hours trying to get the damn thing off to crap. My efforts with Trish's pants were no easier. She must have put them on when she was twelve and let her body grow inside until surgically bonded. The whole thing seemed to be turning into more of an autopsy than a fuck, and if we were to complete our mission, drastic action needed to be taken. We would have to turn Trish over.

Now, turning a woman over with her participation is easy, but when they play dead and have been bulked up on a Lower Clapton diet which offers battered Mars bars as the menu's healthy option, it's well-nigh impossible. Mick shouted out encouragement as Ben and I set to work.

"Come on, lads, put your backs into it."

We pushed.

"Work as a team. You're only as strong as yer mate. One for all."

Years of listening to the sergeant major were finally being put to good use and the battle of the bulge was turning our way.

With Trish on her back, the sex began in earnest. I would like to say I now played a part in a torrid classic of abandon and overpowering lust, and if this was a work of fiction then, sure, it would be my pleasure. Unfortunately, Trish remained as passive and uninvolved as before. I briefly tried the steamy romantic stuff, nibbling her ears, caressing her nipples. No response. I switched to dirty talk but quickly closed that line down when Mick said, "Steady on, Lol, that's my wife you've got there."

Ben was a perfunctory performer at the best of times, and faced with such passivity, his approach was probably the best. Don't get me wrong, passivity can be electrifying. There are women who yield to you, silently saying, "Do what you want with me, I am but a rag doll in your hands."

They are passive, but their passivity is a ploy to enhance the 'active' in their lover, and their responsiveness, their moans and climaxes, pay testament to their desire and involvement.

Trish was the other kind of passive. Her libido was simply absent. She clearly was as indifferent to the sex as a mother might be indifferent to a soiled nappy.

Again, a memory comes to mind. My gran, whom I loved to bits, hadn't been to the cinema in thirty years. I invited her to some art classic at the Screen on the Green.

Within minutes, she was asleep. As the credits rolled up, I gently nudged her. She woke and said, "Very nice, dear. Thank you."

What my gran and the cinema, and Trish and the sex had in common, apart from them both being absent from events, is that they both found a parallel fulfilment. My agenda was to see the film, my gran's, to please me. With Trish my agenda was to have hot sex and blow her mind. Hers was to bring ease to a dying husband by consenting to an intimacy by proxy.

Trish was the kind of woman that my feminist friends from Stokey would have set out to save, to empower. To them, lying on your back whilst strangers are paid to fuck you, watched by your husband, was demeaning, a textbook example of sexual exploitation. What they didn't perhaps understand is that actions are interpreted uniquely by each and every one of us and it's the interpretation we give them that counts. Trish was in no way fazed by events. She saw men as silly boys who spilled things, got into trouble and needed to empty their balls. She knew her husband loved her, and she loved him back.

Anyway, I followed Ben's lead and fucked Trish in the missionary position, kissed her on the forehead, told her she was a kind and lovely lady, and went in search of the Turk.

He had remained watching TV and fallen asleep, lulled by a documentary on mortgage rates in a language he didn't understand. I went and woke him, pointed to my still swollen cock and the bedroom door. He grinned, nodded and followed me back in.

His efforts with Trish are not noteworthy except the following. He never took his clothes off and he ejaculated prematurely. Unfortunately for Ben, Trish had by now been hauled into a position which had brought her cunt perilously close to his folded clothes. As Ben watched powerless, a prolonged jet of cum arched straight for his shirt. Ben was visibly in a state of shock.

I know those moments. I was once sitting at home reading by the fire when I heard the clear sound of someone pissing outside my door. I went to see and, sure enough, a complete stranger was spraying away. Big mistake opening the door, as the stream destined for painted wood ends up on your trousers. When I asked him what the fuck he was doing, he replied, "Sorry, mate, I thought a friend lived here."

So left field was the experience and comment that I said, "OK," and shut the door. Only later did I come to my senses and chase him down the street. Ben's response was identical: stunned immobility. This made matters far worse. The Turk, seeing that spraying the shirt with cum evoked no reaction, must have assumed that the garment was there for cleaning up and proceeded to wipe his knob on the sleeve.

"Wa-wa-what yu-yu-you doin? Tha-tha-that's meh-meh-my sh-sh-shirt yu-you cu-cu-cunt."

Good old Trish came to the rescue.

"It's only cum, Ben. It's still fresh and will come off in a jiffy. When Mick still came, it rinsed off the sheets in no time. Mind you, I've never tried cleaning Turkish cum. Don't suppose there's much difference, though I once had a spicy ketchup stain, and it was a devil to clean. Don't know what they put in it. The normal stuff only needs a soak in Biotex."

Corseted Trish proceeded to gather up the shirt and disappear to the kitchen, leaving us four men alone in the bedroom. Mick, still at his command post on the chest of drawers, seemed to feel a duty to address the troops.

"Thanks, lads. Mission accomplished. No casualties," adding between uncontrollable laughter, "except a shirt wounded in action."

The Turk returned his cock to his trousers, Ben slowly and meticulously dressed, pending his shirt, and I followed Trish into the kitchen.

She was bent over the sink. I stood behind her. I felt horny and cupping her breasts, entered her again.

Trish stopped rinsing and her voice took on a serious tone: "Don't get me wrong, Lol, you're a nice boy and fit, but I'm a married woman and I don't cheat on Mick. I'm sure there are lots of girls who fancy you."

Trish was right. I wasn't here as an alternative to Mick; I was here *as* Mick. I pulled out, kissed her gently on the shoulder and told her that she and Mick were lucky to have each other. I dressed, shook hands with Mick, told shirtless Ben I would doubtless see him soon, and left.

The Turk had already gone, and I found him standing outside looking lost. He saw me and handed me a scrap of paper with the name of an underground stop. In silence we walked together until we saw the station. I wonder what he thought of England? A strange place, I imagine, where men fuck each other's wives and shirts are used as cum rags.

I cycled home in the rain thinking about this latest entrance. On the face of it, it had been gross. But I didn't feel in any way disgusted with myself or diminished. I was on a mission to explore the underbelly of sex. Sometimes that would lead me into experiences which were thrilling and pleasurable. But that was secondary. What I was after was the truth, the feeding of my fascination with life. That took me to dizzy heights, but also to unfathomable depths. It also showed me that sometimes the real horror is found in those heights and true beauty in the depths.

At times I came to conclusions, felt I had a handle on human nature and the scheme of things. But as my adventures continued, I became increasingly aware that the only thing I could be certain of was that there were no correct answers, just experiences which shaped me. If there was to be some kind of revelation then it would be found in what I would become; in me.

I once went walking in the Himalayas with Patrick Bintz, a French photographer and intellectual who went on to become Curator of Sculpture at the Louvre. He didn't use his camera and I asked him why.

He paused and, placing his rucksack against a Mangrove tree, pondered my question whilst eating an apple. When his answer finally came, it helped shape my life thereafter.

"If you use a camera, you are putting something between you and what you wish to see. The relationship is no longer direct and the bond of seen and seeing is broken." Another bite of the apple. "Some things are too powerful and can only be photographed with our eyes. If we use a camera, we believe we can always see what we are looking at later and never fully see it at the time," he said and crouched down to plant the apple core in a hole he had been carelessly making with his boot.

"But what about having something to remember them by – a photo?" I asked.

"Memories become printed on us. If you really look, really feel, they are there as part of you, of the way you think and are. Experiences are not to be collected in albums; they are the building blocks from which we are made."

And with that he shouldered his sack, wiped his glasses, and we began our slow ascent to the icy frontier plateau which would take us into Tibet.

It has taken me thirty years to write about my days of sex for sale. Until now I never felt the need. I wrote the stories into the fabric of my life. They became part of me and to that extent, have been told a thousand times through my daily actions. Like the dancer who never loses his posture, I am imprinted with them.

So why write now?

I'll tell you, but not just yet.

# Cockenomics

My grandparents on my father's side, ghetto Jews from Prague, were exterminated in Auschwitz.

There must have been a particular moment, anonymous and ignored, in the line which stretched from acceptance of the Jews to their annihilation; a singularity which, with hindsight, was the turning point. A glint, if you will, in the über-eye which tells the keen observer that the zeitgeist is on the move. Perhaps a brick through the window or daubed insults on the door? I think not. Something more subtle. An unsettled bill, perhaps, the whisper of a shout to come that 'those marked out to die need not be paid.' If only they had left. All money is small change compared with life itself.

My graduation day. Champers and Vivaldi on the lawn. Amateur dramatics without the drama.

Mere mortals have to go for job interviews or thank an aunt for slippers they would rather walk across hot coals than wear. The Master of the college had it worse. He had to speak to parents. Imagine all the mums and dads of all these newly-weds to life, and he the best man. A bookworm with no book: libraries, libraries everywhere without a word to chew.

No scholar lacks patience. Knowledge needs to be winkled out. But patience has its limits. Maybe one dorkish son too many, some good-for-nothing that had to get his allotted, "Best luck, old chap." Maybe something silly; braces strung too tight, or a rival's crushing comment at high table. Who knows or cares. The fact is, the Master cracked.

Some gushy mum had him cornered, his back to the trestle table, all exits barred, his nod and smile on autopilot. But he was a professional. He stayed on script.

"So tell me, Mrs Perkins, what has David in mind to do?"

"Management. We're thrilled. He's joining Unilever. He starts next month."

He took her hand; he leant a little closer. And then he said it. The stuff of legend. The reason why, if for nothing else, Cambridge paid its way.

"I am so sorry."

No explosion; no human debris on the lawn. His was a time bomb so silent and unexpected that she thanked him, her mind incapable of processing in real time the meaning of his words.

'I am so sorry' is my marker. My flag in world A. The old world where commerce was not quite right, a joke too blue; not the done thing.

We move on. The 3rd of March 1985. The end of the miners' strike. My second flag. World B. The free market's defining victory.

But where's the singularity? What, with hindsight, was the turning point? Though hard to find, they are innumerable, singular only inasmuch as unique to each of us. Here's mine.

I was at the pub, The Earl of Lonsdale, where incidentally Jonny and the other rotten Pistols used to drink. Martin Stone, Alistair Townley and me. Three lads, all friends. Alistair spotted a guy he knew, who joined our table in the garden. Usual chit-chat, jokes to break the ice and test this guy. Dog bum sniffing for intellectuals.

Martin talked about his day, how he was writing a play, almost finished.

"So is there much money in writing, then?" This from the new guy.

That's it. That's my singularity. My unpaid bill. Not the harbinger of death camps but of another form of genocide, one that leaves bodies standing but something of your soul buried in the communal grave of lost society. Six months before, he might have asked what the play was about, even asked to read it. Now he weighed it with a trader's eye. A new bull market perhaps, or a lousy bear best hibernated?

1980 was a good year for orgies. The heavenly bodies were in unique alignment. Syphilis and gonorrhoea were on the run, mere irritations, even badges of honour, the scabs our battle scars. Our only worry was how we would last the ten-day antibiotic's course without a pint of beer. Herpes was too mythological to give concern and the first case of AIDS in the UK wasn't to break for another year – and then the guy was gay and an American on holiday, so not one of us. 1980, a window of opportunity in a wall of pestilence.

But the flourishing of orgies can't just be explained by antibiotics. Sex has never bowed its head just to the fear of death. No, the orgy was a symbol of belonging to world B as surely as wide collars, loud jackets, power shoulders and big hair.

Orgies are quantifiable, something which can be summed and compared as easily as a city bonus, size of car or height of shoulder pad. He had one in his bed, there were ten of us. I am five times the better man. That kind of nonsense. Cockenomics.

I have not seen eternity in a grain of sand, but I have seen society in a mound of butt cheeks. Or, more precisely, the tell-tale signs that Britain was once again turning in the widening gyre, destination not war but the plug-hole. Follow me and I will take you down the drain.

Four weeks had gone past since I played schoolboy to Lady Trocknell's madam. The sex had been heady, the kind that gives you unsolicited flashbacks in the groin. I rang Peter.

"Hello, Laurence. What a nice surprise. Sweet that you could find the time to ring old Peter. Rang to book a massage? Seen the light? I expect I can fit you in."

"In your wet dreams, Peter. No, I was just wondering if you had anything else for me."

"Ah, got the bug, have you! Let me guess which you most preferred. Lady Trocknell?"

"Of course! Amazing!"

I proceeded to reminisce with Peter, adding details passed over in the first telling. After all, if you can't wander down memory lane with your pimp, with whom can you?

"That's nice. Sounds like you both enjoyed yourselves. Nothing wrong in that. We're not here forever. Did I tell you my doctor died?"

"No."

"Well, he did. Fell off my neighbour's roof. Doing Mrs Willows a good turn, he was, fixing her slates on his day off. Next thing you know, he's on the patio. She was well shook-up, I can tell you. She came banging on my door. Bit close that was. I had a client on the table and was up to his nuts in cock. Well upsetting. Gave him his money back, of course. You still there, Laurence? Haven't bored you to death, have I?"

"Listening to every word. Go on, please. Tell me what happened."

"Well, I went round. You've got to, haven't you. She wouldn't go in the garden, just waved her stick at the back door. Said she had seen enough bad things in the Blitz. I comforted her as best I could. The bloke was well dead. His brains were all over the place. Still, it's all part of us. Brains, I mean. Odd thing, though, his glasses hadn't broken. Anyway, you don't want to hear all this."

"Peter, I absolutely want to hear about it. I love stories!"

"Well, OK, but only 'cause you asked. So, where was I? Oh, yeah. I told her he looked peaceful and had died doing something good. Something like that. She had cooked his tea – gammon and eggs – and said that I should have it. Said he would have liked that. I suppose I should have rung the police first, but the eggs were getting cold.

"I was almost done, just mopping up the juice and – would you believe it? – the neighbour on the other side came round. Asked us if we knew that there was a bloke lying in the garden who looked like Dr Jacobs and didn't seem quite right. People round here are so daft! Mrs Willows put the kettle on for tea. She was all sixes and sevens and set a cup for Dr Jacobs. I nipped back home and got the biscuits. Hobnobs.

"The coppers had rolled up when I got back. Mrs Willows said that had she known there would be guests, she would have dressed up proper. Fixed her hair. As though it mattered! We all said not to worry, that the garden looked a treat. That sort of thing. Funeral's next week. Sorry, Laurence, I guess I've rattled on too long as usual."

"Not at all! As I said, I love your stories. They are so real. An antidote to Proust."

"Who's Proust, then, a mate of yours?"

"He wrote a book I'm reading. *Remembrance of Things Past*."

"We could all write one of those. Things past my ring-piece would be mine." He chuckled.

Peter never laughed. The underlying sadness of his life would stifle any laugh mid-throat.

"So, anything on the horizon? Another Lady Trocknell would be nice!"

"How about an orgy? Ever been to one?"

"No, can't say I have, but I fancy the idea."

"Right then. Your first orgy. Makes me proud, that does. Me being the one to sort you out. I'll tell ya. No mistake. However many you have, you'll never forget your first." He proceeded to give me the details, said he would see me there, and that was that.

The Barbican at night. Weird place. Made me feel uncomfortable. A colony for the filthy rich who never seem to come and go. Perhaps they teleport to work or have a high speed tunnel link, each in their own Plexi-pod, whooshing on rubber wheels beneath our feet. Plazas sized to hold the whole of Aristotle's Athens without so much as a dog turd. Modules, sold as homes, piled high: cryogenic storage for the living.

The place reminded me of an abandoned space station. You know the kind. Lost in deep space. The hero and a crew of stellar misfits pick up the mayday beacon. They dock and board. The camera dolly tracks down low-lit corridors, doors hiss, the plasma-maxthon drive humming to eternity. More hissing doors and slo-mo panning until they find the mainframe. It powers up. Some high-tech whirring and then the voice.

"Starship 69785, year of the Barbican 1980. I am a model XZ-847 Quantum Infinitron, but you can call me MOTHER. Your bio-stats do not register with my database. State your purpose."

The voice is always female. Calm. Aural Prozac.

"I am an earthling, here to fuck."

"Failure to compute. What is fucking?"

"It's a human thing. Don't worry your pretty chips about it."

"Am I pretty? Will you dream of me?"

My reverie was interrupted by Peter, who tapped me on the shoulder.

"Where you gone, son, somewhere far away?"

"Deep space, mate, just chatting with Mother."

"Oh. Fair enough. Ready for some shagging?"

"Ready."

"Peter! How nice to see you. And this must be the young man we've heard so much about. Larry, isn't it?"

"Laurence."

"Come in. Come in. Welcome to our little gathering."

Our host was middle-aged with short blond hair, unreasonably white teeth and cultured skin. By this, I do not mean that his skin was an habitué at opera houses or knew the manager of the George V hotel by name. I mean that it looked like it had been grown in a lab. It was just too flawless, too featureless. Or maybe something synthetic, a petroleum derivative he'd traded so long it had enveloped him.

When stoned, I have sometimes poured polyurethane from tin to tin just to watch it flow. Its consistency is mesmerising. Thinner and it would break up, making droplets. More viscous, and it would belch. Polyurethane glides, the varnish world's equivalent of Michael Jackson's moonwalk. Anyway, this guy looked like he had been dipped in the stuff. Plasticised to a faultless finish. I could tell; he wore nothing but a Rolex.

He took an envelope from the hall table and handed it to Peter.

"As agreed."

"Oh, no rush. Thanks, George."

Peter never took a cut and, passing the envelope to me, started to unzip his windbreaker. George edged forward and put a hand on the door handle. Even his armpits were hairless.

"As I said, Peter, lovely to see you. Regards to the wife. Speak soon."

Peter got the message. "Right then. I wasn't going to stay, just see young Laurence settled."

"I'll be all right, Peter," I said, not wanting to see his humiliation prolonged. "I'll call you when I'm home."

Peter held his hand out to George, who took it as one might the loaded nappy of a stranger's child.

"I'm not married."

"Well, regards to your lady friend."

"I'm gay."

"Details, Peter. One has to see the big picture. You've delivered. The client has paid. Time to move on, don't you think?"

Peter left. George wiped his hand on a towel pulled from a passing girl. Off set, the smile retracted.

He had hurt a gentle man, a friend of sorts. Before the night was out, I would have my revenge.

We were ten in all, not counting the Spanish maid. Five men. Five women. I was the only one with any clothes on. Being clothed in a room of naked people is as embarrassing as the other way round. That's what X, née Twitter, now preys on: fear of being marginalised. Being in the buff was trending and I was missing out. I stripped.

So let me make the introductions. George, you have already met. Here's Simon, he works for George. Merchant banking. Tanned head to foot, the hallmark that his beach and yacht were private. He was cutting coke with a platinum Amex card and holding forth.

"I told him, if you haven't got the stomach, don't play in the killing fields. Fucking pussy. Speaking of which, how's my wife? Good head?"

The chap whose ear he had was Colin, Bo-Bo to his friends. A mergers and acquisitions man. Hairy as an ape. The wife in question, Samantha, was sucking on his cock.

In gangster movies there's always a scene of the capo having his shoes shined. Between puffs on his cigar, he gives orders to his second in command. Kill so-and-so, persuade a schmuck to pay, gangster stuff. In this version, a guy bursts in and passes on a message. The capo, ever the man of action, springs to his feet. Black polish smears his patent white spats. He kicks the shoe-shine boy and wipes the polish off on his face. A stooge peels a bill or two. They leave.

Samantha was a cock-shine girl. Ignored, paid not to listen. Polishing off the grime from shafting clients.

Suddenly, she sat up and rummaged around in her mouth.

"What the fuck are you doing, woman?"

"I've lost my gum. I must have swallowed it."

"Lost your gum! Lost your mind, more like!"

And then I saw it. We all did. Peeking out, trapped under Bo-Bo's foreskin.

"God in heaven, woman! Well, don't just sit there. Take the bloody thing off him."

Samantha retrieved the gum. "Sorry, Simon."

"It's Bo-Bo you should be apologising to… Samantha, for fuck's sake! Don't put the gum back in your mouth. Throw the bloody thing away."

"Sorry, Simon. Sorry, Bo-Bo."

Let's move on.

George's trophy, Marcia, and Bo-Bo's wife, Labby (from Labinia, I imagine), were in a heated conversation about a pair of chairs.

"Darling, everyone's demanding I tell them where they came from. But I won't! They're my little secret."

"That's so unfair, Marcy. Who was it that tipped you off when those Armani jeans came in? Meany Meany Meany Marcy."

"Oh, very well, but you must promise to tell no one. Especially that bitch, Antonia."

"Cross my heart."

"Cognoscenti on the King's Road. Frederico kept them especially for me! He's such a darling."

The chairs in question were unfathomable, not in their composition, but in their appeal. Who would design and make such things? I speculated that a plastic surgeon had somehow convinced Dalí to start the project, fallen out with that glorious madman and passed the work to Tinguely. He in turn had left, disgusted with the job, which ended up being finished by a bouncy castle manufacturer.

The seats, of stainless steel, were shaped as woman's arses. The arms were, well, arms, human arms. Not real, just replicas, complete with hands. The backs were his and hers, inflatable pink plastic, one embossed with breasts, the other penises. The contraptions were sat on Perspex boxes filled with money.

"Marcy! They're to die for!"

Marcy called the maid, who was serving drinks. "Maria. Give me some money."

Maria set her tray down and, retrieving a little crochet purse from her pocket, offered up a fiver.

"I sorry, Mrs Pilchard. I no have more."

Marcy took the bill and waved to me.

"Can you be a darling and pop this note into the chair? Either one will do. You'll find the hole."

I did her bidding and, sure enough, saw that the stainless steel bums came complete with arseholes. Which to choose? I picked at random. The contraption came to life. The back lit up. An air pump hummed, and the plastic cocks engorged. As grand finale, a voice from somewhere in its innards pronounced: "Money loves you, baby."

Labby removed her hand from Marcia's cunt and applauded.

"Wonderful. Wonderful. Bo-Bo, have you seen the chairs?"

Bo-Bo was snorting coke off Samantha's breasts, so not the attentive husband.

The maid was hovering, trying to get Marcia's attention.

"Mrs Pilchard?"

"Yes, what now?"

"The money, I have it back, please?"

"Really, Maria, how could you? Don't be such a bore. Now run along and get me a G and T."

I was intrigued. How far did this madness go?

"Great, Marcia. Out of interest, what does the other chair say?"

"Feed the need."

You know me, so that leaves three. Clarissa, Sabrina and Roland.

Clarissa was my reason for being there. Her husband, the boss of bosses, couldn't make it. I was the temp, I 'filled in' for him. Clarissa was nobility. Not the highest drawer, just enough to make her acquisition a useful back to tread on in his climb up to the top.

Abuse, like any sickness, has its phases. It starts with incredulity. How could he be so cruel? Then sadness and despair as the diagnosis is confirmed. A spell or two of anger, the patient's brave fight back. Then resignation and the chronic phase, the learning to live with an incapacity for happiness.

She was barely older than I was. Where the others let it all hang out, spilling their personalities across the room, she was contained, folded inwards. The victim's pose: nowhere to hide but in yourself. I wandered over and said, "Hello."

Like a dog, trained by beatings to roll over when their master touches the buckle of the belt, she assumed the position. Mouth open, eyes lowered, legs spread.

"I thought we might just talk," I said.

"Oh, no! George would tell my husband; he wouldn't like that. Best if we just do it."

"It's OK. What's your name?"

She paused as though trying to remember. "Clarissa. Can we fuck now?"

"Nice name, crisp but spicy."

"I shouldn't… thank you. I really ought to fuck. I must fuck everyone, or he will call me frigid. I need to be home by ten; he doesn't like me out late."

Should I have her, add to her shame, or say no and conspire to give her husband a reason to punish her? And what had Peter said? Don't get involved; don't let the work get in your head.

I mounted her. I was very gentle. What am I saying? 'Very gentle', as though I was being kind, showing compassion. No, gentle or rough, I shouldn't have fucked her.

I climaxed. She folded closed again.

"You should go now."

I leant forward. I should have said, "And you, Clarissa, should leave your husband." Instead, I said, "OK," and guzzled a gin and tonic snatched from Maria's tray.

At the time I felt unbridled, empowered. Now, looking back, I cringe and hang my head in shame. An invisible line had been crossed.

Sabrina and Roland were in marketing. Not quite. Sabby was in marketing and Roland in whatever his wife was in. She was squatting on the coffee table peeing into the ice bucket. George was timing her piss on his Rolex.

"Damn you, Sabby. One minute eleven seconds. Another thousand quid pissed away! Oh, that's fucking good! Pissed away! Attention, everyone, I've got a funny for you."

Paying attention to another human being was not the strong point of the assembled company, but there was always the chance that George would make a fool of himself; his fall, their rise.

"Sabby bet me a oner she could piss for a full minute, and she went the distance. Now, here's the funny part. I then said, that's another thousand pissed away!"

Some smiles and maybe he would have raised a laugh, but Bo-Bo's belch on climaxing in Samantha stole the show.

Maria cleared away the urine bucket.

Roland was the odd one out, a genuine human being who found himself stranded with no way back. I later learnt from Peter that they had married young. They were at uni together, he read engineering, she marketing, and Sabrina had him *encoñado*, which literally translated means 'cunted', enthralled (in the original meaning of the word) by cunt. Latinos have the Saxons beat when it comes to the vocabulary of human weakness. Carlo Levi was spot on in *Christ Stopped at Eboli* when he explained that Catholicism isn't embraced because the Italians shun the flesh, but rather because they are so venal and are making a hopeless attempt to keep their lust at bay. Scientists are easy prey for predatory women. Odd, that. One would think that with such analytic rigour, such impartiality, they would do the numbers.

In September 1980, the female population of the world was 2,491,760,901. Strip out the under-aged and elderly and we're left with a billion active pussies, give or take a lip or two. My guess is that, at the same time, disposable lighters which were beginning to replace the Zippos and Ronsons barely nudged the 10 million. Therefore, women were one hundred times more abundant. I don't remember my first lighter, but I certainly never thought I would never have another. The same, of course, is true when selecting a male.

The appeal was clear from Sabby's side. Roland was rich. I've made up a limerick about her:

> There once was a girl called Sabrina
> Whose mouth could not have been keener.
> She sucked his slide rule,
> Till covered in drool,
> And took the poor sod to the cleaners.

Anyway, she humped him all the way to the altar, gave herself an heir and proceeded to do as she pleased. On this evening, that meant fucking the four of us, all at the same time.

The mechanics and logistics of a four-to-one are complex. Those circus families who form human pyramids on top of monocycles whilst juggling balls would be rather good at it. Three egomaniacs from the city who thought teamwork was for losers and a lad who had never gone beyond a threesome were not.

It's all about timing, working together and protocol. There is a hierarchy of hole which must be respected. The top honcho gets the asshole, the next in the pecking order, the mouth. The third man, her pussy, and at the bottom of the food chain, a hand-job.

Please note that mouth beats pussy. This may seem odd. As adolescents we were drilled in the 'bases' and every schoolboy knew that the holy of holies, or spunktum spunktorium, as a juvenile friend in fifth form called it, was the cunt. Indeed, I recall many a Q&A session with my mates where we would ask 'did she let you shag her?', and get a 'no, *only* a blow job'. I rest my case.

So, how come mouth had jostled pussy into third place? The answer, of course, is that good old-fashioned coitus is just too natural. And nature, by 1980, was on the run. Pussy hairs were falling in their millions, felled by the blade or scalded to death with hot wax. The very language of sex was under siege. Where D.H. Lawrence's gamekeeper had appreciated the earthy natural functions of Lady Chatterley's cunt and arse, we now spit-roasted the MILF (a threesome with a Mother I'd Like to Fuck), DP'd the BL (Double Penetrated the Barely Legal), and my favourite, ATM (Ass To Mouth). There is no greater proof of the nascent power of the financial services sector than the naming of a sexual practice after a cash-dispensing machine. And not just any old practice, but one that summarised the whole financial game as it would become: shaft the client up the arse, then make him clean the proof away.

The aboriginal male, on returning from a hunting trip to his homelands, fucks the earth. The merchant banker, after preying on injured and elderly companies, fucks the cash machine. Not all of them, but enough to bring us down.

So back to holes. Let's summarise. Arseholes win because they are the least natural entry point. Mouths come second, pussies third. Hands were joint fourth. The pussy is fighting back, though. Whilst the hair has gone, ornaments, more associated with the face, adorn the lips and clitoris. A work in progress, who knows where it will end. Future generations of pussy may learn to smile, even talk, inviting men back in.

Imagine the testosterone. Three city swinging dicks, a sex-crazed youth and Sabrina, man enough for all. George came out on top and took the ass. It was his flat, and equity always trumps. Bo-Bo was our anchor man, which means he got the cunt, taken supine from below. You need someone to steady the ship. And then a boardroom coup! I was assigned her mouth. I guessed this was a reprimand to Simon for failing to meet profit targets at work. Remember, George was his boss. Whatever the reason, Simon got the hand.

Then the fun started.

You know that old coordination challenge where you have to pat your head whilst moving your hand clockwise over your stomach? Well, add working a cocktail shaker and blowing up a balloon. Tricky, isn't it?

First the woman mounts the anchor man striding his waist. She then leans forward and takes it up the ass. Mouth comes next. Once balanced, she risks raising a hand to grab the last of the cocks. So far, so good.

But now the trouble starts. To work the cock in her cunt, she has to rise and fall. This throws the sodomy off-line. Imagine trying to open your back door with the key between your legs and the lock on the move.

Let's suppose the banker assigned the butt builds up a head of steam and pounds away. The woman is propelled forward, and the fellatio becomes a-rhythmic. Meanwhile, the hand-job, under ordinary circumstances a walk in the park, becomes well-nigh impossible to keep on tempo, leaving the cock in question as likely to suffer permanent deformity as an ejaculation.

Help was at hand. Labby and Marcia had become bored with licking each other's pussies and had elected themselves cheerleaders.

"And... cunt, ass, mouth, cunt, ass, mouth. That's it. Cunt, ass, mouth. Keep the beat. Come on, Maria, your people like music, clap along!"

"I not know this song, Mrs Pilchard. I wash plates please."

Enough said. Let's fast forward to the money shots (there's another one for the financial lexicon of sex). One by one, the bankers came and like sated ticks, rolled off their bitch.

I have some self-esteem. Not much, enough to see me through. So I would like to report that I couldn't come. With some jobs, honour is derived from failing to perform, from not opening the gas valve, from not joining in the witch hunt's chorus. I would like to say that in that trader's pit, my cock withered, that even my sexual instincts couldn't blot out the smell of greed and simple inhumanity.

I can't. I came. Eyes and mouth hard set. I came and in abundance. I am no Odysseus. I answered the siren's call.

That's when I knew they would win. That the rusty moral compass would be discarded, ousted by the collective validation that greed was good, that doing what you want, taking what you could, was not just acceptable but admired. An autobahn to hell was being built and we were all to get free cars.

More coke, more booze, threesomes, foursomes, allsomes, anal beads and plugs, more booze, dildos, gags, more coke, more… everything.

So, what of Roland? Shortly after I arrived, he skulked off. I found him watching TV in the maid's room. Maria had made him Horlicks. He was sitting on the edge of her single bed, cup in hand, wearing his underpants and socks.

"Oh, hello. Yes, well, I'll be out in a minute. Just watching the news."

The good old BBC was doing a piece on the Queen's recent visit to Botswana. She was attending a show of tribal dancing in the company of President Quett Masire. The establishment soldiered on, oblivious of the waking kraken.

"Oh no, I haven't been told to summon you. Just thought I'd say hello."

We sat and chatted on the bed. Good bloke. He had the enjoyable vagueness of the truly clever: those that know that truth can't be pinned down. I can't remember how the conversation went, but at some point, we got onto the matter of the chairs.

"Have you seen the chairs?" he asked.

"Yes. Ridiculous."

"My view entirely. The pneumatics are all wrong. They went to the trouble of installing separate lines to each of those things, the willies and boobs, so a puncture would be isolated, but no escape valve. If the sensor beams in the holes got jammed by something, the pressure would just keep building up. Nothing to stop it, you see."

Interesting.

Orgies should be exciting, mind-blowing, in fact, a multiplier of pleasure. On occasion they are, believe me. But all multipliers only enhance the essence of the single. Multiply a pile of shit by ten and you get a bigger pile of shit. Infinitely multiply a bankrupt sexuality and you still get zero.

In fact, it's even worse because there's greater expectation. You know what I mean. The gawky, dim bank attendant in a suit and tie becomes even gawkier, dimmer because of his attire. Birthdays are another one. The onus to have fun. The accentuated sadness when we don't.

We've reached it. The bottom of the drain.

We think we're spiralling upwards, each heady spin more encompassing. But we forget the world is upside down, our destination not the heavens above but a crashing down to earth.

There you have it: cockenomics, that pseudo-science that makes donkeys out of all of us. Simple. Let them eat the carrot as and when but replace it with a bigger one each time. Of course, the donkey dies, blown apart by the methane he's ingested. But who gives a shit; we'll sell his bones for glue.

By ten-thirty the guests were done. Spent and drugged, they milled about gathering their clothes and wallets. I looked for Samantha's chewing gum and pocketed it for later.

One more thing to do. Find Marcia. I was all smiles and admiration.

"The chairs, they're so wonderful. Do you mind if I ask how much they cost?"

"Thirty thousand. Each."

"A bargain, as I'm sure you know. Such a brilliant choice. May I try again? Feed the mouths some cash?"

"Of course. Listen, everyone, Laurence is going to feed the chairs."

The assembled crew, half-pissed, full gone, were easy to amuse and watched as I fed alternating chairs my fee from George.

I had been chewing Samantha's gum, palmed it and broke it into two. My economics teacher at school had taught me card manipulation. My next trick was child's play.

I slid the gum to the edge of the bill and as I dropped it in, plugged the sensor beam that triggered the chair's devices. Chair two, the same again.

It didn't take long for the first penis to burst. Pop! In the place of an erection, a sorry strip of vinyl, twitching in the air pump's breeze. And then a boob, swelling dangerously. A second pop. A freaky psychotic film with 'money loves you' and 'feed the need' as soundtrack on a never-ending loop.

I let myself out before the last cock popped, payback for Peter sorted.

What a night! I felt deranged. Pumped up as any chair and utterly confused. The sometimes nifty insights I've strung together came much later. Back then I just did the stuff, driven by a thirst for knowledge and kicks. I felt alive, something not to be confused with happy, and I didn't want to go home to join my other life just yet.

Maria was waiting at the bus stop. She had left with the first cock-pop. How would she react? She had seen it all. What did she think of me?

At first, we sat in silence. I felt increasingly ill at ease. Again, a film analogy. The woman witnesses a murder and sees the killer's face. He looks up, hands still bloody, and sees she's seen. She runs. He follows. She gets away this time. They meet again by chance, but the place is too public to take her out. They stand silently, sharing the knowledge of what's been done and seen.

"You funny. The chairs. Puff," she said, accompanied by her hand uncurling, her fingers spanning out. "Good thing. Bad people."

I laughed. She laughed. We laughed until we cried.

"You talk to nice man. I make him hot drink. You… different. Why you go to this bad place?"

"I like to learn things. Good or bad."

"This very bad. Bad people, bad things they use. Even bad *kiki*."

"*Kiki*?"

"How you say… six?"

"Six? Oh, sex!"

"Sex. Yes. No *alma*, no *duende*."

"*Alma*?"

"How you say? Soul."

"And *duende*?"

"Heart, not heart. Near heart."

I was lost. "Lungs?"

"No. Stupid person, *espíritu*."

"Ahh, no spirit. Yes, you are right."

We lapsed back into silence. A different one this time. Much better. She spoke first. She had come to a decision.

"I show you six, sex, with – how you say? – soul and *espíritu*."

Now that was unexpected!

"I'm your man for that!"

"You not my man. I have man back in Burgos. José Manuel. *Mi prometido*. I show you anyway."

We chatted on the bus. She wanted to study medicine and had come over to find work, make money. Her English was poor. The bars and restaurants had found this an inconvenience. The Pilchards saw her inability to understand and possibly repeat their shady deals a plus. So what if she saw the sex? They had no shame. A sex scandal would be good for business, but being caught for fraud would not.

She missed her hometown. Said the food in England was disgusting, that we ate *porquería*, rubbish fit only for pigs. She talked about her family, life post-Franco, how cold and dark London had been that past winter.

A half hour or so and we reached our destination. A small café bar in Paddington. El Rincón de Juan. The place was packed and noisy. We ordered San Miguel and had a grilled squid tapa. The chairs had taken all my money, so she paid. Her paying carried no significance. She neither sought nor gained power. I had none and she had some. In her world, money still knew its place.

An area of floor had been cleared of tables and a stage set down. Just chipboard. Two chairs were placed at the back. A guitar rested against the wall. At some point, the men who had been drinking next to us at the bar set down their glasses and occupied the chairs. They chatted between themselves as the guitarist warmed up. His friend was rubbing his hands together, maybe preparing them to play an instrument. I wondered what. Another guitar?

A chord. Silence. Another. The rise and fall of exquisite, picked out notes. Another chord. The conversations in the bar began to fade. Heads turned; elbows looked for holds. Where rowdy drinkers stood, an audience was forming, reverent and silent. More chords. A clap. His instrument his hands. A steady rise in intensity, more compressed, more complex by the second. Rippling, tense, proud music. All absorbing. Masterful yet tender. Masculinity at its best. A true man's mating call.

A cry from the back: "¡*Vamos ya!*"

Another. First one, then many joining in the clapping, keeping the beat. The tempo picking up, the guitarist's hands a blur.

She stepped out from the crowd. Heavy set, middle-aged, greying hair tied back and held in place by a rose.

"Now you will see. Now you know sex."

She reached the stage and simply stood. The guitar and the clapping stopped. Silence. Stillness. And then a finger moved. A slight bending of the wrist. A single snap. Bang, a foot stamp. Then another. Insistent beats in answer to the music's mating call. The guitar struck; the beating of the palms grew more persistent. The dancer spun, her thundering feet rippling across the floor, capsizing us. Wave after wave of rolling sound and movement, of unbridled passion somehow held in check, drawn through her burning eyes, steadied in the stomach and driven into the floor.

I left at sunrise. She had danced until her rose had fallen, the red petals her virgin's blood, spilt by the passion of the night. Only her hands and head were ever bare, but I'd seen her more naked than any woman. I'd seen sex with passion and soul. I'd seen my first flamenco.

# Whatever Gets You through the Night

My fascination with flamenco has stayed with me to this day and probably played a part in my eventual emigration to Spain. So has cockenomics, though I now call it monetism, the monetisation of life. A force so deadly should not have a joke name. Over the years, the order of high priests who keep its sacred ledgers have imposed their language on all human activity, not just sex.

So generals now deploy military assets instead of people. We seek personal growth. We invest in relationships which may mature into civil partnerships where we deposit our emotional equity. Where once we bought a second home, we now snaffle up an investment unit. We don't sack employees, we downsize resources. In Facebookland, friends are not counted on, just counted, and a guy I know is setting up a site where artists can leverage their creative equity. People buy into ideas even if it means selling out their integrity. We tweet to economise on words. The fact that a tweet has no meaning, is just a sound bite between ads, is neither here nor there. The endgame of the transmission is not to share knowledge but only to clock up ratings. Why waste time attempting to enlighten the few when you can serve up vapid snacks to the multitude? The list is endless, the language of money written into every aspect of our lives.

Language is never arbitrary. Just as 'awesome', 'good' or 'holiday' pay lip service to the old religious world order, so this new financial dictionary underpins and reinforces monetism. Neurolinguistic reprogramming on a global scale.

In short, we monetise life. Why?

First, money makes such a good unit of measurement. Integrity, excellence, the finding and imparting of happiness, these work on the old imperial scale, too complex to decipher; clunky and unfashionable. Money is metric.

'I have more so I am better' is painfully simplistic and just plain wrong. But simple sells. Why struggle for self-knowledge when you can buy *Ten Easy Steps to Personal Fulfilment*? Why fix the German economy with complex instruments and reforms when you can pretend to do the same with gas pipes and some trains? We all embrace the final solution. It's so easy.

Second, money is a universal game. As with football, anyone can play. Sure, there are professionals and most of us just stay kicking around in the park. But we can all join in. To play the piano I have to study, put in the hours. Even then, I'll never be a Mozart. But to be rich, I just need to scratch the right card.

Communism never worked because it goes against our nature. Monetism works so well because it panders to our nature. Like sugar or trash TV, we can't resist.

In spite of Lady Trocknell's comment, I've never collected stamps. But I have bought them. The transaction is transparent. You need to post a letter. You buy a stamp and pay. Now look at Gmail. The stamp is free but only so the vendor can read your letters. You'll pay, all right.

So does any of this matter? I think so.

I don't believe in God. I don't even want to. Too demeaning, like not being trusted with the key to your own front door. Also, too dull. A rather unimaginative solution to the ultimate whodunit. But I respect those that do. Whatever gets you through the night is fine by me. The trouble with monetism is that it doesn't. It gets you to maybe 4am and then wakes you in a sweat. It's not sustainable. Nothing is that has no upper limit, no reason other than its own perpetuation (except the universe, but let's not go there).

The priest who sees the massacre of innocents, the ravages of plague, may question his belief. But the mysteries of God allow a way back: theological argument to absorb the anomaly. Even such thin ice as faith will get you across the river. Monetism dumps you. It's just a matter of time.

I had a friend called José Antonio. He grew up in Bérchules, a tiny hill village in the Alpujarras, east from where I live. He was born to poverty and struggled to escape. He built a company, Extinman, selling fire protection equipment; extinguishers, alarms and the like. He married a local girl and had a daughter. So far, so good.

Then came the boom and a new financial director, a full monetist party member. The silky-tongued and suited wizard told him to diversify, to let his money do the work. He told him making products was quaint, naively charming, but not business. Antonio, ego pandered to, geared up, leveraging his business until he was a dwarf carrying a mountain on his shoulders.

"The money will do the work." Now, there's a lie! He spun so many plates that he didn't have free hands to grasp his daughter to him. His wife and child left, and the wizard tightened his grip.

2007 and the crash. The FD didn't pick up, the only calls from banks calling in their loans. Where once his self-esteem was built on solid ground – family, friends, community, the making of something by people for people – he had only his money. Now that too was gone.

They found the car idling in the garage. Then they saw the little tube, running from the exhaust into the boot. He was in his pants and vest and held a photo of his parents. He was folded in a foetal position, his only way back to where it all begun, through death. I like to think he chose that way to die to not cause trouble. To be already in the car, all set for the drive to the morgue.

Sure, he's an exception, albeit one of many. What of the rest of us? Do we reach the other side? Do we cross safely? Our bodies do, but many are hollowed out: dead wood milling in stagnant pools, the sap sucked out by greed.

So was I part of it? Was my selling of sex the ultimate in monetisation? Was my hypocrisy unbounded? I don't think so. Monetism isn't the selling of something for money. Nothing wrong in that. My motivation was to give and take some pleasure, learn about people and myself. The money followed on. With monetism, money is the endgame and the product, an irritating requirement to get the wallets open.

You were promised a book about a guy who fucks for money, not one who thinks for free. So why the apparent detours? I guess to show the sex for what it was, a journey behind the walls we pass each day. If this book has any purpose, then that's it. Sharing some thoughts and glimpses of what lies beneath. Beneath and behind. Some sex, but other stuff as well. Stuff far more sordid. But we should rejoin the highway. It's been too many words since that other Laurence came. Let's see what he's been getting up to.

Not all my clients were thanks to Peter. Maybe like career soldiers, I carried a posture which advertised my trade. Or maybe I was just a handsome lad with tight jeans in the right shop at the right time. Either way, Shiaza saw me for what I was, a cock for hire.

I had spent the night in Hampstead and had stopped at a deli on my way home. I picked out an unpasteurised chèvre.

"Good choice," this from the woman standing beside me. "It's my favourite."

"I like my cheese to bite back. Has this one teeth?" I asked, turning to her.

She was not a conventionally attractive woman. Short, heavy breasted with a mass of hair, greasy skin, large ass and full lips, probably of Middle Eastern descent. It was as though her sexual parts had been made first, oversized and enriched with desert oils, only for the maker to find that there wasn't enough material left over for the rest of her. As for clothes, she wore elasticised jeans, which accentuated the girth of her stumpy legs, and a T-shirt as saggy as her breasts. Her make-up, mascara and lipstick, had been applied with a random panache and all in all her appearance announced a woman who had said 'fuck it' long ago.

"You'll find the cheese mature and crude. Very... moist and strong smelling," she said, moving closer. "I haven't seen you in here before. Do you live locally?"

I explained I was a carpenter and had been working down the road. I checked the contents of her trolley, an even better way of learning about someone than going through their dirty linen. Family-sized chocolate biscuits, some oven ready meals, crisps, booze, razor blades, fizzy drinks, ice cream, dinosaur biscuits, fish fingers and a token bag of washed-to-eat mixed leaves. So, comfort food, poor self-esteem, a husband and a child or two.

Picking her words too carefully, she explained that she had a problem at home to do with her son's bed and needed a carpenter's advice. She asked if I was free, and I said yes. She offered a £30 consultancy fee and I accepted.

How did I know she was up for sex? Well, I wasn't sure, but chèvre is never moist, always chalky dry. Her line was probably about her pussy and not cheese.

By now I had been on seven 'field trips', as I liked to call them: Trocknell's finishing school, Barbi-can land, a highly enjoyable second orgy, the good soldier's wife, and three others of little merit as perfunctory and middle class. I had come to know the basic rules.

In this first encounter with Shiaza I applied rule one, namely, once a rendezvous has been set up, there isn't anything to talk about. My work was in the line of no-ties sex, and to have engaged in social banter would have devalued the drama and blurred the otherwise sharply focussed agenda. So after a quickly scribbled down address, an exchange of names and the time of 3pm agreed, we went our separate ways.

In fact, I've applied this rule in my non-professional life as well. Here's how it goes. First, the usual stuff. What an Australian friend of my eldest son calls his 'multi-media show'. You bring on the mystery, the brooding look, strike nonchalant but crisp poses and throw in an elliptical comment which peters out. Any nonsense will do. My most absurd but successful was: "The walls are surprisingly..." Please note that this gibberish should be accompanied by a look into the middle distance.

The reply is a given. "Surprisingly what?"

"Can't you guess?" comes next. Besides maintaining the mystery, this hints at intimacy, of a belief that you share a bond so close that she would know what's on your mind.

Usually, that's the end of it and they collude, nodding even though they are completely bewildered. Sometimes you get a plucky one who says, "No, I can't guess."

Then you play your trump card and say, "Perhaps I'll tell you another day."

Job done. You've delivered the package, contents: brooding mystery, a sense that you are kindred spirits and the fait accompli that you will be seeing more of each other. Not bad, considering that the package only contained bubble wrap.

Right, with that out of the way and with an hour or so of intelligent banter and booze under the belt, it's time for phase two: the proposition that you should sleep together. This is where everything can go horribly wrong. So far, you've been betting red or black. Now it's time to pick a number. I am fearful of rejection as, emotionally, a coward. So no risked kisses, no hand brushing hers to gauge the reaction unless her hand moves first. I quite literally cop out. I leave. But not before putting a note in her hand.

I once knew a guy at school who put a condom on before walking the two miles to the college links to fuck his girlfriend. Now, that's impressive and shows foresight. I didn't go that far and anyway, didn't use condoms. I did, however, prepare the note beforehand. Say you're going to the loo, disappear and count down three minutes. That way the girl will think you wrote the note then and not before. Another thing. Leave a space for her name!

The way it's folded is as important as the text. Scrunched up, and you're saying 'you mean nothing to me'. An origami flower is too mushy, unmanly. Personally, I went with 'the box'. The finished result isn't actually a box, but I call it that because it has a tidy packaged look and is slow to open. That's important, as it gives you time to leave and serves to build up drama and intrigue. Easily done, just take a square of paper and fold the corners into the middle. Repeat twice then turn it over and do the same once. If the exit's far away, add a fourth repetition to buy time.

Now for the message. The handwriting is important and for Christ's sake, don't ever process and print. Not too sloppy nor too tidy. Sloppy makes you look indecisive and too tidy a control freak.

The text is make or break. Keep it simple, strong, with hints of a gentle side. A suitable text would be:

(insert her name)

*I feel odd writing this but better to feel odd than have regrets. I don't want you to feel cornered; I want you to have your space. But standing in this queue I can't stop thinking about you. I don't know what it is, but I know there's something which makes me want this moment to continue. I have to go home now, feed the cat. We could go our separate ways, or you could choose a different destiny for us and come with me. I'll wait outside. If you don't show, good luck with your life. If you come, then who knows where we'll end.*

(insert your name and one kiss followed by '...')

Please note not to exceed one kiss. Two or three imposes a limit whilst one is clearly a sample and with the '...', suggests anything could follow. Shagger's tip: having a cat helps, but it can be substituted with watering plants or anything which suggests you're a caring person.

Nauseating clichéd stuff, but one out of every three ended up in my bed. No woman has ever tried this on me, but I assure you I've been bedded via equally calculated and wily ploys. Here's a sample from my personal collection.

I once had to sell a house and met a potential lady buyer in my flat in Stoke Newington. We got on well, flirted, and she seemed genuinely interested in purchasing. The following day she rung me to ask if I could come over to her place in Dartford to discuss contract details, adding that a friend of hers worked in North London and could drive me over that afternoon. I accepted and was duly delivered around 7pm. Wine was poured, a fire lit and by the time I had answered all her questions it was close to 11pm.

When I said I had to leave she expressed surprise that it was so late and informed me that I had missed the last bus, adding that I was welcome to stay. I, of course, agreed and assumed I would be sleeping in the spare bedroom. No such bad luck, as apparently this room had just been treated for bed bugs and could not be used for the next two days. We ended up in her bed.

The following morning I left, and whilst waiting at the bus stop, consulted the timetable. The last bus had left the night before at 11:45pm. She never bought the house and, of course, the only bug in a bed had been me in hers.

The mating game is anything but a game. Anyway, the other person knows deep down it's bullshit but chooses, providing he or she is attracted to you, not to acknowledge the lie as it's not in their interest to do so. Most great truths are founded on a lie. Most marriages start out as a mutual exchange of sneaky scams.

If this trick works for you, tell your friends to buy my book. Just don't name the baby after me. Bad karma.

As it was now already noon I decided to stay around and finding a local park, ate my cheese and bread and dozed under a tree. I thought about Shiaza and the consultation. Was this to be another sex client as I expected, or was I fooling myself looking for signs where none existed? Was I just seeing everything through sex-tinted glasses or was that description of the cheese really a sales pitch for her body? I enjoyed these prologues of uncertainty and maybe invented uncertainty just to create a tension which, if released, made the subsequent sex all the more powerful. I fell asleep and woke up smiling and with a hard-on.

At 3pm sharp, she opened the door. She wore a see-through blouse, no bra, and a black formless skirt down to the floor which I knew from instinct hid no panties. The skirt, I concluded, served two purposes: to cover legs that were most certainly hairy and squat, marbled with cellulite and decorated with nascent varicose veins, and to allow fuss-free access to her pussy: standard issue choice for a married, middle-aged woman embarrassed about her legs and wanting sex against the clock before a husband and children returned.

I admired her forthright approach. She had decided that we were going to fuck and was making sure that I had got the message. In my experience, when a woman decides she wants to bed a guy, she just gets on with it. They know that rare indeed is the man who would be offended by a woman wanting sex, whilst men carry around doubt, even anxiety, that the woman will be uncomfortable, feel objectified, angry or shame you with their rejection. Women, in general, having made a decision proceed to execute it without further ado. A man can spend months, even years, fantasising about a liaison and doing nothing. A woman, on the other hand, often gives the matter no thought until one day the idea seeds in her head and, hey presto, the next day her toes are around her ears. In short, women seem more cautious but once decided, be it to leave you, love you or have an affair, they are far more incisive. They are so strong, so clearly the dominant sex, that in the knowledge of their supremacy, they can afford to let men think they are the stronger.

I surveyed her home from the doorway. The flat, for all its size, was constricting. Mahogany wood trim, mustard carpets, heavy drapes with discoloured satin linings, a few blunt instruments posing as ornaments. The place was as cold as a politician's handshake.

"Come in," she said, her huge breasts nodding in agreement. "My son's bedroom is through here."

We entered a large room with a set of bunk beds, a wardrobe, armchair and desk. Judging from the posters – a rock band, some gushy Kahlil Gibran wisdom printed over a sunset, Dr Who, but also a vestigial teddy bear – the boy must have been in his early teens. You may well be thinking that such a sterile setting and the choice of her son's room to have sex was a turn-off to me. Maybe you would think better of me if I said it was. But once again, this book, above all else, sets out to tell the truth. So I admit that on the contrary, like hospitals, cemeteries and libraries, the morbidity of the place accentuated the crude sexuality of our encounter.

It would appear that I am not alone in having this particular predilection. I once knew a woman surgeon who always operated naked but for erotic lingerie under her gown and she would masturbate to orgasm in the toilet after each op. I have bought girlfriends drinks but have never anaesthetised them and, during foreplay, slapped and nibbled my lovers, but I personally draw the line at ferreting around in their entrails or massaging their beating heart. All too weird. Anyway, where were we? Ah yes: huge breasts and bunk beds.

I was standing slightly to the left and behind her, so close that I could have run my fingers between her legs and over her pussy. As she turned to face me, I saw that her nipples were particularly dark. We knew each other less than friends on Facebook, whilst we both understood that my cock would soon be down her throat. She didn't want to have sex with me because she was in love or felt it was the right thing to do after a meal and cinema date. She just wanted to fuck a young guy on a Tuesday afternoon. Nothing was going to stop us having sex, and precisely because of that there was no rush.

Later, she would change her clothes, ready for her family's return. They would eat, her husband would perhaps grumble about some client, and then off to surround the TV and watch the nightly soap. But that evening would be different. She would sit a little straighter in her chair, take a second glass of wine and hang a leg over the arm. She would feel herself getting aroused as she remembered our coupling, be heightened, more alive, knowing that she had a dark secret which was hers alone. Like a superhero posing as an office worker, she would feel empowered, the one who knows in a room of the ignorant.

She pointed to the bunk beds.

"My son's getting older and probably bangs his head on the ceiling when he fucks his girlfriend. I need to modify the bed. Oh, and here's your fee. What do you advise?"

So, the game of the carpenter and the middle-class client was to be continued but laced with explicit sex talk. Another wonderful erotic balancing act. I played my part.

Up until now I had been writing freely and without a single edit, a buccaneer approach described by a friend as 'straight out the mouth', and, indeed, I continued to do so for the next eight pages. But when rereading them, I realised that I had gone off-piste. You see in that now discarded draft I detailed with unbridled inhibition the minutiae of our sexual encounter to the edges of obscenity and beyond.

Of course, to date I have chronicled my sexual missions, but I hope only to the point that they provide insight into the people I met and the relationships and social structures I observed. In short, I like to think that the sex has not been gratuitous and has served as alluring packaging all the better to deliver the real content.

Sex is like special effects which, when used sparingly and in context, can enhance the plot and characterisations. But overdo them and the whole shebang turns into candy floss: huge and loud, only to deflate as the credits roll, leaving a stick and sickly taste in the mouth. But why take my word for it? Here's a couple of passages from that draft:

*Silences are like darkness: most are partial, few complete. This silence was absolute. We live with so much noise, we hear so little, the aural equivalent of not seeing the wood for the trees. And then I heard it, coming out of the hush like landfall through the mist. A whisper at first, an acoustic mirage that turns out to be real. Her breathing. Irregular, dry, forced out through clenched teeth, growing in intensity until a metronomic wave of sound, her blood pumping in my ears as she came...*

(And three pages later:)

*My fingers still stretching her open, I bent down and ran my tongue over her mouth. She was hot and pliant with breath smelling of gin and tobacco. I sucked her lips, pulling them between my teeth. I used her mouth as other men might use their lover's pussy. Extending my tongue, I dipped it in and out before letting a little of my spit fall on her tongue. Heated from slaps and pinches, loosened by my fingers and tongue, lubricated by my and her own saliva, her mouth hung loose, slack, ready for my cock. Her breath came in irregular bursts and her breasts heaved as she fought to take in air. Smears of mascara and lipstick decorated her cheeks...* (and so on for another four pages until...), *I massaged her breasts, pulling them up only to slap them down, watching intently as my dick disappeared into that musky well-travelled cunt. Then the phone rang.*

So, I ask my reader, do you now have a better understanding of Shiaza? Have I provided any insights to illuminate the mindset and life of a middle-aged, middle-class woman who needed to feel sexually desirable? I doubt it, and that's why those pages had to go. Anyway, you can always use your imagination, that most powerful of erotic tools. But let me guess. The line that most caught your attention was: *Then the phone rang.*

So, no explicit details this time. But I can tell you that I de-personalised Shiaza and was dominant to her submissive. It made her infidelity so much easier, as a person's ability to forgive themselves is inversely proportional to their ability to have acted otherwise. Where there is no choice, there is no blame. Her body was going to do the fucking. Her pink bits. I left her heart and person clothed. The more carnal, obscene and impersonal our sex, the easier she would rest that night. That's why prostitutes never kiss and why bondage is the ultimate conscience liberator, but let's not get too tied down.

Never ask a lover what they want, is what I say. Do what comes naturally to you, what evolves from the situation, and then see how they respond. Most people, unless they choose to lie to themselves, know if the other person likes what is happening. No words need to be spoken. A sudden emptiness in their eyes, a change in the rhythm of their breath, a tensing in the body, are some of the innumerable and clear ways of saying 'no'. A good person should never ask permission to do something with a lover but will always stop if they get a 'no'.

No part of the body should be out of bounds. Putting your fingers in a woman's nose is for most a far stronger taboo than entering their cunt. Sex is about sharing your body, about letting the other person into your private world, and plays like licking their eyes, fingering their nostrils, resting your balls on their face aren't meant to be necessarily physically pleasurable but rather erotic triggers, signifying ultimate physical intimacy.

Time in such moments stands still, freezing the most insignificant detail and accentuating it: the vein in her eye, the cluster of saliva bubbles which welled up and broke on the sides of her lips, the beads of sweat which gathered and ran between her breasts, all caught my attention. So did the thick hair on her arms, the unusual smallness of her ears, the asymmetrical puckering around her nipples, the mole beside her nose and the smell of her pussy. For what odour is more intoxicating: a silent but undeniable confirmation that your lover wants you?

One of the tragedies of recent years is the mania for so-called intimate deodorants, an absurd war declared on that most primal and wondrous of all smells. The Gitanos (Spanish Gypsies) know this. I was once waiting in a hospital in Granada when an argument broke out between a Gitano and a medic. His wife was in for a gynaecological examination and the nurse had shaved and washed her pussy. Her husband was incandescent and ranting about how they had deprived them both of her natural odour. I imagined one of those 'ambulance chaser' lawyers appearing out of nowhere to press his card into the bereft husband's hand. Interesting case, as how do you assign a value to the quantifiable loss of cunt smell?

I said she wasn't conventionally attractive. But then, I wasn't attracted to the conventional. It seems we are attracted by others who manifest that they have something we want or admire. A person who always wants the same thing is a sorry soul indeed. That day I was delighted to be fucking a woman whose external beauty was absent and thus no distraction to the appreciation of her crude sweaty sexuality. Anyway, women who see themselves as unattractive usually make the best lovers. Maybe they are more inclined to see a man's attentions as a gift rather than a birthright.

The women I fucked in the course of my work were not going to be my soulmates, far less the mothers of my children. They would not be paraded in front of my friends or in any way would my status be judged by their point score (not that I cared) using the agreed parameters of the day.

Let's face it, most people are as concerned about how their friends grade their lovers as they are about what they themselves think of them. If they can bag a beauty, they have ticked one of the boxes of public success, not only in the eyes of other men, but also in the eyes of competing women, who see them as the sort of man pretty girls should aspire to. This is the stock cube syndrome. Once a top babe validates a certain man as fit for her stew, all aspiring women want him. Demand spirals. The same, of course, is true reversing the genders. But this is just insects boring away at the veneer of life.

We're on this ball of dust and taxes just the once, and to make choices and perform only to please the hecklers in the stands is simply pathetic.

Maybe with age I have doffed my cap to social convention, even bent the knee, but in those days of sex for sale, cloaked in anonymity, discharging private missions (or do I mean emissions?) behind closed doors, the only pressure was not to conform but rather to perform.

Doing things in bed just to please the other person is sweet and charming, tokens of love like washing the dishes or going out in the rain to get your partner's favoured snack. But there is nothing sexual about kindness. No. Big mistake. Sex is about doing what you want and, in so doing, pleasing the other. And if it doesn't please them, then you are with the wrong lover.

I cannot understand a man who, after years of whining and pleading, gets his wife to accept anal sex even though she grimaces throughout the act. Surely, he must be left with the overriding feeling that he has been offered charity and caused unwanted pain, the antithesis of the pleasure derived from being party to a complicit act of lust. I despise such men and feel sorry for them both.

*Then the phone rang.*

Now, if this were a work of fiction I would proceed to tell you that after a few moments the phone stopped and our afternoon proceeded to ever lustier indulgences. But this is real life and so the phone didn't just stop and go away. Instead, a voice spoke out from the answerphone in the hall.

"Shiaza," this from a 40-something male, "I feel like shit and am coming home early. Can you pick David up? And why aren't you at home?"

I extracted my cock. "Do we have a problem?"

"Fuck, yes, we have a problem. I have to go right now to collect my son from school. Fuck it!"

I climbed off her.

"I must look a complete mess."

"No, you look like a woman who has been having sex."

"Sure, that will go down well with the school." And with that she vanished down the hall.

A good call boy knows when to make his entrances and exits, and now was the time to leave. To have chatted, loitered or showered – even had there been time – would have probably made her uncomfortable and definitely tarnished the sparkling intensity of the experience.

That's one of the big differences between casual sex and love, where the cuddling and post-fuck easy conversation can be more memorable and valuable than the sex. With carnal paid sex, it's just an irrelevance.

We had four subsequent encounters, but as no money changed hands, they don't qualify for inclusion. Did I feel used that first time? Of course. We are all used all the time. Used for love, used for emotional support, advice, money, a shoulder to cry on, a hand to rock the cradle. I want to be of use; to be validated as useful. Whether by my cock or my mind, my mouth to cheer my son on at school or to bring a woman to orgasm, I have been and will, I hope, continue to be used.

Did the sex get even better over the subsequent four meetings? No. Sure, we had no intrusions from answerphones as we met at a friend's flat. But something far harder to ignore intruded: a competing reality. The essence of anonymous intense sex is its anonymity. We knew nothing of each other; we had no shared past or future. Just a duet of lust performed in a bubble. Over the following weeks, I got to know her and even saw a photo of her son. The parallel intimacy of two beings floating outside of daily routine was shattered, the bubble burst, and by mutual agreement we never met again. But I did think about her. What was life like for her? She must have been about forty and as I learnt, her son was fifteen, so she probably married in her early twenties. There she was, in that asphyxiating airless flat, waking up each morning knowing exactly what the day would hold.

She had told me that her husband had lost physical interest in her, and she would read in bed with earplugs so as not to hear his snoring. She had given up caring for her body and the further it declined the more she sought comfort from biscuits, buns and chocolate: a trio of best friends who were there for her and never criticised.

Worst of all, the knowledge that this was not a passing phase; that there would be no remission, only accelerated decline; that the template of monotony would be replicated onto every page of her diary till the last entry. So what if one of those pages was different? What if *fuck a young man* was written in a careless hand between *make lunch* and *make dinner*?

Yes, for some reason I often think about Shiaza and when I do, my thoughts turn to hunting that most elusive of mythological beasts: sustainable love. For the bar of love is set so high that most of us are bound to snag it as we leap. And so I look for clues as crusaders searched for fewmets, the turds of dragons, or as those in search of immortality pass their hands over the boughs of trees looking for the scars from the horn of a wandering unicorn. But for this prey I will go into the forest I know best – my mind – and restrict my search to my memories.

I had been in the little Spanish village I call home for perhaps a year when a neighbour announced that he was soon to marry. I asked him what he loved about his bride.

"Her father's almond groves border mine, she cooks well, is frugal and has wide hips, so will bear me many children," was the gist of his reply.

A few days later at the market, I found his bride in the queue for tomatoes. I asked her the same question. She told me that he didn't drink much, worked hard, was strong, that he owned the adjacent fields and that his father was a *funcionario* (civil servant) and thus guaranteed a good pension.

They are together to this day and have five children, and I see them as and when walking in the village. Lourdes, the wife, has a limp and Antonio, her husband, adjusts his step so they can walk arm-in-arm. The almond fields are now ploughed as one and the *funcionario*, recently retired, collects their youngest son from school.

Their oldest son married three years ago. I asked him the same question I asked his parents. He set the bar high. He wanted and expected a soulmate, a passionate lover, a good mother to his children, a friend, a good sense of humour, tolerance, respect, shared interests and common values. He is now divorced and back living with his parents.

Another memory, again from my early days in Spain. I had decided to bite the moral bullet and go to a bullfight. I asked a friend what best to see. He asked me if I was taking my wife or my lover. I didn't understand what bearing this had on the choice of fight, so he explained that there were two 'performances', Saturday for the wives and Thursday for *la Querida*, the lover. He also told me a wonderful anecdote.

His wife, more daring than most, had accompanied him to a Thursday fight. She surveyed the men and their *Queridas* and, turning to her husband, announced with pride, "Our *Querida* is the most elegant."

Remarkable! Her self-esteem was bolstered by the quality of her husband's lover, a woman of such class that the wife gained status by his association. Now let's dig deeper into the past.

When wandering in India I visited Auroville to do an article for the *New Statesman*. This experimental city of wonder and madness was set up by 'the Mother' and brought a couple from every country on earth together to create a new society whose values would be based on her teachings. Whilst there I stayed in a seven storey pyramidal hut made of timber and banana leaves. My hosts were a Bulgarian revolutionary named Grozdan and his two wives, one Australian and one French. Level four was for guests, five had beds for the women, six was for sex and seven reserved for meditation. Each wife would rise from level five to six three days a week and spend the night with Grozdan. Sundays he slept alone (the guy must have been exhausted).

Both wives agreed that the arrangement worked well. Grozdan was a larger-than-life character with a penchant for bomb-building and turgid revolutionary folk songs from the old country. Half a Grozdan was apparently the ideal dose and on Sundays they would lie in bed together with the banana leaf awnings lifted, sharing anecdotes about 'Grozzer' and watching the birds flying in the tropical tree canopy.

As all social and emotional preconceptions – or should I say prerequisites? – had been left at the entrance to Auroville, they custom-made their own. Again, expectations were achievable and understood by all the players. Incidentally, both women particularly liked their nights 'off' and the chance to get a good sleep.

P.S. Auroville is still going but probably not worth a visit as it's now too sanitised and ordered.

I feel that I am moving too far from the core focus of this book, and as worthy a mission as deciphering true love might be, I better stop. No? OK, one more, and this time personal.

On the way between then and now I had a relationship during which I visited prostitutes on a regular basis. I have to thank my lawyer for this foray. You see, over wine and legal argument I confessed to being randy and in need of an away game. This itch was making me tetchy at home, but I didn't want to end the relationship nor seek anything serious elsewhere as everything else about the relationship was perfect.

"*Putas, mi amigo, putas!*" (*Whores, my friend, whores!*) he declared.

I took his advice, selecting only those who worked for themselves and never visited the same one twice. It was great and when I told them that I, too, had been in their line of work, they sometimes gave me trade prices, which was no small deal as prostitutes are even more expensive than plumbers.

I never fell in love, was always home for tea, and neither felt nor inflicted any kind of conflict of interest.

Interestingly enough, I made the fatal mistake of telling my girlfriend. She was furious and told me that she had known all along that I was screwing prostitutes (the lawyer told his wife, aka the world) and hadn't minded, but now that I had told her it was like a third person in the room. In short, she was angry that I hadn't had the strength of character to keep it to myself. At the time I thought this an absurd argument but now, looking back, I realise that she was right. For, after all, we tell the other person our embarrassing secrets not to help them but rather to selfishly assuage our perceived guilt.

There seems to me no magic formula for emotional happiness, just mutually agreed structures that work for certain people at certain times. But what the successful ones have in common is that the expectations are realisable.

My bullfighting aficionado and his wife had just that. She did not expect him home on Thursdays and he has stood by her through thick and thin on the other six days, and when a year ago she contracted cancer, he gave up his job to look after her. Theirs was a socially accepted set of expectations which were in consonance with the possible and the limitations of human nature. So, too, with the other examples I have dredged up.

Today in much of the western world, we have been told to expect twenty-four-hour bliss and strive to live life as though an album of delirious selfies. No wonder the average marriage only lasts eleven years and over twenty-five per cent of children are in single parent families, as the expectations drilled into us by the media, both social and editorial, are simply unobtainable and not in any way predicated on our nature. Indeed, nature is so far out of the picture that anyone born without what is apparently the perfect body and face feels victimised and demands that plastic surgeons and beauticians immediately rectify this 'mistake' and return to them that dinky nose and pouting lips or the six-pack and chiselled chin which apparently are their birthright.

Shiaza got it right. She used a prostitute to scratch the itch and not a lover. A lover would have threatened to tear down a relationship she was not ready to leave. Perhaps she valued the comforts her husband's income provided or maybe his kindness, sense of humour or ability to empathise. Maybe he was good with their son, who would be hurt and damaged by a divorce. Who knows. What is clear is that she needed sexual release and physical endorsement and set about finding them in the most efficient way possible and without collateral damage.

An old Persian saying comes to mind: 'A woman for duty, a boy for pleasure and a melon for ecstasy.' I guess I was Shiaza's fresh fruit of the day.

There are no universal laws, no right way. There is just stuff that works for a given time and place and stuff that doesn't. Monetism, that endless drive with no direction home, doesn't. Shiaza being throat-fucked by a stranger did. As I said, whatever gets you through the night.

Real sexuality can't be bought in a shop, or its language cut and pasted onto your tongue. The only manual is locked within you. With the release of *Fifty Shades of Grey*, sales of sex toys in the UK rocketed, particularly in Hull. Does this make the citizens of Hull the Lotharios of Britain? Probably the opposite as they try to paper over their erotic bankruptcy with vibrating bananas and miniature vacuum cleaners. There, I've had my rant. Now for some golf.

In the light-hearted film *Tin Cup*, Rene Russo is learning to swing her club. I can't remember exactly how the scene went, but the gist is as follows.

She arrives for her lesson loaded with gadgets to correct her swing. Kevin Costner, her coach, throws the lot away and grabbing her club, drives the ball over the horizon.

"How did you do that?" she asks.

"I just let the big dog bark."

The whips and cuffs, the dildos and ball gags have their place, but they don't help the mute find a voice. They don't help the big dog bark.

# Dipping the Woodwork

Life in Glading Terrace had reached a compromise with chaos, a workable balance of madness and responsibility. We still did our experimental stuff, vying with each other to top the loony list, but the creepers of the grown-up world were beginning to snag our feet.

We had a house food kitty: a jam jar for our fivers. A rota was established for the washing up. A first argument over who had eaten all the eggs reserved for a private breakfast. Little singularities, turning points in the transformation of carefree youths to responsible adults. We thought we were part of an ongoing experiment in new ways to live, funded by our dole money and free accommodation. I know now we were just playing house, putting a toe in the door of the family homes to come.

To begin with, there was 'us' and there were 'the others', the people who ran and maintained the world, who kept our playground working. They drove the buses, kept the food stores stocked, built roads, cooked in restaurants and generally kept the ship afloat. We just sunned ourselves on deck.

But then it starts one day taking you by surprise. You look at the bedroom, and those dirty clothes strewn on the floor that up till then had gone unnoticed begin to irritate. You find yourself walking to the launderette, even asking the assistant what best to clean them with. Two weeks on and you're folding them on shelves, another month and a wardrobe somehow materialises in the room. Before you know it, you're on a bus to town to buy wooden coat hangers, having noticed that with the wire ones your trousers get a crease. A household meeting is convened, the only point of order to purchase a washing machine. The vote in favour is unanimous. Some friends knock on the door to invite you to the pub, and you find yourself saying, "No, not tonight, I have to do the washing."

Another year and they stop knocking, too busy themselves for the pub.

The process is so slow, so evolutionary, that it goes unnoticed. We see time though telescopes. Looking forward, we hold it the usual way and everything is huge, the landscape of time expanded. But when we look back, we place the other end to our eye and everything is tiny, compressed.

Today I am man with two ex-wives, three cars, of which one sometimes works, five children and various professions on the CV. I dust the telescope and, looking back, see a lad with a bike, living in a squat with two lesbians, no job, and the only wives, the ones of other men I was paid or inclined to shag. How did I get here? Fuck knows. In a time machine? Woken from the deep freeze to stand gawking at an unfamiliar world? No. I just floated down the river, conveyed along the rite of passage we all pass down, making tiny, incremental strokes.

I learn a little carpentry. I make a bed for me and then one for a friend. I buy some more tools to do a bigger job. I work for a friend of my friend. They pay and recommend me. Can I also paint the kitchen? Why not? I ask Colin to help, and we share the money. Two other people ring and, as I don't know them, I call them 'clients'. Another mate is roped in to help us with the work. We do another job, but this time I pay wages, not a split of profit. I hear one call me 'boss', as a joke at first, but somehow the title sticks. I employ people who aren't friends and a client, when speaking to a neighbour, calls me his 'contractor' where once my name was Laurence. Tiny incremental steps from 'us' to 'the others'.

That brings us on to clients. A necessary evil or God's gift? I've had both. From Princess Valium, who wept because the apple white of her radiators wasn't the right sort of apple, to those who knew their apples from their pears but didn't care either way. I'm talking about my other clients, the ones, ostensibly at least, who were after another sort of handyman.

Business was good and I had assembled a team. The 'Z' team.

You know that famous photo of the New York steel erectors having their lunch sitting on a girder high in the sky? You remember? Tough, hardy pros with no fear of heights. Hold that image and let's make a few changes.

Firstly, make one of them a woman. Next, colour one of the bloke's faces and hands black, and make another a bit fat. Shrink a couple of the others to three-quarter size. Swap some of the fags for spliffs and leave some wine and beer within hand's reach. Randomly select clothes from army surplus stores, men's outfitters, jumble sales and auctions of deceased effects and go about redressing them. Insert one ghetto blaster. Now, last step, gently lower the girder until it reaches the ground. Gently now, one of the lads is asleep. Welcome to the 'Z' team.

Let me make the introductions.

Pepe the Knife, a Cypriot and one of my two labourers. On his first day I told him that our punters were middle-class and liked their tradesman to be clean. He impressed me by arriving in a freshly washed sweater and new jeans. All good until the day warmed up and he took the sweater off. The T-shirt underneath was imprinted with a simple message. *Fuck off and Die*. It was clean though.

He had tattoos, back in the day when they were not essential bodywear. A client asked him where his favourite one was. I dreaded he would take his dick out. Instead, he pulled back his lower lip to reveal *Fuck off*. Like all good advertising, he kept his message simple and repeated.

His teammate was Big Dave, otherwise known as Animal Dave or Davy Croquette. The first two nicknames are easy to explain. He was big and, in the best possible sense, an animal. We were once having lunch in a café. Over steak and chips, he suddenly reached out and plucked a hanging hair from inside my nose.

The last nickname requires a longer explanation. We were camping in the Sierras, Big Dave, myself, Tom Ling and my dog, Natty, brought along to warm our feet in the freezing nights up there. I woke up: the moon was full, and I wanted to see the snow. Dave was sitting outside eating. My God, he had an appetite. He had a bag in his hand and was flipping morsels into his mouth. Peanuts? Bite-sized biscuits? No way, we didn't have any.

"What you eating, Dave?"

"Heey, Laaurrence." He had a languid way and paused a lot. "Don't... know. Found them in... the rucksack. Tasty."

They were Natty's dog food. Get it? Croquettes?

Ed Walls. Bomber Ed. Not really a terrorist, we called him that because he was Irish and a plumber. Come on, if anyone's the terrorist on a construction team it's got to be the plumber. If we're talking cybercrime, the electrician, but for terrorism, the plumber. Flames and gas, expansion tanks. They're halfway there.

Never Hurry a Murray. Colin, if you were pressed for time. You met him in chapter one. The skinhead with the paintbrush. His surname was Murray. One day he sat in the only site toilet for over an hour. A couple of the guys started banging on the door. When he eventually came out, he wagged his finger at them.

"Never hurry a Murray." More finger wags. "Never hurry a Murray." The name stuck.

Sparkie Dave. All electricians are called 'sparkie'. That's the rule. Most are speed freaks. Juiced-up. They seem to like getting electric shocks. I wouldn't want to see a drugs stand-off between one of them and Colin. Never Hurry a Murray would take a huge drag on a reefer that needed scaffolding. Appreciative nods from the crowd.

Sparkie steps up to the crease and rams a 2000-volt live cable up his nose. The house erupts. So all the stranger that our Dave was a sparkie. He was only addicted to P.G. Wodehouse and tea. Instead of a GTI, he drove a Beetle, and when not at work, lived in his Rupert the Bear dressing gown. We expected him to say any day that he was off to open a sweet-shop in Wensleydale.

Young Mick. Named so because he was incalculably old, which probably meant he was fifty. Everyone seemed old to us. He was our brickie and started every sentence with: "If I was still a young man," followed by such gems of wisdom as: "I'd leave her looking like a plasterer's radio," or, "I'd stick a shovel through his ears," or, "I'd drink all your pints and then some." Thank you, Mick.

That leaves Liz. Ever since the 'incident', everyone was too scared of her to suggest a nickname. She'd been our plasterer for a couple of days. Huge woman. The lads had been gawking at her breasts, snickering. On the third day she'd had enough and, downing tools, strips off her overalls, T-shirt and bra.

"Right, lads," she said, "you've got three minutes to stare at my tits. Then I'm going to put them away and you're all going to stop your nonsense."

Utter silence. For three minutes everyone looked at the floor. No one ever mentioned her breasts again.

We were more of a circus troupe than a building crew, but somehow we got the work done and the clients queued up: the necessary evils and the godsends. It's easy to spot the difference. It's all about that old theme: money. Money and the motivation behind acquiring things.

Way back in the day, people exchanged goods and services. They swapped things of equal value. I've got chickens you want to eat. You know how to roof a hut. Let's swap. In this exchange there is no hierarchy. But we all know what happened next.

The guy with the chickens didn't need a roof but the roofer was still hungry. So they agreed that in exchange for chickens, the poultry farmer could call in the debt by asking for a new roof when he needed one. He never did and passed the credit note to a farmer in exchange for grain. The farmer then asked the roofer to fix his hut. These matchings of wanted and offered became more complex until someone came up with the bright idea of unitising value: chickens, one credit; a new hut roof, ten credits; and so on. Now the roofer could eat and give a credit, a coin that the poultry farmer could swap for whatever he wanted, when he wanted. Money had arrived and, on the face of it, a golden age. But all that glitters…

The God-sent clients understood that money only represented a way of matching needs over time. The door my carpenter hung is worth a mini-break in the Lake District. I can't provide a cottage, so I'll give him money. He can then swap it with a house owner and have his holiday. No hierarchy. These were the ones who understood that trade is the exchange of things of equal value and, thus, the parties to the trade are equals too.

But sometimes we worked for the others, the ones who thought that money ruled, that somehow, just because they didn't have the cottage and closed the swap with little bits of paper, they were superior and we, by default, inferior. A bad taste in the mouth.

The other dividing line that sorted the good from the bad was what made them commission the work. Some practical examples.

I had been doing a job for Michael Palin, an incredibly sweet man. A friend had tipped me off that a church was being demolished in Sussex and that the spire was a jewel worth salvaging. I mentioned this to Michael over tea. Did he know of anyone who might like a forty-feet church spire? He didn't think twice.

"Terry Gilliam's your man."

He was and commissioned its retrieval and installation at his home in Highgate by the cemetery. I remember what he said.

"Sounds exciting. Could be fun. Have you thought of what we could do with it? A folly, perhaps, for the garden?"

Not much spoken but everything conveyed. The essence was the fun, a possibility of adventure, the thrill of creativity and saving something fine from the knacker's yard. Then there's the 'we', 'what *we* could do'. One word that drew me in, made me part of the project, his understanding that there are always two owners, the one who pays but also the one who makes, the biological father of the child adopted by the client.

Wonderful man with an equally splendid wife, Maggie. They treated us as friends and actually made Davy Croquette godfather to one of their children. I was as green as the oak I used to patch the tower and did a job unworthy of his trust. He shamed me with his kindness, choosing to let my under-dimensioned columns pass muster, even though they must have been an affront to his artist's eye. Thanks, Terry.

The folly was built, and not long after, they opened their gardens to the public for the day, an initiative repeated every year. All sorts came. But the avid gardeners checking out the blooms were few. Most came to pry, to gain vicarious status, their garden, so many pop-up pages in a *Hello* magazine. And then there were the ones who came with calculators. Who weighed and measured. If the garden was smaller than theirs, they went away contented. If bigger, then a challenge, a record that had to be beaten.

The folly was big, a monumental gauntlet not thrown down but rising up to touch the sky. It cast a shadow that no self-respecting social climber could live under. Three offers followed, three neighbours wanting one.

But what did they really want? If a tower at all, then only one from Babel. In fact, it could have been anything which ticked the boxes of power and status. No bonding with the object and its making and, through that bond, transcendence to the creativity and love beneath. They were simply parking their money like energy is parked in matter, given temporary form to return to the bank one day. More cockenomics. It's not the things we have which count. It's not their weight and price which sums and judges us, but our relationship to them.

Of course, these lost souls are full of fear. When your only reason for acquiring something is the status it conveys, it must be right. Not right for them, right in the eyes of those that matter. Their friends, a euphemism for competitors, will come and see it, bringing their own calculators to value their social equity.

My coterie of clients contained some famous names, making me an arbiter of what should and should not be built. These other clients, the ones from hell, never had an opinion, they simply paid for mine. But they were always left with nagging doubts.

"Tell me I've done the right thing."

"What do *you* think? Do *you* like it?" I would naively ask.

"I don't know. That's why I'm asking you."

They looked so fragile, not in spite of but because of their money, that I would comfort them. Their inner selves were terminally ill, locked up in a hospice somewhere, so I did the rounds of the beds, administering solace.

"Of course you have. Everyone will love it."

They always questioned the bill. All fears forgotten on pay day, they returned to their comfort zone, the trader's pit. In their world, someone has to lose for there to be a winner. I let them beat me down a token sum. A cheap price to give them so much pleasure.

I wasn't always so gracious. The story of the radiators is true. I really had a woman cry because the apple white was not the hybrid she'd seen in a rival's house. I lost it and said she should sell the central heating system and use the money for therapy. I was so naive. I didn't know that all tears are real, however sham the cause. I'm sorry.

All in all, we were lucky bastards and had for clients, in the main, the best of people. One such gem was Simon, an art director in the film industry. He was a rogue with an angel's pencil. He was also one of only four people I have even told about my other life, the sex for cash. I knew he wouldn't be judgmental. He laughed and slapped me on the back. I felt good telling someone; relieved.

Reading back through this book, I seem to give the impression that I was in control, dissecting experiences but rarely bloodying my hands. That's not strictly true. I had the innocence of youth which makes you bold and gives the appearance of bravery. I just didn't know enough to be frightened. My sensibilities were not sufficiently evolved to really see the pain that others were in and that sometimes I was the cause of. But it did get to me all the same. Doing what I did and carrying this secret took its toll. Telling Simon brought the relief that always comes with confession. It also brought me my next sex client. Her name was Sarah, and this is her story.

I was lying on my back, head in a cupboard, screwing on some cabinet doors.

"Did you mean it when you said you fucked women for money, Laurence?" This from Simon.

"Of course I did. You don't think I would confess to such a thing and not even get the pleasure of doing it?" I replied from the cupboard.

"Well, finish the doors and come to the kitchen. We'll open a bottle and I'll tell you about Sarah."

She was his neighbour and recently divorced. A 30-something, middle-class magazine editor, she was taking the separation badly, her self-esteem somewhere below ground. I don't think Simon actually wanted to help her or even particularly liked her. He just wanted to be part of something naughty. He wanted to get the ball rolling, as it were, and see where it ended up. He also wanted to hear all the details of what happened. So maybe a voyeur as well.

His proposition was simple. Sarah was down and needed a little pick-me-up. Not vitamins or a holiday in Greece. A good shag from a young bloke. He had it all planned out. Obviously, I couldn't just roll up at the house and say, "Hello, Sarah, Simon says you need a shag," so he proposed a little subterfuge. She was having a lunch party the following Saturday, a rallying of friends to bitch about the ex, and he had been invited.

"I'll ask her to come over for a drink this Friday evening. Are you free, Laurence?"

I nodded.

"Good. Now, she's a total house junkie. Like most middle-class arty women, she's a frustrated interior designer. We'll get the *vin* flowing and you start dropping names and talk designer talk. Agree with her thoughts on kitchens. That kind of stuff. She'll love the attention and see you as a bit of a find."

"What, like an old chest of drawers or something?"

"What bollocks are you talking?"

"A bit of a find like a cheap antique."

"Yeah, yeah. Exactly. Right, bla bla bla, I say I can't make it on the Saturday but why doesn't she invite you? Fingers crossed she'll ask if you're free, you say yes and we're in."

"Well, not exactly in, Simon, just an invite to lunch."

"Yeah, yeah. The rest will be up to you. Come on, she's recently divorced. Child's play for a man of your experience."

I was thinking the proposal over when Simon added, "And I'll pay, of course."

"Simon, you don't have to do that. Sounds more like a blind date. I could do a freebie."

"I want to pay. It's all part of it. Christ, it's the most important part. It makes it all so… different."

"OK, Simon, I'll let you pay. Thirty quid all right?"

"Fine."

"But I have a condition of my own."

"What's that?"

"You have to go through my pimp."

"Fabulous!"

"You don't mind?"

"You kidding? The script's getting better and better. Out of interest, I can see the plus for me, but why do you want him in the middle?"

"Oh, he doesn't like me going behind his back. He likes to feel useful."

"Weird, but whatever. Right, that's sorted. Give me his number and I'll ring him now."

Two bottles of Beaujolais, a hummus dip, and only an anecdote about me having my first client meeting with the lovely actress Julie Christie whilst she was sitting on the loo, and I got the invitation.

Saturday. Sarah lived in Hoxton Square, Shoreditch. It was an up-and-coming area, recently discovered. Odd, this business of discovery. As though Shoreditch had lay hidden until some intrepid middle-class explorer had found a secret passageway and stumbled on it. I wonder what the locals thought, drinking in the pub, when overhearing some newcomer hold forth that he or she had 'discovered' where they had always lived? I'm surprised the invaders didn't change the name to something, shall we say, less grubby.

Stoke Newington didn't escape that fate and was rechristened 'Newington Village'. Neither did Sagarmatha, degraded from a name meaning 'Earth Mother' to the boring Everest we know today. I mean, really, how can anyone pretend to have discovered the world's highest mountain? It's not exactly something you can hide. I can't see a group of Nepalese replying, when the peak was pointed out, "Oh, thank you, Mr Surveyor, we hadn't noticed it."

The house was as expected. Even from the outside it said out loud, "I've been yuppified."

You can always tell. Yuppies are so industrious but deeply predictable. Maybe they were drilled as sperms and eggs to fulfil the yuppie holy mission of doing up a house according to the sacred *Home and Garden Book*. I see them as foetuses repeating their instructions.

"I shall go forth and seek a working-class district near the city and there buy a run-down house. All glory to the Thames basin brick that I shall sand-blast. The windows must be gloss, forgive my sin, but eggshell will reign supreme in bathroom, loo and kitchen. All praise to the OG architrave and matching skirting board that I shall strip, revealing the grain of truth beneath. The doors I vouch shall be cleansed in caustic soda and Briwaxed, adorned with spun brass knob and hinge. I will smite the dividing wall twixt dining and living rooms to bring in light, to better see the sanded wooden floor that I shall spend the Sabbath varnishing till satin. I shall tear down the hardboard, revealing original features in their splendour. Oh, may the cast iron fireplace not be cracked! The hearth stone shall be slate, and I shall scrimp and save to buy the marble mantelpiece and Victorian tiles. All glory to the First Yuppie! My table shall be scrubbed wood; my kitchen, hanging gardens where garlic and the herbs of Provence shall reign supreme. I shall make the sacred pilgrimage to Habitat and buy the allotted yards of sisal for the stair, rough cotton fabric and an Italian coffee machine, all in accordance with the word. Plain will be my worktops of English elm, all the better to praise the chrome Toastmaster, Bodum plates and mugs. No cup and saucer shall corrupt my path. May my nails split picking the years of heathen paint from the ceiling rose and cornice. May my back break carrying the ball and claw bathtub up the stairs. I shall not find rest until the toilet seat is wood. In the name of Le Creuset, the Aga and the holy Fired Earth, amen."

Thank your personal God I didn't give you the full version.

Back on planet Earth, I pressed the bell. Sarah answered the door in Laura Ashley. A simple cotton dress and espadrilles. Her only jewellery were two bracelets of dulled silver of indeterminate form and some glass earrings that looked like bits of tagliatelle. Her mousy hair was cut straight at neck nape height and tucked behind her ears. She was slim, a product of salads, reduced onions and ratatouille. There must have been a dessert or two inside her somewhere, but yoghurt would have replaced the cream, honey ousting sugar. She was not unattractive. Not quite 'thinking man's crumpet', more like 'holiday in Tuscany man's bread stick': a bit dry and prone to cracking up.

Come in. Take a seat. We're going to perform a play and you're invited.

## *The Divorcee's Lunch*

The Players:
   Sarah: A divorcee
   Jon: An advertising executive
   Chloe: A graphic designer and married to Jon
   Ben: A French wine importer
   Tinka: An aromatherapist and married to Ben
   Laurence: A male tart and observer

*The Scene.*
   *A yuppie dining room. Lunch is under way. White plates and skinny cutlery, tall stemmed wine glasses, rough cotton napkins. Brown bread has been cut and laid out on a slab of stone. A pepper grinder the size of a newel post takes pride of place. The four bottles of Italian white wine, once set out with a surveyor's precision, now litter the table. Three are empty. The guests, having finished their charred*

*Camembert with wild fruit coulis, are tucking into the spaghetti alla putanesca. Van Morrison plays quietly in the background.*

Jon: I told him, with 100k to spend, he'd end up living in Stoke Newington.

(*Laughter all round.*)

Ben: Or Brixton.
Chloe: You can't compare the two. Brixton's so colourful.
Ben: You mean black?
Chloe: Really, Ben! You shouldn't use the B word.
Ben: Sorry, Chloe. You're right. I meant to say Anglo-African. Just slipped out.
Jon: But are they? I thought they were mostly from Jamaica. So Anglo-Jamaican, I suppose.
Chloe: But why should the Anglo come first? I mean, surely it's the other way round? I mean, first they were Jamaicans. Aren't we being insensitive to put the Anglo first? Shouldn't we say Jamaican-Anglo?
Ben: Sounds like a question: Ja make an Anglo?

(*The diners look down at their plates. No one laughs.*)

Ben: Get it? Ja make an Anglo?
Chloe: Yes, we got it, Ben, but it's just not funny. I mean, we're talking about real people. Not everything's a joke, you know. You could hurt their feelings.

Tinka: If we could all just get in touch with our chakras then there wouldn't be black and white or rich and poor. We would just be spirits of the One.

Sarah: More wine, anyone?

Ben: Chloe, I think you are being unfair. My dentist's coloured but perfectly clean. I mean, it must be hard, eating with your hands and being a dentist. Hard to keep your hands clean, I mean. So I hardly think you can call me prejudiced.

Tinka: Eating with your hands connects you with Gaia, the Earth mother. Martha from work eats with her feet and she's never had a period pain. There's so little we understand.

Jon: Mind you, there are bargains to be had in Brixton. Did I tell you that Chloe and I went to see a place there last weekend?

Chloe: Two weekends ago, Jon. Last weekend we were at the pro-abortion rally.

Jon: Of course. Well, two weeks ago, Chloe and I decide we'd go and have a look at a place that was coming up at auction.

Ben: But I thought you had struck Brixton off the list?

Jon: Oh, we have. We didn't go planning to buy, just as a fun day out.

Sarah: How exciting. Peter and I loved going to the house auctions. He proposed to me at one. He said, 'Will you buy a house with me and spend the rest of your life restoring it?' He was so romantic. *(Sarah starts to cry. Tinka offers her a serviette.)* No. Thank you, Tinka, not the Egyptian cotton. *(Laurence hands her a Kleenex and she wipes her eyes.)* I'm sorry, everyone. It's just all this talk about houses. Brings back memories.

Chloe: Perhaps we should stop.

Sarah: No. No. Go on. It's good for me. My therapist says I need to confront the past to move on. Please. Jon, darling, do go on.

Jon: Well, if you're sure. It's a jolly good story, actually. Anyway, we take the Citroën, get to Brixton all right but can't find the street. We're parked up looking at the *A-Z* when these two… what did we decide to call them in the end?

Ben: Off-white?

Sarah: Oh God, Peter's favourite colour. Well, French white, actually. We mixed it ourselves using tar. So cheap. We did the whole spare room woodwork for £10. It would have made a lovely nursery. I suppose now I ought to rent it out.

*(More tears. No Kleenex left, so kitchen roll.)*

Tinka: You should burn sandalwood. The Hindus use it to cleanse the house after a death.

Chloe: Tinka, Peter's not dead, just gone to live somewhere else.

Sarah: With that fucking woman! Not even a fucking woman. Just a girl. Let's see how she manages with his little temper tantrums. I can't see

|        | fucking Susan putting the records in the right order. Then she'll see the real Peter. |
|--------|---|
| Chloe: | Anglo-Jamaicans. |
| Jon:   | Right. Well, these two Anglo-Jamaicans tap at the window. You can imagine. Total terror. Luckily, Chloe had her pepper spray. |
| Ben:   | My God! What did you do? |
| Jon:   | That was the problem. What to do? We were parked behind a bus, so any attempt to make a run for it in the 2CV was out. I just kept my nose in the *A-Z* hoping they would go away. |
| Ben:   | Did they? |
| Chloe: | No! They kept tapping on the window. Jon had to open it. |
| Ben:   | What were they like? |
| Jon:   | Bob Marley, only bigger. |
| Ben:   | (*Singing*) Everything's gonna be all right now, everything's… |
| Chloe: | I think you should stop that, Ben. Nothing's all right for Sarah. You're being insensitive. |
| Ben:   | Sorry, Chloe. Sorry, Sarah. |
| Sarah: | Thank you, Chloe. Having you all here helps so much, you know. At a time like this, real friends make all the difference. |
| In chorus: | Of course. |
| Ben:   | So what did the two Jamaicans want? |
| Jon:   | Well, at first we didn't understand. Something about did we want blow. |
| Ben:   | Oh my God, he wanted Chloe to suck him off! Or maybe he wanted to suck you off? |

Tinka: Blow is pot. Marijuana. It's sacred in their country. Helps them astral plane.

Jon: Tinka's right. But we didn't know that, not until one of them pulled out a lump of hash the size of an egg. He wanted fifty quid for it.

Ben: Did you buy it?

Jon: Yes. We felt we had to.

Ben: How much did you end up paying?

Jon: Oh we didn't haggle.

Chloe: I wanted to, but Jon said it might not be right. Could cause trouble. Jon, show everyone the hash.

*(Jon takes out the hash which is passed round for inspection).*

Ben: Looks like a good deal. How exciting! And did you get to see the house?

Chloe: Of course.

Ben: What was it like?

Jon: Two up, two down, good original ceilings, turned balusters, three broken, but General Building Supplies have perfect matches, sashes shot, nice hydrolysed lime tile floor motif in the hall and height in the attic for a loft conversion. Fielded panel doors except to the kitchen, which was a rip-out. The bathroom would have needed a total refit as well. Maybe we could have saved the taps. All the wood would have needed dipping. Thirty to thirty-five would have sorted it.

(*Sarah sobs uncontrollably and is comforted by Tinka.*)

Sarah: Peter and I dipped all our architraves and skirtings. We set up a caustic soda tank in the garden. We'd put on our rubber gloves, and he would say, 'Let's go skinny-dipping.' What a summer that was. We did the whole ground floor. The only skinny-dipping that bitch could do wouldn't need rubber gloves. It won't last, you know. Peter will tire of the sex. He did with me. And then what will they have? No proper home. He'll come back.

(*The guests look uncomfortable.*)

Chloe: Look, Sarah, there's something you should know and, as we're your friends, you should hear it from us.
Sarah: (*Blowing her nose.*) What?
Chloe: Peter and Susan have bought a house.
Sarah: (*Between sobs.*) Where? When (*sob*) did this (*sob*) happen? No one (*sob*) told me.
Jon: We didn't want you to get hurt. Whilst the funds were in escrow, we felt it best not to tell you. The sale might have fallen through. But now they've closed, you have a right to be told.
Sarah: So you all knew?

(*Nods.*)

Sarah: What's it like?

Chloe: Are you strong enough to hear?
Sarah: Has it got an Aga?
Chloe: I'm afraid so.
Sarah: And high ceilings?
Jon: Ten feet four on the ground floor. Nine-eight on the other two.
Sarah: Oh, my God, it's a ground plus two. We always said that if we moved it would be to a triple-decker. And the garden? Don't tell me they've got a Yorkstone patio?
Jon: Yes. Reclaimed stone, I'm afraid, from Benjamin's architectural salvage.
Chloe: Come on, Jon, you don't have to make this harder than it is. This will cheer you up. The bath is avocado.
Sarah: You, you're just trying to be nice.
Tinka: Avocados are an aphrodisiac.
Ben: The bathroom can be fixed. Peter said they had their eye on that cast iron one we saw on the weekend at Le Bath.
Sarah: Hang on. How come you know so much about the house? Have you all been round to see it?

(*Embarrassed silence.*)

Chloe: Sarah, I know this is difficult, but Peter asked us round. We couldn't just say no.
Sarah: Yes, you could. It's easy. *No.*
Tinka: I said no. I was meditating in Brighton the day of the dinner party.

| | |
|---|---|
| Sarah: | A fucking dinner party. Jesus Christ! And you all went? Fuck! Did the bitch cook? |
| Jon: | Poached salmon with lemon grass and a vinaigrette made with Italian vinegar and a virgin olive oil. |
| Sarah: | Balsamic? |
| Jon: | Yes. |
| Chloe: | But not the best. |
| Sarah: | And the oil? First cold press? |
| Chloe: | Why are you putting yourself through this? |
| Sarah: | I want the details. The whole sordid lot. |
| Jon: | First cold press. Extra virgin. Picual olives. |
| Sarah: | And the wine? |
| Ben: | Chianti. |
| Sarah: | Not one of yours, I hope. |

(*Silence.*)

| | |
|---|---|
| Sarah: | Oh my God, it was. You supplied the wine! How could you be so insensitive? |
| Ben: | Sarah, be reasonable. Peter is a good customer and Susan's brother owns Friglani's on the King's Road. |
| Sarah: | Dessert? Crème brûlée? |

(*Jon nods.*)

| | |
|---|---|
| Sarah: | Peter's favourite. Individual portions? |

(*Another nod.*)

Chloe: But not as good as yours. Too… gelatinous.
Ben: Oh yes, absolutely. We all remarked on it.

(*An unpleasant silence descends, punctuated by the Van Morrison record which has stuck on 'someone like you keeps me satisfied'. Sarah gets up to change the music. The guests look at each other. Chloe whispers something to Jon.*)

Chloe: (*Getting up.*) Darling, we really must be heading off. The traffic's going to be ghastly with the protest on.

(*The other guests follow suit.*)

Sarah: Oh. Yes. Of course. Can't you at least stay for coffee? I've bought Lavazza, it's just come into Regagio's.
Jon: Another time, Sarah. If you keep it in the airtight French jars we bought you for Christmas it will stay fresh.
Sarah: Peter took the jars. I kept the garlic crusher and pasta machine.
Ben: Well, use the spaghetti jar you bought at Conran's, it's got a rubber seal.
Jon: Yes, what a good idea! You see, life isn't all bad.

(*The guests make their way into the hall, awkwardly hug Sarah and file out. Chloe is last and turns at the door.*)

Chloe: So, Sarah, who's that young man? Bit quiet, but maybe you don't need him for his conversation?

Sarah: *(Having paused and come to a decision.)* Let's just say that two can play Peter's game. And he *can* talk. Went to Cambridge. And he's a designer. You wouldn't believe some of the clients he's working for.

Chloe: You dark horse! We must meet for a latte, and you can tell me all about it, girl to girl.

Sarah: I will on one condition.

Chloe: Anything.

Sarah: Tell Peter.

Chloe: Of course.

I was clearing up the dishes when Sarah returned. Jon had forgotten to take the hash which Tinka had left in the fruit bowl.

"You don't have to do that, Laurence."

"Not a problem, glad to help. You look tired. I'll do the washing up."

"How sweet of you, but you'll tell Simon and he'll think me a bad hostess."

"OK, so let's wash up together."

"All right."

"But first let's roll a joint."

I had decided halfway through lunch that I wouldn't try and seduce Sarah. She was too vulnerable, and anything started would have to be followed through. I didn't want a relationship with her and the last thing she needed was to feel used. I had some morals, you know. Not many, and perhaps mostly particular to me, but morals all the same. Or maybe it wasn't morals, just my selfish concern that it would all end up a hassle? Either way, what I hadn't counted on was her seducing me.

I lit the spliff, took a toke and passed it on to her.

"Oh, no. No, thanks."

"You've never tried it?"

"Only at uni. But uni doesn't count, does it?"

"Everything counts. Fancy a puff? A trip down memory lane?"

"Umm... oh, what the hell."

She inhaled and coughed. I washed and she dried and put away.

In most flings, the order of events is flirting, sex, and if all goes well, then maybe the washing up, a sort of rite which consolidates the intimacy. What I hadn't counted on was that with yuppies, the washing up *is* the flirting and the sex a prize in recognition that you know how to rinse glasses and that cast iron pots should be oiled before stored.

As I soaped and rinsed, I could hear her humming. She had a man in the kitchen wearing a striped apron, the yuppie equivalent of a man in the bathroom showering after sex and coming out in your dressing gown.

The locking nut on the mixer tap was loose and it wobbled when I swung the spout to rinse. She apologised, as though her fault, something to be ashamed of. Apart from that, our little domestic scene seemed to please her.

Once the kitchen had returned to magazine perfection, we went and sat by the fire. I relit the spliff. She showed me her albums of photos which chronicled the refurbishment of the house. It was her portfolio, her CV, which vouched that she had been a good wife.

The fire, the spliff, the booze at lunch, a lonely woman with a young guy, the need to seek revenge and to bolster self-esteem, the fact it was a Saturday, so no looming weekday work, they all conspired to make what happened happen. We had exhausted the five albums and two spliffs and were standing by the door. She was well and truly stoned. It was getting late. That's what I said, anyway.

I loitered, looking for an appropriate farewell comment, something complementary about the house perhaps, when she said, "Stay... Oh God, I shouldn't have said that."

"I—"

And she kissed me, pressing me against the bull-nosed dado moulding which divided the reclaimed panelling from the sponge-effect paintwork.

"Stay. If you can. If you want to."

Another kiss.

"Oh God, I'm stoned." She laughed and pointed at a particular section of random scumbles on the wall. "Look. Beside the painting. Can you see the cat? I've never noticed it before."

"Yes, but it looks more like four men carrying a heavy ball to me."

"And there, up a bit, to the right, can you see the ship?"

"Where? Oh, I see it... and there's a whale, just below."

My arm just seemed to find her waist, her hip my hip.

"Ha ha... and there's a dog pulling something, a banana or a canoe."

I turned to look at her but instead of meeting her eyes found her lips and tongue.

West is west and sex is sex,
No prizes for what happened next.

She had a good body. Yuppies usually have. She just didn't know what to do with it. Just like their living rooms. They make the perfect room but fail when it comes to the living. She was industrious, ticking off positions like items on a shopping list in Sainsbury's. Not mechanical, just diligent. She took her earrings off and placed them on the bedside table, next to the alarm clock set for six and a book on French cuisine. She had a mole on her shoulder and red indented circles at the base of her breasts where the wire stiffeners of her bra had dug in, that and some marbling from cellulite on her thighs, the thing of shapes to come.

We fucked in silence on the futon, the window shutters half closed. She smelt of soap. We kept the duvet over us, our bodies the frame of our feather tent. Not furtive, just private. The walls still had too much of her husband in them to risk coming out from under. She shut her eyes when I licked her pussy and held my hand. She didn't squeeze, just held it lightly, a second point of contact to close the circle. When she came, she called me Peter. I held her in my arms until she was asleep, dressed quietly and went downstairs.

I found the toolbox in the basement, along with skis and a chair waiting to be restored. It took me perhaps five minutes to tighten the locking nut on the kitchen tap. I left the spanner on the worktop, my lover's parting note.

It was raining outside and chilly, the autumn air already whispering premonitions of winter. I walked home, passing house on house: little yuppie castles. We do the best we can, learning the rules and trying to abide by them. They built their matching fortresses to bolster the pretence that life was permanent, an enduring thing and not a one-line joke. I did the same, using experiences for bricks, building high and deep my little Laurence fortress, my house of thrills. Not built to last, but it would see me through.

# Sweet and Sour Porking

"So what's the verdict?" asked Alistair.

We were sitting in Sam's Malaysian restaurant on Church Street, a ten-minute walk from Glading Terrace. It was one of our favourite haunts. Cheap, filling and tasty food. No frills, dubious sanitation and a loud and friendly atmosphere.

I've never liked 'fine dining', where you tremble at the sommelier's approach and struggle to keep your elbows down. No one ever talks in those places, too frightened, perhaps, that the waiter will declare their conversation too ordinary for the dish, their jokes as out of place as red wine with fish. Marco Pierre White and the other wizards may cast their spells and turn ice into fire, bringing magic to the food, but in so doing they rob us of another kind of magic. A simpler kind, conjured out of nothing: the timeless wonder of a group of humans breaking bread together, at their ease, alive to feed another day.

Let's face it, few of us will ever know the real pleasure food can bring. We will never run with others through the forest, acutely aware of every sound and smell, belly empty, straining our muscles until within reach to throw the spear and end another life. The perfect simplicity of it all. The hunter's return, the open fire, one life taken so another can go on. The lying under the stars, sated, a little blood and fat still lingering on the lips. We can't go back to that, but hey, there must be a middle road, something better than a deconstructed endive foam, which the waiter tells us will bring back memories of shopping in New York.

Then there was Sam himself, an alcoholic who had told his wife – a diminutive and feisty woman whose sari trailed on the floor– that he had stopped drinking. The restaurant didn't have a license to serve alcohol but allowed the regulars to bring in booze, bought two doors down at the off-license. Sam and I had an arrangement. When taking our order, he would slip me a pound. In exchange, I would buy an extra beer and leave the can of Special Brew open on the table. When his wife wasn't looking, he would take a swig as he worked the tables. At the time, I prized our special relationship as setting me apart from the other diners. Now I look back and see it for what it was: a drunk and a liar to his wife being aided in his vice and deceit by a guy who did it just to score cheap points.

Alistair was my oldest friend. I first met him aged fifteen at school. I was wandering about in break and went into the library, a sacred room reserved for sixth-formers. He was sitting alone reading. He looked so mature. For a start, he wore glasses. Then there was the book, Aristotle in the original Greek. Finally, the boy himself, so self-contained. All my peers were doing Monty

Python silly walks and lighting their farts, and here he was finding good company in words spoken by the long dead. We became friends and he catapulted me into some semblance of maturity. He was shy and had his share of nervous ticks. He would clear his throat compulsively and would slightly raise and shake his left leg after every fifth step. Our friendship continued through university and on to London, where he shared a house down the road. He brought me reason and I brought a touch of madness which perhaps thrilled that gentle man.

That evening we were joined by Martin Stone, another Cambridge boy and fully paid-up member of our little band of brothers. Alistair, over ice cream and exotic fruits, had set the following problem.

A psychopath has been on a killing spree, downing seventeen women. The eighteenth gets away. A police photofit is distributed, and two men found to match. Same height and build, same hand and shoe size – he had left a glove and footprints had been measured. Same blood group. Same facial features, or near as damn it. DNA testing was still years away and a positive visual identification was needed to convict the killer. The two line up, and the victim is called. She can't tell them apart but knows for sure it's one of them. Two men, one innocent, one a ruthless killer who will strike again. So what's the verdict?

Martin, scriptwriter and self-therapist, kicked us off.

"Yeah, good question but, you know, the judge, he's got to let them both free. Presumption of innocence. It's fundamental. Any other verdict would have a fifty per cent chance of convicting an innocent dude."

We swigged our beers. I wasn't sure I agreed with Martin.

"He should convict both. OK, one guy gets to take a fall unfairly, but who knows how many innocent women will be saved from being murdered."

Alistair hankered after living in a world where self-sacrifice was still the norm.

"Ideally, the one who's innocent should offer to be imprisoned, provided the other is convicted as well. I'm reading this book on the First World War. Really interesting. There's this account of going over the trenches. The soldiers knew that most of them would die, so one or two could get through and breach the enemy line. Amazing bravery."

"Or stupid to have gone to war," said Martin. "No, I don't mean that. It's the war that's stupid."

"Maybe the judge, like Solomon, should acquit the one who gives himself up?" I proposed.

Martin was quick to point out that anyone capable of killing was also capable of lying and so my judge might well be freeing the killer.

The problem Alistair set went to the heart of the question: Whose interests does justice serve, the individual's, or the collective?

We had been born into a world where the collective came first, the individual's interests subordinated to the well-being of the group, which in turn looked after the individual. Yet by the '80s, the individual was claiming centre stage. It was happening all around us and fast.

Birth rates were falling as adults found neither the will nor the need to procreate. With the welfare state and mobility of labour and opportunity, children were beginning to lose their appeal. They were being relegated from labour in the family business, cheap care in old age and token immortality to a burden on money and time. Where my mother's parents scrimped and saved to finance the next generation, seeing the success of their children as their own, we were committed to leaving nothing behind. Sex, that instinctual guarantee of procreation, had been separated out, thanks to a little pill, and was a sport in its own right. The unit of consciousness had moved from tribe to extended family, then nuclear, and finally, if you will, to atomic: the individual.

I remember standing in the square of a little village in Spain some fifteen years ago. I had my daughter by the hand and a puppy held in the other. A Spanish family saw us and made a fuss of my child, completely ignoring the puppy. Then an English couple approached, enthusing about the puppy but paying no attention to my daughter. People still need to feel capable of offering love and getting some in return. But puppies provide those services at a fraction of the cost of children.

The truth is we assign little value to a human life except our own and those of a cherished few. The reason why we can't bear to see the judge condemn the two, and in so doing condemn the innocent, is that it could have been us found unfairly guilty. The women who might die if both go free touch us less. Their deaths are more remote, hypothetical. We'll buy a T-shirt made by enslaved children, and only have a twinge of guilt, quickly wiped away, as we admire our shape in the mirror. We'll upgrade the TV till it spans the wall to better see a documentary on Africa before we send a tenner to save that very child we saw. That's human nature. But let a tiny child get caught in a well in Surrey, let the TV stations set up cameras, and the nation will be glued. Politicians will cancel holidays; the Queen might send a message. An all-night vigil will be held around the well. Why? Because it could have been our child, one of the cherished few, down that dark hole. We will not sacrifice the individual because we are the individual. Society can go fuck itself.

We've always had our concentric circles of care, but at least they used to reach out as far as our community, county, even a whole country. Now most people's outer circle barely strokes their own front door.

We talked and drank our beers till Sam shut shop and carried on in my tiny living room. We concluded nothing, but the matter of what was justice had been raised and led to my recounting the following story.

For the last three weeks I had been working for Anthony Claire, a brilliant historian and deeply damaged man. He had bought a four storey house in Islington, complete with lodger, and the 'Z' team were doing the place up in preparation for his forthcoming marriage to Jennifer, a research student from Oxford, his old university. They were professional academics after fame and power, and knowledge was a means of achieving both.

Their obsession wasn't the house – no yuppies here – but rather a constant need to optimise time. Dr Claire would always run. Up and down the stairs, through the hall, shouting instructions to his bride or workmen. He was also paranoid, and we would have site meetings in the downstairs loo, a tiny space, so no one could overhear. Utterly surreal and deeply disturbing. He scrunched up between the wall and basin, I sitting on the loo taking notes. His bride calling through the door to remind him to take his tranquillisers and detailing plans for the wedding. Thank God there were no mobile phones back then, or he would have had six and used them all at once.

He once went berserk because Pepe the Knife had left the front door open.

"Anyone passing by could look through. Jennifer and I could have been making love in the hall. This really won't do!"

I suppose it's possible that they could have done the deed in the hall to save on time, joined and waddling in tandem from the foreplay area on the landing, via penetration on the stair, to climax somewhere near the umbrella stand. But I don't think so. Ad hoc copulation would not have furthered their career of marriage or the marriage of their careers. More likely and simpler to surmise, Dr Claire objected to the limitation of his possibilities, however remote and absurd such possibility.

He acquired knowledge like a rancher might ever acquire adjacent fields, extending his dominion. The cowboy magnate then goes to town and demands a special beer in the saloon. They don't stock it and don't know why he's asking, as he only drinks whisky. Of course, they've missed the point. It wasn't the beer he wanted, just the right to have it. So, too, with Dr Claire.

Imagine his frustration with having a lodger! If being denied the possibility of sex in the hall at 11am blew his composure, what agony the man must have been in because a whole suite of rooms was closed to him. Again, the fact that he had no use for them was irrelevant. They were a beer he couldn't drink.

A meeting was scheduled in the loo. Claire wanted the lodger out. His name was Nigel Wilson and he lived alone. An old-school homosexual, he would feed the birds in the park each day on his way to work in the bowels of some civil service building. He was shy, gentle, middle-to-late aged and adored opera. He would play *Aida* as he sat in his armchair, cradling the cat, a little glass of Amontillado at hand. I speculated that the arias brought back memories of some unrequited love. Perhaps of a tenor he bought tickets to hear night after night until he saw the man kissing a chorus girl and went home, never to risk love again.

He was also rather deaf and played his gramophone loudly. Far from annoying Dr Claire, who was rarely at home, the man saw this debility as an opportunity. He drew up a new contract for the tenant, including a clause on noise. He then held the rent at a low price to sugar-coat the ploy. For my sins, I was the one who delivered this Trojan horse and got his signature. I am ashamed to this day.

All was set for phase two. He hired a decibel counter and measured the sound from the rooms above. Readings were marked down with dates and times. My workers were called as witnesses and paid a little extra to sign the entries. We all played Judas for Claire's gold. With the contract signed and proof of breach, he delivered the coup de grâce: notice to quit.

I was there when Nigel was served. He was on his way to work, sandwiches and a KitKat in his lunchbox. He offered me a stick of chocolate. I turned him down. The thought of taking food from the man I had betrayed was all too much.

Claire was waiting for him, lurking in the copulation hall, clutching his pills and the notice to quit.

"Mr Wilson, a word please. This won't take long. I have a document you need to sign receipt of."

Nigel set his tired leather briefcase down, removed a woolly glove and took the papers. He fumbled for his glasses, saying sorry to the end, set them on his nose and read.

"What's this? What are you playing at? Look, if the music disturbs you, I'll turn it down. All right?"

"No, I am afraid it is not all right. You are in breach of contract. Clause seven. You can't deny it, I have your signature on the contract, you see. Now, kindly sign receipt and we can all get back to work."

"Come on, Anthony, you can't be serious. You've only just renewed the lease. Why didn't you say something? We can sort this out, you know. I… I've been living here for twenty-six years. You can't just throw me out. I have nowhere to go. And my cat. The birds. I'll just lower the volume on the amp. This is a joke, surely!"

"No, Mr Wilson, not being able to complete my work on China for the BBC because of your infernal racket is not a joke. Look, mindful of the fact that you have been here quite some time, you will note that I am not seeking punitive damages for loss of earnings. I think, in the circumstances, I have been more than fair. Do you follow?"

"No, I don't... follow! You planned this from the beginning, didn't you? Getting me to sign the new agreement. You had it all worked out, didn't you?"

"Now, Mr Wilson, my time is limited, and I would remind you that your tone and words could be construed as slander. You have two choices, either sign now or I will have my lawyers serve you with notice at your place of work. Why not avoid a scene and sign? I have less than a minute left. What is your reply?"

"My reply? My reply? This is my reply." And with that, he hit him. Punched him in the face. Not much of a blow. An old man who had probably never hit a soul, striking out, cornered by a growling legal document. A glancing blow, but enough to seal his fate.

A doctor, lawyers and the police were called. Claire made an indignant statement. Two pages on the brutal lodger, whom he had tried to be kind to allowing him tenure for a charitable rent, the raucous homosexual prone to violence that made his life hell and was now a physical danger, who could pounce when he and his bride were vulnerable in bed. Criminal charges were added to the civil case.

We completed our work a few days later and the 'Z' team moved on. A month or so passed and I was wondering what had become of Nigel. I knew his habits, what time he left, what bench was his by custom in the park. I brought some bread with me.

He was there, all right, gloves folded through the handle of his briefcase set beside him, lunchbox open and an egg sandwich in his hand from which he broke off bits to give the cooing birds. They milled about his feet, seeing not a lonely homosexual living in an attic, but a benefactor, a god on his slatted wooden throne dispensing food to the faithful.

I kept my distance, wanting him to see me first and decide to talk or not. That's the least I could do. I sat two benches down and watched him. He was so ordered, rituals for everything, from how he double-knotted his shoes to the way he wiped his hands after each triangle of sandwich.

I never knew exactly what he did, down there in the depths of Whitehall. I imagined him sitting in a little office with a hook for his coat, a photo from his days at sea with the Navy, some filing cabinets with labels neatly written with a fountain pen. I saw him holding documents for 'pending review' or 'to file' and stamping each accordingly. He would have his sleeves rolled up, two folds, no extra creases, and would read and stamp till one and lunch, in a corner of the canteen, alone with his arias and thoughts of what he and his cat would have for tea. Then back to view and stamp, fold down the sleeves, take up his coat and leave for home and the luxury of dreaming in his chair, a little music and a friendly puss. Not much to ask.

Sandwiches gone, hands wiped a final time, lunchbox lid pressed down and double-checked before stowing in his case, he stood up to go and saw me. I was feeding the birds with a bagel. A peace offering.

"You should make the pieces smaller; they like it that way. If you hold a few crumbs in your hand and keep still, they'll sit and take them from you."

*Trusting*, I thought, *like him*. We chatted and of course the matter of the eviction and charges came up. I told him I was sorry for the part I played.

He said that there was nothing to forgive, that I had done my duty by my client. That was kind of him to let me off, but the judge and jury in my heart have never acquitted me. He could see that in my eyes, perhaps, my genuine remorse, and gave me strange solace.

Both the eviction and the criminal charges had been dropped. Dr Claire had committed suicide. He had jumped under a train on the Bakerloo line.

Solace, but what a mess all the same. I had conspired to help legal argument try and win over morality. The police and lawyers had upheld the letter of the law and shut their eyes to human nature. The 'letter of the law'. That says it all. The pen is mightier than the sword, but those without pens or untrained, perhaps unwilling, to wield such a dirty weapon have no other recourse than the blade. Dr Claire drew up and dropped a deadly document, drafted with poisoned ink, designed to strike at the heart. Nigel's pen was only filled with Waterman's Royal Blue so, searching in his armoury, he only found a fist. What a messy business. Blood on the tracks and we the fools joking about a twitchy nutter and not seeing a man so deeply sad that his pain could only be drowned out by screaming steel issuing from a gaping black tunnel.

All in all, a sour porking.

Shortly afterwards I was given my most curious assignment. One so extraordinary that to this day I have to check the scar it left to be certain that it actually happened. Above my left eye, a little line where the hair won't grow. A path through my facial undergrowth that takes me back to Marilyn and our madness.

I should have turned the job down, taken note of Peter's reticence to my accepting a mission he saw as 'smelling like trouble'. But at twenty-four, armoured by the invulnerability of youth, emblazoned with 'no pain, no gain', trouble was a fashionable and irresistible scent.

"Another divorced one. Everyone seems to be doing it. Divorcing, I mean. Right bastard of a husband, or so she says. It's the kids that I feel sorry for. Always get caught up in the fight. I mean, they ought to have the love. Not much about later on. Get the love in when you're young. Sets you up, doesn't it, you know, for all the shit after."

"You mean like a good cooked breakfast?" I suggested.

"Blimey, that's good! Exactly that. A good full English to see you through. A love fry-up. Great, that!"

"So what's she after, this divorcee? The usual comfort shag? A bit of revenge, perhaps?"

"She says she wants to have a talk with her bloke. He'll only communicate through lawyers' letters, and she says there are some things she wants to tell him face-to-face."

"No sex then?"

"Seems not. Well, maybe sort of. You see, her idea is that you ring the bloke up and say you know who's fucking his wife and—"

"Hang on, I thought you said they were divorced?"

"Deary me, so I did. Well, actually, they are in the middle of it all. Fighting over all the stuff. He wants the lot. The kids, the house, the lot. Got the nanny on his side to say Marilyn's not a fit mum. Apparently, the bastard's shagging her. His new missus all lined-up. He's got preliminary custody of the kids and kicked her out the house until the trial. Anyway, as I said, she wants to talk in private with him, get a few things off her chest, I imagine."

"Fair enough, but how do I fit in? And how come she came to you? Branching out into marriage counselling, are you?"

"Give over, mate! Having a laugh? Peter, a marriage counsellor? Now, that's rich, that is! I can't keep a boyfriend for more than a week! Anyway, she didn't come to me. Not directly. Came through one of my regulars. Bit of a private dick. Ha ha, private dick! Small stuff. Ha ha. Photos, recording conversations. Not your Sherlock Holmes. I had him on the massage table. I asked him how business was and got down to lick his balls. He says he's making a living, enough to pay his daughter's riding lessons. Then he says a job's come up that didn't square with him. That's when he told me about Marilyn.

"He'd done some dodgy stuff for her lawyer in the past. You know. Planting evidence, taking pictures of husbands being naughty. Says she's looking for a bloke to tell her old man that he knows who's knobbing his missus and for him to come round if he wants to know. He's up to show that she's been naughty, done adultery, so she's certain he'll accept. She'll hide at the place of the meeting and gets to talk to him in private."

"So why doesn't your regular want the job?"

"Says it's too up close and personal. The blokes he uses keep their distance and just as well. He says there could be a barney and his lads don't know when to stop. Said it all smelt iffy, that it would end up messy. Particularly as the husband's a journalist, the sort who'd call the cops. I'm only telling you all this because you asked what was going down. You should let this one pass. It's not even what you signed up to do. Wait a few days and Uncle Pete will sort you out something with a bit more cock involved. I shouldn't have even mentioned it. So what you been up to, anyway?"

"I'll do it. I hate bullies. I've been involved with one and didn't do the right thing. Didn't stop him. Maybe this is my chance to redeem myself."

"What are you talking about? You've lost me good and proper."

I told him about Claire, the lodger and my shame.

"Blimey! What a mess. Poor sod. Well, both poor sods. One dead, the other in the closet. But I don't like to see you beating yourself up about it. Can't help everyone. Let this one pass."

"Come on, Peter. You know I can't. Give me her number and I promise to be careful."

"You better be. You're employee of the month, you are, and I can't have you out of service. Promise to be careful?"

"I promise and I tell you what I'll do, I'll meet her first. See the lie of the land and if she really is the victim. I'm not going to back the villain another time."

He gave me the number.

We arranged to meet at her place, a basement flat near the Angel tube. I arrived at eight in the evening.

"Hi! Come in. Sorry for the mess."

She was a refugee from her marriage and in transit, the flat her temporary camp. Not a home, as such, no sense of consolidation over time, just a halfway house to pass through on the way to higher, firmer ground.

Everything about the place was neutral, designed to not be noticed. Built for all of a certain income bracket and thus a match for no one. White, of course, throughout. Flush doors; knobs, not handles, as handles ask a question, and knobs are conciliatory. Small skirting boards devoid of mouldings, all function, no form. Ceilings set to British standards, one foot above the outstretched arm of homo average. A ceiling rose per room, sockets for TV, the kettle, oven, fridge, one by the bed and an extra for a hairdryer. Tolerant-of-stains beige carpets, neither thin enough to cause complaint nor thick enough to settle into. The human equivalent of a cage in a centre for abandoned pets. Sure, the bedding's clean, two scoops of food arrive at dusk and a volunteer pats you once a day. But it's not home.

She had her children with her. Three, five and seven. Two boys, one girl. The older two were watching TV, cartoons. The little one was drawing in a book, coloured crayons in a mug. All new. All factory sharpened. The remains of their dinner were still on the table, some juice in a plastic cup, a finger joint of fish and some ketchup on a plate. That and abandoned peas, the mother's serving exceeding her children's tolerance of veg.

I know these places. All divorced parents do who lose the family home or visit from abroad and have to stay in halfway houses. It starts with standing outside the door that once led to your erstwhile life. You ring the bell and put on your happy face. The other parent, once someone with whom you exchanged the vow to love, calls out, "Who is it?"

Good question. Who are you now? A retired employee visiting his old place of work, tolerated but not welcome? No longer part of the team? The children are called.

"It's your father."

Not 'daddy' with connotations of cuddly. Not that wonderful word that baby said, looking up at you, and in so doing changed your world. Just 'father', a definition of biological status.

You announce, "We're going to have fun."

Do they believe you? You don't believe yourself. You've done your research and have a list of events and places to fill the weekend.

"There's a concert in the park. No? Not tempted? How about a swim? Oh, Mummy says you've got a cold and can't. Well, what about the science museum? There's a new show on beetles. No? Too creepy? So let's go shopping and have some lunch. We'll have fun, just you see."

Refugees, you buy some toys and make lunch last as long as possible. Then back to the halfway house, the TV and the fiction that all is well. You tell a joke over tea but try too hard. You ask your oldest how is school and he mentions a friend you've never heard of, placing a little distance between you.

You are dispossessed, in transit, your life flight cancelled, trying to sleep on a chair designed to sit an hour, clutching your voucher for the courtesy breakfast, watching the clock, counting the hours till you can cash it in. Filling time when once there never seemed to be enough.

"Sit down. Thanks for coming. I'll put the children to bed and then we can talk. Can I get you anything? A drink, perhaps?"

I sat on the sofa, and she brought me a glass of wine. I watched her as she went about her business. She was of an indeterminate age, somewhere in limbo between youth and middle life. Was she beautiful? Ugly? Neither. With most people their features trigger a valuation. Such small eyes! Did you see her nose? Tiny breasts considering her bum was so big. But Marilyn's eyes were just eyes, her nose a nose, breasts, breasts.

I spent some time in a convent near Sevilla. Where nuns had once contemplated the whims of God, the new owner was setting up an arts centre. There was a painter in residence, and I spent my lunch hour watching him work his canvas. He was painting a nude from memory and grew her from the inside out, like a baby in the womb.

First a few loose pencil lines; then a little detail, the rough shape of the face, some curves, a place for hands but no fingers yet. Each day his woman grew, nourished from his palette, fed through the invisible umbilical cord which binds the artist to his work. After two weeks, the woman was all there, all her bits in the places bits should be. I had to leave and asked him what would happen next.

"Now the hard part. I have to make her specific. Right now she's any woman. I have to make her live and be the person I remember."

With Marilyn, the artist never finished, never made her specific. She looked tired. Not the kind of tiredness that comes from a missed night's sleep. No. This was long term. The kind we learn to live with.

These days I like to tinker with my house. I have a wireless drill. Sometimes I'm in a rush and don't have time to recharge it. I keep drilling away on half-power, the work so much harder. That's deep tiredness, living on half-power, all tasks exhausting.

But more than tired she looked… how can I put it? Extinguished?

I once visited a brothel in Calcutta. It was my birthday, and the district Chief of Police was showing me around. We were in a market when he stopped between the stalls of spices and pointed out a door where men were loitering.

"That's where they use the women," he said.

I asked to look inside. I wish I hadn't. He came in with me, his presence parting the throng of waiting customers until we stood in a corridor of little cubicles with curtains. A shanty town of women waiting to be used. He shouted something and one by one each cubicle disgorged its whoring man. Poor workers sneaking an orgasm before going home to pray and eat. Some came out quietly, ashamed to be caught in that place, others ready to complain until he touched his night stick.

We were left alone in the corridor.

"You pick any you like. Five rupees, twenty minutes."

I pulled back curtain after curtain until I couldn't stand it anymore. Each cubicle was tiny, just the space for a single bed. No sheets or pillows, just a concrete ledge and a blood-and-cum-stained mean-mouthed mattress. There they were, chained to their beds by the wrist, one hand free to work the cocks. Some were dark and squat, perhaps from Kashmir, others tall and slender as women are from Kerala in the south. They were too far gone to look at me, their eyes the only part of them they could keep safe from further humiliation. All except one. She was younger than the rest, maybe sixteen, barely older than my daughter now. Perhaps she thought I was there to liberate her, that the hurried departure of her client meant salvation was at hand. I wish I'd never seen into those eyes. They had no anger, no fear, not even tears. Oh, how much better to have seen emotion in them, however sad. But I saw nothing. Emptiness.

It is said that eyes are windows through which we can see a person's inner self. Those eyes offered a view of nothing, only the void where a person used to live. Beyond anger, beyond fear, beyond the hope of hope. Where once those windows showed a little girl who dreamt of gold-threaded saris and dancing Bollywood princes, of afternoons painting swirls and constellations on her mother's hands with henna, of gossip and splashing by the river scrubbing clothes, there was nothing. No past, present or future, all rubbed away by the lecherous hands of strangers. Extinguished.

I ran into the street and vomited.

So no, we can't use 'extinguished' for Marilyn. It would diminish that Calcuttan girl. Let's say… inured. Inured to suffering.

Marilyn told me everything. I am lucky, if that's the word, that people confide in me. I think they confuse my fascination for their lives with care. Or perhaps they somehow know that I've seen enough, done enough, fucked up enough, not to criticise? Listening is like sex. You need to be attentive, catch the subtext, the important stuff hidden in the pauses. Or maybe I was like the hitch-hiker who gets the life story of the driver who picks him up knowing that two junctions down, the traveller will leave, and with him any criticism? For whatever reason, Marilyn told me everything.

She had been raised an Appalachian mountain girl in Bluefield, West Virginia. Born to Baptist parents, second generation settlers from Sweden, she grew up to do her duty. A no-nonsense girl who rose at six and took care of her little baby brother in the evenings. She had had three lovers. A boy from the town who took her virginity in the woods, a brief fling with a ski instructor twenty years her senior, and David Snelling, the man she married. She had met him at Salem International, the university where she studied Land Management for a year. That's all it took before the smooth-tongued foreign correspondent had her hooked, wheeled in and back to London.

A girlfriend and I once set about creating categories of men. A hierarchy of males from Top Geezer, down through Good Bloke, Dude, Bloke, Boy, Unfinished Dinner, Tampax, Disposable Lighter Flint, and at the very bottom, Bidet Plug. David would have made a harlot's fanny-washer proud. I could tell, not so much by what she said about him, though damning through and through, but by what she had become. A footprint tells us the weight and build of the person who passed that way. So, too, with her, imprinted, trampled by his brutish ways as surely as with a hobnailed boot.

I have this mental picture of why and how he chose her, an analogy I want to share. I see him at a horse fair. He's come in from an outlying farm and is rarely seen in town. He's thrifty and has brought some mutton with him to save the cost of a meal. A group of men are admiring a fine mare, prizing her splendid haunches, her glistening mane and coat, the fine turned ankles and flaring nostrils.

He sniggers to himself. *What fools*, he thinks, *that mare will never stand the winters.* He moves on, dismissive of any animal with pride and spirit. At the furthest point of the fair, behind the last stalls, tied to a tree, he sees her. A dray mare, a one-year-old. Not a looker, just a worker.

"Interested in the mare, are you, sir?"

"Maybe. Does she eat a lot?"

"No. Most economical."

"And will she work and take the winters?"

"Oh, yes. You'll need to break her in, though."

"Not a problem. I like to break them in myself. My way." He checks her teeth and haunches, punching the muscle. "I'll take her if the price is right."

So it was with Marilyn. David went to market with his shopping list:

- ✔ Limited experience with men so I can set the rules of how a woman must please her man.
- ✔ Can cook and clean without complaint.
- ✔ Must bear me children and rear them as I require.
- ✔ Must not have any personal wishes, get sick, or otherwise annoy or incur costs.
- ✔ No friends or family near at hand.
- ✔ Strong and big-boned, to take the pain.

He bought her, paying with promises of London and sophistication. He chose well and for ten years Marilyn served her purpose. But the bully needs to see the suffering he is causing – or where's the fun? And Marilyn became inured.

"At first the things he did to me – you know, sex things – really hurt. He liked that, the bastard. He liked to see me cry. But then I somehow got used to it. I thought about the children or what I would cook the following day to disconnect. I just took it. He couldn't handle that. Couldn't get it up. That's when he started beating me. He used to drag me by the leg on the basement concrete floor. Said I was only useful as a mop."

"Why didn't you call the police?"

"I did once. They said it was a domestic and that I needed to be sympathetic."

"Christ!"

"He got furious with me after that. I didn't bother to try again."

One of the children started crying and she went to sooth him. On returning, she asked me if I wanted to eat and proceeded to cook lemon chicken. She was so efficient, just got on with it.

Over dinner she explained about the nanny.

"He started having sex with her about a year ago. She's only twenty-six. I felt sorry for her, in fact. I tried to talk to her, warn her. But she said I was jealous because David loved her and not me. I didn't care. It was a relief. That made him all the madder. He started divorce proceedings and got the nanny and a couple of his friends to say I was unfit as a mother. He wants everything, you know. The house, the children, the lot. I just want to have a talk with him. Will you help me? I really need your help. I can pay you, of course."

"Yes. But don't pay me. We'll get David to pay."

We spent the rest of the evening planning the meeting down to the last detail.

Our squat was moving up in the world. I had opened up the loft, slapped a spiral staircase in and made a bedroom. It was really just a hut set up on the roof, but it gave me some extra space.

The setting up of the meeting went far easier than I had expected. But then again, when the prize on offer – in this case, a lover's name – is sufficiently desired, the punter will silence his own suspicions. I called him at his work.

"Is that David?"

"Yes. Who are you?"

"My name is Laurence and I have some information you definitely want."

"What have you got? A lead for a story? Are you a journalist?"

"No. A lead to help you with your divorce."

"What? I don't even know you. Is this a joke?"

"No, no joke. I just happen to know that your wife is having an affair and I know who with."

"How did you get this number?"

"The guy who's shagging her told me your name and where you worked. I just rang reception and asked to be put through."

"So why tell me?"

"You guys pay for information, don't you? I need some money. Anyway, I don't particularly like the bloke who's doing her. So I get to piss him off and make some cash. Now, are you interested or what?"

"Suppose I was interested, what do you want?"

"A hundred quid. Bring it to my flat and I'll tell you his name and where he lives."

"A hundred quid. Forget it."

"OK. Nice talking to you, bye."

"Wait. Wait. You've got proof?"

"No, but I can tell you where they meet, and you can get the photos done."

"Seventy-five pounds. Last offer."

"A hundred."

"Eighty."

"A hundred."

"Oh, fuck you. OK, a hundred. But if this is a joke, you will not be laughing."

"No joke."

I gave him the address and we agreed he would come round in two days' time at 7:30pm, when I knew my 'sisters' would be away.

I meticulously prepared for the meet and the possibility of violence. First, I covered the only sofa with coats and books. Then I placed a kitchen knife and some spoons and forks on the only other chair, which I set next to the cupboard in the living room where I kept the plates and cutlery.

At 7:15pm, Marilyn went upstairs to the bedroom with the promise that she wouldn't make a sound until called. When the doorbell rang, I grabbed a tea-towel and let him in.

He was as I had imagined. Not the details, just the general miserable effect. A small man with mangy hair, beady eyes and a little moustache. Big tashes can enhance a face like horns do a stag. Waxed and sculpted moustaches, too, adding as they do a certain style and idiosyncrasy. David's tash was measly, grubby, like a smear of grot formed on the wall from a dripping gutter.

"Are you Laurence?"

"Yes. Are you David?"

"Yes."

"Come in. Sorry, I'm just drying up. Please, sit where you can. On the chair. Can you hand me the cutlery?"

He picked it up and I was careful to use the tea-towel.

I put it away with his fingerprints on the knife. So far so good.

"I am sorry, but I have to take precautions. I will need to search you. You may have a recorder or whatever and what I have to tell you is only for your ears."

"That is quite unnecessary."

"My rules. No search. No name."

"Fuck you. OK. OK. But I don't want your hands on me. Here." He handed me a cassette recorder.

"Anything else? Do I have to search you?"

He proceeded to extract from his coat a viscous little cosh with a flexible springy arm ending in a large steel ball.

"Here."

"I'll take that, thank you." The cosh was a bonus I hadn't planned on.

I've often wondered since that evening why he gave me the cosh. I mean, if a guy comes armed, why hand the weapon over? It's only now, when I am revisiting those times writing this book, that I know the answer. Basically, he just copped out.

Thinking about hurting someone isn't violence. The reality of blood and guts, of inflicting pain, is suppressed by the intellectual game of planning. On leaving his house, I can imagine David tooling up, even making a downward swing or two with his cosh in the hall mirror. But standing in front of another man with a backdrop of books, the cosh became absurd, a prop from another show which had been delivered by mistake.

He probably should have kept it.

"So, can I have the money, please."

"Give me the name first."

"People who bring coshes to meetings get to pay in advance."

I could see his mind twisting and turning, searching for a way of keeping the money, and his frustration on realising he couldn't.

"Here. Take it."

He tossed a bundle of old fivers onto the sofa. No envelope. No unnecessary expense.

So, crunch time. Marilyn and I had, of course, pondered what I should say when the question came and decided that I was to call her and get the business of the evening under way. But what I hadn't taken into account was my personal disgust for this man. That, and my stupidity. Marilyn would get her moment, but I wanted mine. I wanted to goad the man, to put my boot in too. I lied.

"I'm fucking her, it's me."

It just came out, unpremeditated. Oh shit!

At first nothing happened. I stood there with my washing up cloth. He sat leaning forward in the chair. The fucker and the fucked. It's always the same, isn't it? When we hear the unexpected. The delay as our mind double- and triple-checks what we've heard and searches our databases for the right reply. It came, all right.

He lunged forward, arms outstretched, making straight for me. No words, just a physical response to a confession of physicality.

I'm not a good fighter. I don't think I'm a coward and am quite strong, but I lack experience. How hard should you hit? What are the rules? I know the weight of words but not of punches. I can strike with my pen and precisely calculate the damage it will cause. I can lightly wound a person's self-esteem or drive my adversary to question his right to live. Most people can't. They cannot weigh their words. But I fear physical fights, not for the beating I might take but for the excess harm I may cause. It's not that I care for the other chap. I just don't want to go to prison.

Anyway, he pounced on me, dragging me back against the wall. He was a crap fighter and got far too close to throw a punch. We wrestled, exhausting ourselves to no effect until he tripped, and I had him down and beat. I knew I ought to punch him, and I did. Right on the nose, drawing blood. I hit him again, but without conviction, and he swung a Stanley knife he had concealed and cut me above the eye. Next time, I punched him properly and bit his wrist until he released the knife.

I once went to a village bullfight at a place called La Calahorra. The matador couldn't kill the bull and the locals booed him off and beat the poor animal to death with the church door. Our fight was equally graceless and clumsy, ending up with me on top pinning his arms down, blood dripping on his shirt from the cut above my eye. I was out of breath, gulping in air. I felt good though. I had bested another man. The beast had been let out of his cage. How easy it is to loosen the moral restraints which check us! How intoxicating and dangerous when we slip the bonds! To tell you that I liked the taste of my blood as it ran against my nose and snagged on my lip tells you everything.

I felt calm.

I have a cherished cartoon of a Vietnam GI. He's standing over the body of a man he's shot. His speech bubble asks this question: "Why do I always get an erection when I kill?"

The question is surely rhetorical.

Time for Marilyn.

"Now, if you move, I'll punch you again. Stay still for your own good. There's someone who wants to talk to you. Marilyn, you can come down now."

At the mention of her name, he struggled to get up. I could see a new level of fear in his eyes. The look of the torturer knowing he will face his victim at a disadvantage.

"Get a knife from the kitchen and keep him still," I called out to Marilyn as she descended the stairs. She did and held it to his throat.

"Don't leave me with this woman. You don't know what she is capable of. Please. Really. Please."

He assumed she would treat him as he had her. He wasn't wrong.

"Now I'm going to tie you up and Marilyn is going to have a little chat with you."

He struggled, nothing serious, now a beaten man: the victim for a change. Whilst Marilyn pressed the point of the knife to his throat, I got the upright chair from the bedroom. We tied him to it, arms behind his back, legs spread and bound.

You have to remember it had been twelve years. Over a decade of abuse, of taking it. You have to be forgiving or at least have some understanding that not all justice can be metered out in court. That the old ways are sometimes best and have a sanguine purity. You have to understand. I need that.

Marilyn rained down her pain on him. She punched and bit. Kicked and slapped.

"Take that, you shit."

Punch.

"That's for the time you beat my head on the oven door."

Kick.

"You fucking bastard. You fucking fucking bastard."

Punch, scratch, spit, kick.

More talk of past suffering. More blows. The chair fell over twice. She stamped on his chest, spat in his eyes.

His beating lasted at most twenty minutes, less than two minutes for every year. Not much, but enough to shout large and loud: "It's over, and I am free of you."

She stopped, flushed, the detail and the colour finally applied to that half-finished nude, a person emerging, crafted out of blows.

I had managed to stay the blood from above my eye, though it would need stitches later. Now what? We had a tied up and beaten man in the living room and we were high on adrenalin and street justice. What next? Marilyn knew. Maybe knew from the beginning. Knew how and where to strike to end all this.

"You fucking maggot of a man. You think I actually enjoyed the things you did to me. The filthy sex, you little shit. Your pathetic little cock. You think I meant it when I repeated the phrases you made me learn? You shit. You think you even caused me pain when you put that little maggot of a cock in my ass? Do you? You fucking loser. You were never man enough to fuck me properly."

She lifted her skirt and stripped off her knickers. She gagged him with them. Then she reached down and unzipped his fly, exposing his wrinkled cock.

She got the knife. He pissed himself.

"Marilyn. Don't do that. Maybe the guy deserves it, but you don't."

A tiny part of me wanted to see his cock sliced off and stamped on. But enough of the nurtured me was left to try and check the other.

"Don't do it, Marilyn. Put the knife down."

She pulled on his cock and raised the knife.

"Don't do it!"

I could have grabbed her arm. Taken the knife. I could have played no part in all of this. Instead, I stroked her hair and whispered one more time, "Don't do it."

The knife came crashing down as she drove the tip into the chair just below his balls. He pissed again and whimpered to himself.

Marilyn stood up and whispered in my ear, "Now fuck me," and then, turning to David, said, "Watch, you little toad, whilst your wife gets fucked properly for the first time in twelve years. Watch a stranger give me what you never could."

Maybe I should have guessed that this would be her parting salvo.

I let her take control. It was her show, her well-earned time. She had me strip her right in front of him, each garment, gesture and movement catalogued for David. It wasn't enough for him to see, he had to hear and taste and smell as well. She fucked me to wipe clean all memory of his use of her. She fucked me so this night would be his only memory.

"Now take my bra off, Laurence. Can you see, David, how he cups my breasts? Can you see how my nipples are hard under his fingers? It feels good to have a man's hands on them."

And later: "Look how I wrap my lips around his shaft. Why, it must be twice the size of yours."

And spitting on his face: "Can you taste his cock in my saliva?"

And rubbing her crotch on his nose: "Not the dry cunt you had to grease with Vaseline. A smell you've never known. What could it be? Laurence, tell David what he's smelling."

"An aroused woman."

And riding my cock: "Look, David. Can you see? How virile he is, how much he wants me. He doesn't need to beat me to get hard. Can't get it up, David? How come? You get it up reading your dirty mags. You wank at pictures of women getting fucked? Not the same with a real woman?"

And me licking her cunt: "Mmm, that's good. When you licked me out, I used to think what needed ironing to stop myself getting bored."

And sucking my cock until I came in her mouth: "Look, David." She got up close to him to show the cum in her mouth. She swallowed and smiled. "Very nice. Quite a sweet taste, actually. You know, I never swallowed yours. I would just pretend and keep it in my mouth. You always fell asleep within minutes of coming and I would go to the bathroom and flush your seed down the toilet."

And finally: "You know, you never really hurt me. I used to fake the tears to get you off me quicker. You never had the strength."

I think by the end we could have untied him and asked him to jump out the window and he would have. She had struck a death blow to his self-esteem, and he would not recover. The only pride a torturer may have is that he inflicted pain. Instead, we cleaned him up a little, got dressed, drank a glass of wine and rang the police.

We were sitting on the sofa looking suitably agitated when they arrived. Two sergeants, enormous in my tiny flat. I gave it to them straight, not hiding the anxiety in my voice.

"This is Marilyn, she is my client. I am helping her find a house to live in. This is her husband who she is in the process of divorcing. She came round for a meeting and this nutter must have followed her. He came in a rage. Crazy. Said I was having an affair with her, which I'm not. He even brought a tape recorder. It's over there. I was washing up. He had a cosh."

"May we see it, please."

I handed the sergeant the weapon.

"This is a nasty weapon you have here. You're lucky he didn't use it on you."

"Yes, I know. He went for me, but I was fortunate and disarmed him. That's when he grabbed the knife. I've kept it clean of our prints in case you want to use it as evidence."

"Thank you. Bob, take the knife."

"Again I brought him down. That's when he slashed my eye with the Stanley knife. Marilyn, can you remember where we put it?"

"On the mantelpiece. I'll get it... here you are, Officer."

"We had to tie him down so we could call you. That's about it."

The policemen conferred.

"Right. Leave this to us. Bob, untie him. Careful now, though he doesn't look like up to resist. Read him his rights, Bob."

The rights were read.

"So what happens now?" I asked.

"We'll take him down the station and take a statement. We'll need to see you both again, but now I suggest that you get down the hospital and have your eye seen to. You'll need stitches."

They left. Marilyn and I finished off the wine. I've never, ever, felt so alive, so exhilarated.

The police came round to see me the following morning. They had kept him in the cells overnight and wanted to know if I was going to press charges. Whilst I was considering what best to do, the sergeant told me the following story.

"Odd one, that Mr Snelling. He told us this extraordinary bollocks about how you and his missus planned all this and beat him up. He also claims you had sex in front of him. He was ranting like a loony to the desk sergeant, demanding we arrest you both. Real nutter. We all had a good laugh. No truth, I suppose, in all that?"

"Not a word."

"We thought not. Anyway, you can press charges any time in the next two years. Or you can let it go. Looks like he got a fair beating, after all. Your eye got stitched up, I see."

"Yes – yes about the eye. The charges? I think I'll wait. You say I've got two years?"

"Yes."

"OK. I'll think about it."

I rang David one last time. He picked up the phone. I didn't wait for him to speak.

"It's Laurence, the guy who fucks your wife. Any time in the next two years I can press charges against you for ABH. You'll probably lose your job and will have a criminal record. If you don't lay a finger on Marilyn and let her have the children, no charges. If I hear from her that you've touched her or are pressing for the kids, you go down."

A week later he threw a brick through my window, but he never touched her again and she won uncontested custody of the kids.

A very sweet porking.

# Chitty Chitty Gang-Bang

*Men in Black*. That's the film I'm thinking of. You know, the one where alien creatures live amongst us, taking on our forms and uniforms? Antiquarians, schoolgirls, waiters, regular members of the community, their compliance belying the beast within.

And so it was with me. My mask, that of the fresh-faced graduate. Tennis in the park, Hughes and Plath read over Earl Grey tea.

The building work was in a lull, and I dabbled with journalism. After all, if that shit David could pull it off, then why not me? I wrote a critique of a Tamil play for the *Guardian Weekly*, interviewed discarded London dockers for the *New Statesman* and kept the company of ethnic curiosities.

All generations and their subcultures have their rules, their handbook, as surely prescriptive as any Edwardian tome of etiquette. I bought such a book at a Conservative Party jumble (we were, of course, all socialists but knew the Tories offered the better pickings). We giggled and mocked the tight decorum of our ancestors, their right and only way of doing each and every thing. We took turns lolling by the canal, Sue, Nina and I, to read out passages from *Etiquette for Women: A Book of Modern Modes and Manners*, each vying to find the greater proof of our emancipation. But emancipation is a snake that discards its worn-out skin only to reveal the one below. Sure, the colours and pattern may change, but skin is skin.

Of course, we were revolutionaries, what generation aren't? But our manifesto? Only a demand for recognition of our own status quo, of the right to impose a new conformity. What band of brothers, years from now, would rummage Amazon for books on us? What passages would have them wet-eyed with laughter? Our pretensions, their validation? Our uniform of mismatched second-hand clothes? The obligatory roll-up and Doc M's? The token black friend? Tarkovsky films we slept through, to later claim amazing?

The watchdog of history stays the same. Only the fleas are different. But I had my beast, and beasts transcend the whims of history.

I once spent seventeen days walking in a rainforest. Long walks are intensive. It's thus with all travelling. We can be extensive and visit a hundred villages and spend three hours in each, or intensive and visit one and spend three hundred hours there. The problem with extensive is that we end up knowing nothing. If we just shake hands with life, all that rubs off is sweat. But if we really delve and spend the time, by understanding one, we understand them all.

What's true of villages is even truer of deep nature. The first few hours we're not even there. Our body might be, but our mind is back in the city or wherever else we came from. It takes time for us and the moment we are in to coincide.

After a day or so, we begin to understand the pallet of colours and range of shapes and textures of the world we are travelling through. We begin to differentiate where before we saw no variation. Sounds that frightened, then surprised, become familiar and comforting. We stop looking down and let our feet feel the way. What required a conscious effort, we reassign to our body to get on with. Even longer – maybe five, maybe more days – and loneliness gives way to understanding that we have travelling companions everywhere. The clouds going about their business, fat cumulus in no rush, skittish cirrus, high-strung spirits who never touch our food. The rustle of the leaves delivering gossip to be passed on. A log is overturned and a city in full swing revealed. Fat beetles sluggish after a business lunch on their way to the club. Busy ants racing here and there, trampling each other to be worker of the month. Traffic jams, epic building projects, births and deaths.

That's how it begins, but then you leave the analogies behind, ceasing to compare this world with yours and seeing it as it is. Beetles become beetles, ants, ants. Day by day you move from tourist to resident. Step by step you are closer to getting your real green card. It's the process of becoming what you only barely noticed. Of moving forward through the crowd, ever closer to the stage, of reaching up, rising and turning to see that instead of a member of the audience, you are a protagonist and somehow know your lines.

I had no map. Stupid thing to take no map. Near the end my path was blocked by a waterfall. I couldn't get around it and started to climb down. Halfway and crouching on a ledge, I realised I was stuck with no way back or on. At first, I was immobilised by fear. I screamed for help, the only answers the raucous calling of the birds. Death was nothing special in the jungle, just a creature returning to the mulch.

I crouched there for two days as the fear gave way to resignation, even a willingness to die. The intense heat, the lack of water, the million shades of green all calling out, climbing on each other to reach the light. Life stripped down to its very essence, existence, the core compared with which all else is just fashion. I stopped thinking. How delicious that was! The edges of myself began to blur, dissolving into the jungle, into the simmering air. I can't explain it. I don't want to even try. This was the world of the beast. Non-verbal, instinctual, dimensions beyond the intellect. I won't demean it further with words. I jumped.

The fall should have killed me. I knew that. But, of course, it didn't. Somehow my hands wrapped round a creeper, and I descended alive to the dry river below. I stripped naked and ran through the jungle. I primal-screamed. I met and talked with snakes. No words, of course. Real communication. Three naked creatures, two coiled, one crouched. All touching the earth, hearing its rhythm through skin. I ran until dusk, finally returning to my discarded clothes and my backpack. I dressed and, in so doing, locked the beast back in. Two days later, I broke through the forest onto a road. I hitched a lift. I drank beer and ate burgers in a nearby town and woke up on someone's lawn with a sprinkler dousing my face. There's no going back. Our evolution has made sure of that. We're trapped by our consciousness. But the beast is there, buried deep, waiting to be summoned as and when.

We see intellect as setting us beyond the beast. It does. But only beyond understanding, leaving us with its poor relation, knowledge. The beast will always jump from the waterfall. Always has. The rest of what we do is an endless Sudoku, all directions summing to the same number.

Yep, I had my beast. Not running free but taken out for walks from time to time. Enough to keep me feeling alive, but not enough to have me hunted down and shot.

My spell spent interviewing the dockers got to me. I saw them as our urban equivalent of an Amazonian tribe. I don't think that's an exaggeration. Under Thatcher, working-class communities were driven to extinction, and for the same reasons as those tribes. They were in the way of commercial progress.

The Amazonians live on land valued for its timber and fertility. The dockers, on land valued as real estate. They both had customs and rituals which didn't require the purchase of commercialised products. You can't buy a sing-song in a pub just as you can't a ceremony to bless a river. You can sell iTunes, though. But first you have to atomise the community and lock each individual in a world of one, so they each seek solace in a stranger's voice that only they can hear.

Of course, the docks were inefficient. But inefficient at doing what? Emptying the hulls of boats? Yes. Filling the hearts of people. No. Of course, they had their restrictive practices, but we replaced them with restrictive lives.

I have in my mind a group of children playing in the dirt. They only have a tin can and some sticks – street hockey on a budget. The wicked witch descends, disguised as Father Christmas. She gives them each a mountain of toys to play with. They are thrilled, tearing at gigantic boxes with tiny, hungry hands. They are too busy to hear her say, as she melts into the air, "But you can only play alone."

Above all else, communities are communal. Amazonian hunters work in groups, sharing out the kill. So did dockers. Stabbing the bales with their hooks and sharing out the contraband. Optimisation of production requires workers to compete, to win, to beat the others. So Margaret Thatcher broke them in the name of most of us. Bring on the meritocracy. Let the best man win. But win what? The right to enjoy your spoils in a corner? The right to play alone?

Back in Australia, there is a special place. It's a big chunk of land with a fence around it. No people are allowed in. I mean *no* people. No one. Ever. It makes no money, produces nothing we can use. It exists like a Buddhist monk exists to pray for us, to salve our guilt. Perhaps we should have kept the dockers just for that. To salve our guilt.

I talked this over with Peter. He said I shouldn't let it get to me. That I spent too much time thinking. That everything would be all right. Then he chuckled.

"You want community? Then roll up next Thursday. You're going to a gang-bang."

Earl's Court this time. No Earl, no Court, a borough between identities, part of the corridor from Kensington to Chelsea, a prosthetic leg from well-heeled to hip.

I had been to the cinema and arrived late. The venue of the shagging, a '30s block of serviced flats, had fallen on hard times. A porter's office but no porter. Wilting Wilton carpets. Grand mirrors with spots of black where the silver backing had given up, tired of the same old faces. Art Deco frosted glass shades with burnt-out bulbs, like vases with dead flowers.

I took the lift, though the stairs would have been quicker. It trundled upwards, a decrepit beast of burden, its mangy coat of burr walnut veneer blistered, varnished now with only sweat from the hands of sallow middle managers and OAPs. It juddered to a drunken stop at floor three. I battled with the concertina mesh door, once, I suppose, a statement of prestige, now more like an outmoded girdle, and stepped out on the landing.

Four doors. Three would lead to couples drinking tea, watching TV, spinsters ironing blouses whilst the macaroni warmed. One to sweat and sticky cracks, pigs gorging at a living trough. Did the others know? Had pussy pilgrims lost their way and asked directions?

"Yes, dear?"

"I'm here for the gang-bang. Is this the place?"

"No, dear, my Joe was quite enough. That'll be Mr Simmons, two doors down."

I can't think otherwise. They must have known. But known in the way the English know of sodomy at boarding school or that local ads for a 'large white chest' will provide no storage for their socks. Known but best forgotten. Relegated to a euphemism like, "One of Mr Simmons's little get-togethers."

I found the door. No name. No indication that here men came to fuck. I pressed the tiny plastic buzzer. I waited. Peter opened the door.

The dictionary definition of a gang-bang is copulation by several persons in succession with the same passive partner. There were nine of us, including Sue and the Hoover.

"Hello, Laurence. Find the place OK?"

"Yes, thanks, Peter. You all right?"

"Mustn't grumble. Alive and licking, as they say."

Peter was stark naked. Actually, not quite. He did have some contraption, a sort of low-cost parachute harness, where other men might wear underpants. It was made of patent black leather and comprised a belt, some straps which went down each side of his ass crack and up in front where they were attached to a steel cock ring. Two more straps connected the ring across his thighs and back to the belt. Oh, and he was also wearing flip-flops.

He had unusually large little toes. It's odd, you know, what we notice. Toes should have names. Our fingers are Thumb, Index, Middle, Ring and Pinky. But toes are just toes. Sad, that. A testament to our hopeless attempt to forget we are attached to the earth. It's an insult to evolution. It all began with feet, you know. This walking business. Then everything followed in their footsteps. So I will give them names. Bruiser, Snoopy, Digger, Grabby and Titch. My Titch is a pathetic pallid slug with a nail you'd need a magnifying glass to paint. I know that evolutionists tell us that the Titch is on the way out, an unnecessary appendage with no place in our modern lives. But what a bummer that I was born in the waning years of Titch. Better to have come earlier, when Titches were fully-fledged members of the foot, or much later when they had gone. I suppose it could have been worse. Imagine those poor bastards who were born in the twilight years of tails. Neither that appendage of sensual delight nor the little bump we have today. Only a sort of oversized dag, like my dog sometimes gets when he eats too much grass and shits. Anyway, Peter's Titches were sterling specimens.

"Come on in and meet the Dagenham boys."

"Dagenham?"

"Yes, Tony comes from there. When he was made redundant, he got a job as nightwatchman down the road and moved in here. It used to belong to one of the managers' mothers who died, poor girl. Every so often the lads come round for a good old shag and natter. The rest of them are married, all except the Hoover, and their missuses aren't up for a gang-bang in the living room."

"The Shag and Natter." Good name for a pub.

"Nice one!"

"So what's with the Hoover?"

"Oh, you'll see. Now, come inside and meet the lads before I catch a chill."

The flat was tiny and the men huge. Their blobby bits filled the place. Big bellies and wobbly asses all over the shop. Three of them were in the kitchen. One was doing a fry-up and the other two were sitting at a little Formica table drinking beer. The bloke on the fry-up was telling a joke.

"There was this toff, a fancy chef and a lad from Dagenham down the pub. They'd had a few and were giving it some about their birds.

"The toff says, all proper, 'After I make love to my woman, I cover her body with rose petals from the garden and pick them off her with my teeth. It drives her crazy!'

"In steams the chef and says, 'After a night of passion, I take my whipped double cream and baste her breasts with it. I then lick it off with my tongue. She goes crazy!'

"The Dagenham lad sets his pint down and says, 'Load of bollocks! After I shag the missus, I wipe my dick on the curtain. She goes fucking crazy!'."

General laughter of a type which says they'd heard the joke before.

"So that's why your Betty took the curtains down when I knobbed her," said one of the guys at the table, "frightened I might starch them up so much they wouldn't open again."

"That excuse for cum that drips from yer knob wouldn't stiffen a vicar's collar," said the other. "Hello, Dazzer! Whose yer mate?"

Peter made the introductions. "This is Laurence. He's a bit posh, but all right."

"Laurence? What kind of a fucking name is that? Supposing I'm about to shoot me load and you're standing in the way, I can't say, 'Laurence, get out the way.' It would put me off. We'll have to give ya a proper name."

Peter, or should I say, Dazzer, came to my defence.

"Go easy on the lad, boys. Let him settle in, Minute Wonder."

"Now, you see, Minute Wonder, that's a proper name."

"So how come Minute Wonder?" I asked.

The guy at the fryer, who was now serving up eggs and bacon, beans and fried bread, explained.

"He was born Steve, he's fuckin' obsessed with sunglasses and shoots his load in a minute."

"I don't get it," I said.

"Christ Almighty, Lol, what do they teach you at school? Steve, Stevie Wonder, the blind bloke with the glasses? Wan' a drawin', do you?"

"And this is Half Bob," said Peter, pointing to the other guy at the table.

"I s'pose you want to know how he got 'is name an' all?" said Minute Wonder, who, without waiting for a reply, told me anyway. "Bob from Richard, a cunt's name. Half Bob 'cos he's as tight as a duck's arse. Goes round lookin' for one-eyed women to marry. That way, if they die before him, he only 'as to use a penny and not two to cover their eyes."

"Don't pay any attention to Take the Mick, he's just pissed 'cos he said to his ol' lady on their wedding night to keep her eyes shut until 'is cock was in her and the poor bird hasn't opened them yet."

Minute Wonder, Half Bob and Take the Mick were tucking into their fry-up. They all had their socks on and variants of dainty slip-on shoes. Elephants with ballet pumps. Apart from that, they were naked, except Take the Mick, who had an apron on and Minute Wonder, who had a serviette round his neck.

"Before you ask," said Peter, "they call me Dazzer because I'm so white. Dazzer from Daz, the washing powder."

"So, Lol," asked Half Bob with a mouth full of beans, "what's your game?"

"I do a bit of building work and some writing."

"What you doin' on the tools? You sound a proper educated man."

"I don't know. I just like it. Good crack."

"You'll be getting good crack when Sue comes out."

"More like good Grand Fucking Canyon, the amount of cocks she's had."

"So where you live then, Lol?"

"Stoke Newington."

"I don't get it. You went to university, right?"

"He was at Cambridge," this from Peter, who was prouder of my education than I was.

"And you weren't born in Stokey, were you?"

"No."

"So what the fuck are you doing? Every cunt I know who lives in that shit 'ole wants to leave and there's you, who could live in the Queen's fanny, choosing to go there. Are you sure he's right in the 'ead, Dazzer?"

"I know it must sound odd, but I like the place. I used to live at my mum's flat in Kensington, but it was so boring. You know, my mum has lived there for sixteen years and doesn't even know the name of the neighbours."

"If you lived in Dagenham you wouldn't want to know your neighbour's name."

"Oy, Mick, I'm your fuckin' neighbour."

"That's what I mean. Anyway, you being so educated, perhaps you could explain this to us. How come we're letting all these blacks into our country? We don't go and live in their place.

"Don't get me wrong. The coloureds are all right, I'm sure, but what the fuck are they doing here? I mean, Lol, seriously now, the way I see it— Minute, you've made a right fucking mess of that serviette. The way I see it, a country's like a house, right. Well, you're not going to let any old cunt you've never met live in yer house, are you? You've got yer ways, haven't you? How you like to keep things just right. Well, yer not going to let some stranger in, are you? I mean they've got their ways and we've got ours. Nothing wrong with dogs and nothing wrong with fish, but you don't see 'em livin' together, do you? I mean, like it's taken, like, thousands of years for us Brits to get things how we like 'em. Our songs, our beer, what we like to eat, our jokes. You know, it may all be shit, but it's our shit. It's what makes us, us.

"Me and the lads went for a weekend to Calais. Took the ferry and 'ad a right booze up. The frogs ain't like us. No bitter. No proper fry-up. Couldn't get a cup of cha for love or money. But I ain't about to go live in frog land and try and change 'em. It's their country and they can do what they like. So what's all this immigration about, Lol?"

Good question.

"Cup of cha, Lol, to get yer bonce working?"

"Erm, yes. Thanks. Do you really want an answer? I mean, not a joke one?"

"Of course he wants an answer. We all fucking do. It's like World War Three round Dagenham. The last one we all understood. Hitler was a cunt and we 'ad to stop him. This time we've invited in the enemy."

"OK. I'll tell you what I think. The immigrants haven't gatecrashed your private party. They came with written invitations. And the reason is we wanted cheap labour to do the crap jobs no one here was willing to do. We became too lazy thanks to the empire and couldn't be bothered to do shit like clean the public toilets or drive the buses."

Take the Mick got up. He had enormous balls and a fat but short dick. His genital ensemble reminded me of the head of a snowman, though with a furry cap in lieu of a trilby, and the eyes were obviously missing.

"Oy, Lol, are you tellin' us the British working man is a lazy cunt?"

Peter had left a while back, saying he was going to check on Sue's progress, leaving me alone with these large representatives of the British working man. *Tread carefully, Laurence.* I was thinking what best to reply when Mick sorted the matter.

"'Cos if you are, then you're right. You should 'ear our dads talking about work back then. Fuck me, it makes my back ache just listening to them. Up at six when any proper bloke should only be up his wife's fanny. Worked Saturdays and all. What me and the lads don't get is why the fuck we made them British? Why not just ask a few to come over, do some work, pay a decent wage and send them back 'ome? What's yer suss on that, Lol?"

"I think that the Brits imagine that anyone coming to our country would want to be like us. You know, fit in and do what we do, like what we like. It's called the delusion of cultural superiority."

"So that's what's wrong with me. It's not a hernia like the doc says, it's... what you say, delusion of what?"

"Cultural superiority."

"So what's that when it's at home, Lol? Talk fucking English, will ya."

"Basically, the British think what we've got and our ways are the best, and anyone who comes here would want to be like us and adapt. The trouble is that the people who come over have got their own ways, as you say, and don't want to be us. They want to be them."

General nods of agreement.

"Let me ask you a question. If the blacks were just like Half Bob and Minute Wonder, just with different-coloured skin, would you have the same problem with them?"

"What, you mean if they were stupid cunts who got pissed up and couldn't find their own dicks?"

"That and all the other stuff. I mean it seriously. If Half Bob was black but everything else about him was the same, would he still be your mate?"

"Can I still shag his old lady?"

"You can still shag her."

"What you asking him for?" said Half Bob. "Since when does Lol here decide if you're gonna shag my Mary. I'm the bloke you should be asking."

"Fuckin' 'ell, Bob. It's a fuckin' joke. Keep yer hair on! For a start, you're not fuckin' black, you daft cunt. It's what you call… what the fuck do you call it, Lol?"

"Hypothetical."

"Coor, sounds painful. Can't go to work today, I've come over all hipootetical."

"It means imaginary."

"I know what it means. We're not daft, you know."

"Sorry, no offence meant."

"None taken, Lol. Now get on with what you want to say or by the time we get to Sue's cunt there'll be enough spunk in it to drown a fuckin' cat."

"Here's your tea. Sugar's on the table."

"Thanks, Tone. OK. So what I'm getting at is that, more than being black, it's the fact that they don't want to be like us that pisses you off."

"I dunno. Sounds like bollocks."

"Hang on a minute."

I went and rummaged in the kitchen draws and cabinets. Perfect.

"What the fuck you up to, Lol? You haven't got some fuckin' dwarf in there, 'ave you, who tells you the answers?"

"Here." I held out a tin of black boot polish. "Let's try an experiment."

"What's this, Lol?"

"Let's black up Half Bob and you two can tell me if you still feel the same way about your mate."

"You bunch of cunts ain't blackin' me. No fuckin' way."

"Good fuckin' idea, Lol. Now, Bob, it's for science. You always said you wanted to go to the moon. Fuck knows why. Nothin' fuckin' up there. Well, a soppy dick like you can't. But you can do your bit by blackin' up. Who knows, your dick might grow and then you don't have to borrow your missus's tweezers to have a wank. Everyone knows blacks have big knobs. Lol, tell Half Bob here that the boot polish will make his knob grow."

"Well—"

"I'm not doing it. You black up."

"Come on, don't be a cunt. Lol picked you, not me."

"I said—"

"I'll give you a fiver."

"How long do I have to be black for?"

"Not long."

"Give us the fiver then."

"Don't know about you, Bob, but I don't keep my dosh up my arse."

"No dosh, no black."

"For fuck's sake. I'll pay yer when we get home. All right?"

"All right, but just the face."

"Green light, Lol. Bring on Black Bob."

I started to apply the boot polish to his face.

"Careful now, Lol. Oy, it's not going to take my tan off, is it? Cost me a bullseye down the salon."

"Shut it, Half Bob, or we'll get Lol to do yer dick and all."

"Can I have a fag?"

"For fuck's sake, Bob, you've got less patience than a nun in a footballer's locker room. Just let Lol finish."

A couple of minutes more and Bob was done.

"There, I give you… Black Bob."

Both his mates cracked up with laughter.

"What's so fucking funny?"

"You are, you cunt. And yer dick's no bigger."

"So what next, Lol?"

"I think Bob should do something you're used to him doing. See if he's the same old Bob."

"What this cunt's used to doing is not getting the beers in when it's his shout."

"Anything else?"

"And his bloody songs. He's a walking gramophone, this one."

"Well, let's have a song, then."

"I'm not singing for you cunts just to have a laugh."

"Tell Bob you won't laugh," I said.

"Bob, we won't laugh."

"That's two quid more if you want a song."

"Fuckin' 'ell, Bob. I tell you what, you can borrow me porn mags for the weekend. But I don't want the pages stuck together."

"All right."

Bob sang.

"*I like pickled onions, I like piccalilli,*
"*Pickled cabbage is all right,*
"*With a bit of cold meat on a Sunday night,*
"*I can go tomatoes, but what I do prefer,*
"*Is a little bit of cucum, cucum, cucum,*
"*Little bit of cucumber.*"

Bob repeated this chorus three times with his mates accompanying him on the third. He actually had a good voice. The singing brought two of the other Dagenham lads into the already cramped kitchen, where they stood laughing.

"What the fuckin' 'ell's going on in 'ere? What you cunts up to?" said the taller of the two.

"So who is he, then?" asked Minute Wonder of the new arrivals.

"It's that daft plonker mate of yours, Half Bob, but with a black face. Still as fuckin' ugly."

"I think he looks better black. I think he should keep it."

"Well, I'm not. You've had your fun and I'm off to wash it off. Let me at that sink."

"At least have a look at yerself, mate. Cop a gander in the bathroom mirror."

"All right. I s'pose I might as well."

Black Bob set off for the bathroom.

"You got a point, Prof," said Take the Mick, "same old Bob. So maybe not the colour then, or at least not just the colour."

"The Prof. That's yer name," said Minute.

"Yeah, that'll do. The Prof. So what else, Prof? Is that it? Is that why we let them in?"

"No, not everything. The people who make decisions are high-ranking politicians and civil servants. The immigrants aren't a threat to them. Not in competition, or at least not yet. They don't live in their neighbourhoods, don't go after the same jobs. Don't try it on with their women. There is no downside. You used the example of a shared house. Well, they don't share theirs. Let's see in thirty years' time, though, what they think. All depends if they integrate or stay different. Right now the decision makers can get all the praise and votes for seeming to not be racist without any of the downside."

"I'm not waiting thirty years, but you're a clever cunt all the same."

Half Bob returned at this point to the kitchen. He was still blacked-up.

"I thought you was goin' to wash that off?"

"Sue was coming out the bathroom when I got there. Funny thing. She says I looked a treat and asked if I would keep it on until after I'd shagged her. Said she'd always fancied a bit of black."

"I think under the circumstances you should give me back the dosh. We've done you a favour, mate. You should be paying us!"

I left them squabbling about the fiver and went in search of Peter.

The living room had a couple of sofas, an armchair, three shelves arranged on the wall like flying ducks and a TV. The sofas had been pushed back, leaving space for a single mattress, set out on the floor. The two guys who had come into the kitchen sauntered back in, beers in hand, and occupied one of the sofas. The armchair was already taken by a slightly built man who had kept his pants on and who I knew instinctively would be The Hoover. The other two were naked. I stripped off.

The two on the sofa introduced themselves. Tone it Down, from Tony, whose flat it was, and his mate, Big John. When asked my name, I said, "The Prof."

"So what mo-a do ye drive, Prof?" asked Big John.

"I don't have a car."

"So how you get about, then? On the buses?"

"Sometimes, or on my bike."

"My dad was on the buses," said Tone, "he was a conductor for thirty-three years. Did most of the routes out of Victoria, though the seventy-three was 'is favourite."

"Mine too," I said. "It stops just by where I live and goes right through town."

"That's the one. He said it was 'is round the world cruise. Said all sorts got on and off. Tourists at the station, the old dears in Kensington who thought he was their chauffeur, the Knightsbridge birds all dolled up, shoppers in Oxford Street, some tarts round King's Cross and those nutter Jews up your way, with the furry hats. He would come 'ome for his tea and always tell me mum the same. He'd say he'd gone round the world but hadn't found anywhere as good as 'ome or a girl as pretty as his Bettie."

"Can I tell you a story about the seventy-three route?" I asked.

"Course, Prof. We like stories, don't we, Big John?"

"We do, Tone, we do."

"Well, OK. It's very short. I've got this friend called Jeanie. When she's got nothing better to do, she takes the seventy-three from Dalston. She makes sure she sits next to one of those Jews with the hats. She settles in, and when she feels it's right, she rubs up against him a bit and tells the bloke she's got her period. Now, those Jews are ultra-orthodox and their religion says they can't touch a woman when she's on the rag. So he has to get off the bus and go home to have a shower."

"It wouldn't bother Tone an' me. We're all-weather men. Just a bit of ketchup on the burger. I'd rather 'ave that than one of these shaven bints. Not natural. 'Ad one once. Like stuffing a plucked chicken."

"I agree. A hand in the bush is worth two in the bird."

"Say that again."

"A hand in the bush is worth two in the bird."

"That's good, that is. A hand in the bird— no, a hand in the bush is worth two in the bird. That's clever, that is. Did yer just make that up?"

"Yes."

"Oy, Hoover. Did you hear what the Prof said?"

"I don't get it. Isn't it meant to be a bird in the hand is worth two in the bush?" said the Hoover.

"That's the point, yer stupid cunt. The Prof's changed it round."

"But why would he wan' to do that?"

"Leave it, Hoover. So, if yer 'ad a mo-a, what would yer 'ave?"

"But why did your mate rub up against the fella on the bus?"

"Give it a rest, Hoover. Save yer puff… Me, I drive a Rover. Proper British car. The SD1. Sometimes I think I should 'ave gone for the 3500 with the V8 but 2.6 litres is enough for most trips. Mind you, it would 'ave been nice to 'ave the V8 seeing as 'ow I worked on it. Beautiful mo-a that one. Last car I ever worked on."

"Dazzer says you got made redundant. How come?"

I never got to hear the answer, as Peter and Sue made their appearance in the room.

Their arms were linked, and they looked for all the world like a couple about to have the next waltz. Mind you, even stretching reality TV to the max, I don't see an anorexic homosexual wearing a cock ring accompanied by a peroxide hooker with stockings, suspender and see-through knickers making it past the selection process. Not unless Berlusconi avoids prison and buys the rights to *Come Dancing*.

"Listen up, everyone. Sue is ready. Can someone get her a sherry, please? Hoover, give up your chair for the lady."

"Sorry, Dazzer. I'll get the sherry."

Sue settled herself down in the armchair. She was perhaps thirty-five, which would have put her of an age with the younger men. Her lingerie was all white and she had no shoes on. Big, slightly saggy breasts, pale skin, too much lacquer in her hair, her only affectation, nail extensions. No plastic super babe, just a regular, standard issue woman. Comfortable and comforting.

Take the Mick and the others came in from the kitchen and settled themselves on the other sofa. The Hoover returned with a mug.

"You can't serve a lady sherry in a mug! Who brung you up?" said Big John. "Now take your sorry arse back in the kitchen and find a glass. And not a beer glass. Get one of them little ones from the top cupboard. Go with 'im Prof, or we'll be 'ere all night."

The Hoover was nervously studying the label on a bottle he had in his hand.

"Prof, is this sherry?"

"Let me see. Yes."

"It's just that it don't say sherry."

"It's Fino de Jerez and Jerez is where sherry comes from."

"You don't mind me asking, do you? It's just that the lads would give me stick if I got it wrong and I'm really only a stand-in for my bruvver anyway."

"So normally your brother comes?"

"He did when he was alive. Died last Christmas. Pissed coming 'ome on leave from the Army and crashed his car at the bottom of our street. Got from the Sudan to outside the paper shop but couldn't make it to our house. At least he died somewhere he knew."

"I'm really sorry."

"He was the life and soul of the party. That lot in there all loved 'im. At the funeral, Tone and some of the others said I had to fill his shoes, and come March they invited me to a gang-bang. I can't get it up, but I help out in other ways."

Big John appeared in the kitchen doorway.

"Are you two planning a bank robbery or pouring a fucking drink? Gi' me that. Well, at least it's sherry. Last time Hoover tried to give 'er fucking cooking oil."

We all returned to the living room.

"There you go, Sue. A nice little sherry."

"Thank you, John. Always the gent. Cheers, lads."

"Cheers, Sue," from the assembled blokes.

"Right. TV off, I think. Ready when you are, Sue," said Big John.

"I'll just finish my tipple."

"No rush, Sue. In your own time, luv. Did Bernie do a good job on the kitchen?"

"Oh yes, John. Thanks a million for sending him round. He did the lot in a day. Looks brand-new. I owe you."

"Nah, a pleasure, girl. You're good to us, you are."

"No, I mean it. One of my regulars gets duty-free fags, I'll sort you out a carton or two."

"That'll be nice. A smoke always tastes better without the duty."

"Right, I'm ready now, John, just wanted to wet me whistle. Come on, boys, who's first?"

When I retrieve the memories of that evening, I don't look in my mind for files marked 'sex'. I look elsewhere, in the least expected places. A fragment may be buried under 'songs', another under 'friendship'. Bits have found their way to boxes reserved for jokes, others to images of actors' waiting rooms or rhinos wallowing at a water hole. Above all else, I look under 'community'.

It's 2am and the house sleeps. My son spread out like a starfish in his cot, dreaming of buses and tractors, his mum with the sheet over her ear and her PJ top tucked into the trousers. The dogs, curled as furry pretzels, wheeze and twitch, reliving the chasing of poor bikers up the hill that looms above our house. I am alone with my fragments. Shall I weave them into a story? Create a beginning, a middle and an end? No. Let's keep them as they are.

I once did an article about the British Museum facsimile service, a wonderful place where they make plaster copies of the marbles. I spent the day there wandering past busts of Hephaestus, watched by vying Aphrodites. There were shelves reserved just for hands, others for feet. An emporium of classical body parts, the place had the air of an android assembly plant. At the back was a room containing the friezes. Some were complete, others fragmented with the bits laid out like an unfinished jigsaw. One in particular drew me in. Two-thirds had been lost. Here, a hand, a rump and leg of a horse. There, the base of a column, a corner of a chariot. An eye, a nose, a spear tip. It made me look. Properly look and see in a way that a completed picture never does, attending to detail otherwise passed by. So here's my fragmented frieze. No glorious battlefield, no pantheon of gods. Just fractured memories of an Earl's Court flat, some mates, and a bit of a shag and natter.

Fragment 1: Poached Salmon

"Thank you, Stevie, that was nice. Now, have a rest and maybe you'll be up for seconds," said Sue. "You've lost some weight. Suits you."

"Ta, Sue. You're looking trim yerself. It's her indoors, me better half. She's joined a gym, would you believe it, and says we got to eat all healthy. I come 'ome from work last week and bugger me if she ain't made a salad. What's this? I say. A salad, what you think? she says. I says, I know it's a salad but what's it doin' on my plate? We always have fish an' chips on a Friday. Always 'ave as long as I can remember. Off to Blackpool tonight. That was our little joke. Meant fish 'an chips for tea. So what's this, I say. Seaside night, not allotment night. She says I've got to watch the co-lester-ol, that me tubes will get all clogged an' I'll drop down dead like me da at fifty-five. Whatever fuckin' next, eh girl? She says I should go down the gym with 'er. No fuckin' way, I says. You're not gettin' me in shorts. Even if I 'ad some I wouldn't put 'em on. What if someun saw? Well, no one but our Tom and Trace is 'ere to see you eat the salad, she says, so stop yer moanin' and tuck in. Well yer can't tuck into a salad, can you? You can a pork pie or a plate of eels, but not a bloody salad. So what else you made, I says. Poached salmon, she says. Poached salmon? I says. You've gone to see Mick the Fence and got a nicked fish? Don't be so fuckin' daft, she says. Not that kind of poach. It's the way I's cooked it. No oil o' nothin'. Proper healthy. Bloody 'ell, girl, I says, how's I goin' to have me beer with that? That's another thin', she says, no beer. Bollocks to that, girl. What's the point of living to a ton without me beer? I put me foot down. Mind you, the fish was tasty like."

## Fragment 2: Left Hooker

"So I says to 'im, twenty quid tops. I mean, it's only the starter motor, not the lump. Oy, Tony, why do you use your left 'and to wank?"

"Nothin'. No reason."

"There's got to be a reason. Oy, Big John, 'as Tone always wanked with 'is left 'and?"

"What's that?"

"Is Tone a left hooker?"

"What you asking me for? Ask his cock."

"It's bad enough asking a cunt like you. I'm not talking to Tone's cock. What if it answered? I'd 'ave a fuckin 'eart attack! Mind you, I'd get more sense than out of you. Oy, Dazzer, what 'and does Tone wank with?"

"His right."

"All right, all right. I used to use me right but now I don't. Nuff said."

"No, not nuff said, John. A bloke just doesn't change his wankin' 'and for no reason. A bloke might change 'is motor but not 'is wankin' 'and."

"I can see you cunts won't leave me alone until I tell, so shut your gobs and listen. Pete's right. I never used to use me left. But then our Doris passed away. God bless her soul. Tossing me off was 'er department. She used to say it wasn't right me doing it meself. Said it made her look bad. Who's to know, I said. The fuckin' cat's not goin' to tell the neighbours. She says she would know and that it wasn't right. So when I started wankin' again, after she passed away, with me right mitt, it felt all wrong. Like I was betrayin' 'er. Daft, really. But I kept thinkin' of 'er up there in heaven with Tracy from number ten, lookin' down and seein' me doin' it. So I use me left. It feels like our Doris's 'and that way."

"That's very romantic," said Sue. "Who'd 'ave thought our Tone so sweet? Your Doris would be proud. No, Mick, you know the rules. Only the one finger up the arse and no rings."

"Sorry, Sue. Got carried away."

"Well, I think our Tone done good. Come on, lads, left hands on cocks. Solidarity. Get your dicks up and let's salute his Doris."

"Fuck sake, lads. Don't be tossers. Well, not left hand tossers, anyway. It's not right. That's Doris's 'and, and the only cock she ever stroked was mine."

"All right, Tone. Point taken. So Bob, what you end up payin' for the starter motor?"

"A tenner and some cassettes from Mick the Fence."

Fragment 3: London Burning

"Oy, Bob! You're on bloody fire tonight! Go easy on our Sue, she's got to last the night. You'll wear 'er out. It's not natural goin' at it so long."

"Not natural! Mind you, everyone would go on too long compared with you, the fuckin' Minute Wonder."

"You're meant to be stokin' the fire, not burnin' London down. Prof, what's in that boot polish?"

"Shut it, John. You're puttin' me off. Shut your cake 'ole or I'll never shoot me load."

"All right, all right, keep your polish on!"

"All right if we change positions? My leg's got pins and needles," says Sue.

"Sorry, luv, you should 'ave said."

"Naah, you was enjoyin' yerself. A little bit of tingle, that's all. 'Ave I got to wear specs or 'ave you had your dick enlarged? It feels bigger."

"It's the blacking up that's done it. I told you, Bob,

you're dick would grow. No way I'm forking out a fiver for you to 'ave a bigger cock."

"Will you lot shut up? Does it really look bigger?"

## Fragment 4: Rug Munching

"I don't know 'ow he does it. Not natural. Chewing the rug's all right, I suppose, but not what Hoover does."

"Leave 'im be, Tone. Every bloke's got 'is tipple," said Take the Mick.

"I'll grant you that, but it's one thing to go all poncy and have a glass of wine, but sucking another bloke's cum out of a fanny is more than an unusual tipple. It's not dignified. His brother would never 'ave done it. Reggie would turn in 'is fuckin' grave to see his little bruvver gobbling cum."

"Let it rest, mate. I don't disagree with ya, but Hoover's Hoover. 'E's one of us. We made a promise to Reggie that if anything 'appened to 'im, we'd look out for 'im. Way I see it, 'e's doin' a service. Cleanin' Sue out like that."

"Oy, Hoover. How come with all the spunk you eat that you ain't bigger? They say spunk's protein. You must have guzzled the equivalent of a fuckin' cow by now, but you're still a scrawny cunt."

"I've never kept the weight on," says Hoover, looking up. "Reggie made me eat ten meat pies once. Said I 'ad to beef up. That I looked like a girl. He weighed me before and after. My weight went up. But then my tummy started rumbling something terrible. Dad said I should 'ave a crap before I blew up and sent us all 'ome to God. I bunged up the shitter and was thinner than ever."

"I'm tellin' you. It's not right. One of us should 'ave a word. Stop the spunk gobbling."

"Bit short on the old memory, Tone. Remember when you was sick and couldn't get it up?"

"Yes, but that won't me fault. Fucking virus."

"Of course not yer fault, but what did we all do?"

"You let me come all the same, said I could watch and stumped up for me when Sue sent the hat round. I won't forget. You were all proper mates."

"Well, it's the same with Hoover 'ere. We're all mates and mates look out for each other. He can't shag but enjoys 'imself as best he can. The cunt's not got much else going for 'im."

"Still not right, though. I don't like to think of me load in his gob."

"Christ almighty, Tone, if that's what's botherin' ye, cum in 'er mouth. Hoover never sticks 'is tongue in there."

"Not a bad idea, that."

"You'll 'ave to square it with Sue. You know she's a fussy eater."

## Fragment 5: My Doreen

"Sorry, Sue. Don't know what's the matter."

"Could happen to anyone. Don't upset yourself about it. With blokes it happens, you know," said Sue.

"It's not you, Sue. I mean, you're a cracker and any bloke would fancy you."

"Perhaps if I sucked you off a little. That might do the trick?"

"Go on then."

Ten minutes pass.

"Thanks, Sue, but let's give it a rest. Not my night."

"Everything all right with you, John? No problems?"

"All right, I suppose. But my Doreen's been poorly. She's got to 'ave a test. Cervical smear, they call it."

"I'm sure it's nothing, John. No point in worrying, eh?"

"I don't know what I'd do if anything 'appened to my Doreen."

"Come 'ere and have a cuddle, John. There, there, can't have a big bloke like you all sad. Maybe try a bit later, eh?"

"Thanks, Sue. You're a mate, you are. Fancy another sherry?"

"Go on then."

Fragment 6: Stumping Up

Peter masturbated whilst watching me fuck Sue. He stood against the wall, his eyes fixed on me. They all did. Like aspiring actors waiting to be called to audition, they practised their parts. I guess Peter went unnoticed by the others. Just another bloke fiddling with his bits. But then, of course, he never had his turn with Sue. That and the fact that he stared at me, whilst the others only chatted amongst themselves. Oh, and the matter of the payment. When the hat came round, I heard Peter say, as he dropped the money in, "A tenner for me and another for Laurence."

At first, I felt uneasy to be the object of his sexual desire. I was effectively being paid for by Peter so he could have sex with me by proxy. But that's just intellect talking. What had Take the Mick said? "Mates look out for each other." So I put on my best show, all the positions. I could choose to have my psyche damaged or see it for what it was, a friend tugging at a strip of flesh fantasising about a guy he could never have. It was his fantasy, not mine, and I had no right to take that from him. He came into a tissue, timing his orgasm with mine. I had looked after my mate. Bit weird all the same.

## Fragment 7: Flying Cars

"Comin' down the pub Saturday, Steve?"

"Naah, Bob, promised I'd take the kids to the cinema. The Odeon's got *Chitty Chitty Bang Bang* on and they were too young to see it when it first came out."

"A flyin' car, now that would be somethin', eh? Oy, Prof, you reckon it's possible to make a flyin' car?"

"Maybe. Cool thing to have."

Bob starts singing.

"Oh Chitty You Chitty
"Pretty Chitty Bang Bang
"Chitty Chitty Bang Bang
"We love you."

One by one, we all join in, even the Hoover, who pauses in his cleaning duties, though he didn't know the words and just said, "Bang Bang," once in a while. A gay voyeur, an intellectual call boy, a vacuum, a prostitute and five

Dagenham fat boys. We made a tasteless, but functional, choir, though the Sherman brothers who wrote the song might not agree.

I left at ten in the company of Sue. She was going my way and we decided to share a cab. We talked on the long drive back to North London.

"So we're two of a kind, according to Peter. You're one of 'is boys, ain't ya? How did you end up in the game?"

"I'll tell you if you tell me how you started."

"All right."

I explained about the bath and steam rooms, the proposition, and gave her glimpses of events thereafter. Lady Trocknell made her laugh; she said, "Good on ya, girl." The soldier and his wife brought out the tears and the rest she summed up with, "Takes all sorts."

"Now your turn."

"Me mum was who got me in the game. She used to put it about for the Yanks stationed over 'ere. Started out with them bungin' 'er some nylons, a bit of soap, fags and the like. Stuff what was rationed. One day a bloke was meant to bring a side of beef. He said he couldn't find any an' could he pay cash. After the war she just carried on.

"I says to 'er, Mum, why don't you marry? Me dad's not coming back, that's for sure. She says she never fancied marriage and, anyway, men are all the same. Not worth the bother, she says. I must 'ave been nineteen when Reg, one of 'er regulars, comes round. Me mum must 'ave forgotten and was visitin' me nan. I ended up doin' 'im meself. Me mum went fuckin' crazy when she got 'ome. Well, not then. Later in the pub when Reg says he didn't know her Sue was in the family business. She kicked me out, she did. Just for a week, mind. Then comes round an' says, all casual, comin' 'ome for tea, are ya? She'd cooked me favourite, ravioli. 'Er way of sayin' sorry, I suppose. That's 'ow it started."

"Get any trouble?"

"Naah. Some of the other girls get into right messes. But I 'ave me regulars. I've known this lot from school. Most of my blokes just want a chat an' a cuddle. Sad, really. That they 'ave to pay to get someone to listen. Yeah, just a natter and a bit of slap and tickle. I did 'ave one bloke, mind. A proper skank. Now 'e was a nasty piece of work. City bloke. Trade was a bit slow. Always is over the Christmas holidays. I suppose the lads think God's looking all the closer round Christmas time. You know, it being 'is son's day an' all. Anyway, I did what I've never done before or since. I advertised in the *Standard*."

"What did you say in the ad?"

"Funny question, Lol! 'Ang on, let me think. Err, *Private French Lessons from Experienced Teacher*. That was it. The bloke down our paper shop helped me write it."

"So what happened?"

"Well, it stared out all right. He says to come to 'is 'otel. Dead posh. Blimey, you should 'ave seen the looks they gave me. The porters an' all. They knew. I could tell. Bollocks, I thought, and walked straight past them like the Queen of Sheba. Mind you, I got in a tizz in the lift and tipped the boy. The lads later told me that was daft, that lift boys don't get tips. 'Ow was I to know!

"He was a proper piece of work, that one. Thought he owned me. All me regulars are gentle lads. They give it a lot of lip, I know, but they're soft as eggs. Say something nice about their cocks, let them 'ave a feel 'an a bit of a shag and they're good as gold. This bloke – Simon was 'is name – what a cunt 'e was. Banker, no less. Slapped me about, he did. Wanted to 'ave me up the bum and I don't do bums. And the sod short-changed me when he paid. Did me out of a fiver, he did. Not doing that again. I've got me regulars and that's that."

The taxi pulled up near Dalston Junction, where she lived. She got up to go and ferreted about in her purse. I wondered if it was the same Simon I had met at the Barbican.

"Three quid. That should pay me part. All right, Lol."

"All right, Sue."

She got out of the taxi, turned to go, thought better of it and leant through the open window.

"You're a nice boy, Lol. If you ever fancy a bit, 'ere's me number."

"Thanks," I said, "but who pays who?"

"You'll 'ave to pay. It's not proper if you don't. Ta ta, then."

# Away Game

I needed a holiday. I hadn't been burning the candle at both ends, I'd napalmed it! I did what I always did when needing to think something through. I went and sat on the roof.

Roof is not terrace. Altogether different. Terraces are rooms without a ceiling. They have been tamed and incorporated into the house, to live under the disciplined rule of its owners. Terraces don't allow you to escape the limitations of your daily life. They are an armchair safari, your hand always in reach of the phone. But roofs are outside the constructed envelope, beyond, in all ways, your habitat.

I was lucky. I had a window in the shack I called a bedroom which gave access to the up and over pitches. I loved it there. Like Batman high up in Gotham City, I would sit, knees up, feet firmly planted on the slates, and look across the roofscape.

It's amazing how quickly you leave people behind. Down there, on the streets and in the buildings, is where it all happens: all human endeavour. But dig down or climb up and we've gone. We appear to be everywhere, but, in fact, we're just a thin layer of dust between earth and air. You get a different view from roofs. A different perspective. Less petty.

It's a fact that when walking with a friend, the conversation changes, depending on the altitude. Stay in the valleys and you'll get the gossip and routine stuff, an argument at work, how such and such a child is getting on at school. You'll also get your share of pettiness, some grumbling about a guy who took their parking space or never returned a book. Go higher onto the hills and the talk will move to wider issues – politics, the economy, a little literature and cinema, perhaps. A token largesse will permeate the talk. Now move up, go even higher and listen. Pensive silence is the norm, though when punctuated, the conversation is magnanimous, forgiving and insightful. But go above the snowline if you really want to get to know the person you are walking with.

So it is with the urban landscape. The roads and streets are our valleys, the buildings our hills. But for a place to see the bigger picture, you need to find the roofs, our urban peaks.

When once up there, on my Victorian slates, nestling in the shadow of the chimney pots, I saw a fellow thinker. She too had her roof to crouch upon, a few streets north of mine. We looked at each other, I nodded, so did she. We shared the sky between us. I almost fell in love with her, there and then. I fantasised about her. I even went and tried to find the house, made enquiries when people opened doors.

"Sorry to trouble you but is there a girl staying here who climbs up on the roof?"

"No, why?"

"Oh, nothing. Not a problem."

I sat on my slates each afternoon for four days. She never showed again. Silly, really.

So, first choice to make. Travel alone or in the company of others? Both have their advantages. I excluded safety from my mental check list of the pluses assigned to a companion. To travel with another, just to limit the risks involved, is all too dull and a bad way to start a trip. Anyway, it smacks of cruelty, to take a friend just because you want to divvy up any future trouble. A problem shared is never halved; it's doubled.

No, the virtue of being more than one is the possibility of sharing an experience, not trouble, and in so doing, making it that much more real. They witness the event. They vouch for it. The sharing also builds a bond. We were there together. We shared a common moment.

All good, but travelling in pairs or more makes you less accessible to the world and vice versa. It makes you self-contained. No tendrils sticking out that can attach to life around you. Like wearing a wedding ring that says 'I'm taken so count me out if looking for a mate'. Of course, it's hard at first. A bit lonely. But loneliness is the spur to making friends, to connect with others. You have to be a little vulnerable, incomplete, to engage with life.

No, I'd go alone.

Next question, where? I had three weeks and not much money, so somewhere near at hand. These were the days before cheap flights. Very sad, this business of low-cost travel. At first it seems a boon. We can all reach out across the globe. A new age of equality of adventure. But travel isn't defined by distance, but by the degree of change. What's the point of crossing half a world to find the same you left back home?

My grandfather on my mother's side, having argued with his guardian, walked from the Midlands to London, eating turnips pulled from fields along the way. What a story he had to tell. What wide-eyed wonder! "I felt I had arrived on another planet," he would say of London. Now we have the global village. Sounds catchy, doesn't it? Global village. Quaint but bold, ethnic, almost tribal, but on an epic scale. Now look again. In reality, the global village is just that: a world reduced to a village. But isn't the point of travel to leave the village? To go beyond the borders of what you know?

Shangri La is a mythical paradise approached, or so the old soldier in the tavern said, by impenetrable mountain passes. Soon Ryanair will fly there. Next, Virgin will build hotels, a golf course where once the locals celebrated rituals. Souvenirs will flourish. T-shirts emblazoned with *Shag an Immortal*, little bottles of water branded *Eternal life 2 Go*. Six months, at tops, before we overhear in the queue at Gatwick, "I'm off to Shangers, ten days at the Hilton Forever." McDonald's will market the Eternaburger and *Shangri La La* will top the charts worldwide for a week. So much more exotic to eat turnips by the roadside.

And then there's the time it takes to fly. Too short. The Iraqis say, "The soul only travels at the speed of a camel." Meaning, by implication, that if you travel faster, you only have to wait for your soul to catch up.

This compression of time and the increment of ease devalue the event or destination. Werner Herzog, that madman film director, walked from Germany to Paris to say farewell to a dying friend. He walked in homage, his way of saying 'you are of value, not a stopover between closely scheduled flights'.

When once standing in the queue for the Uffizi in Florence, I heard the following exchange between Americans:

"I've checked the guidebook and we can do the Fizzy in an hour."

"Don't be silly, this is one of the greatest museums on earth. We'll need two."

I was there to see one painting.

They would fly away with nothing. Just a catalogue of names and the right to tell their friends they'd been there, done that. With luck, I might take home a glimpse of the artist's world, some paltry understanding of how a miracle of creativity had been achieved. Nothing to tell, but everything to keep and cherish. You have to make the choice. Live to tick the boxes or outside of them.

OK. So somewhere not too far away. Next choice. A place I might like or one I would find interesting. The two are not the same. It's thus with everything we do. One of my favourite dishes is leg of lamb. The one I most remember, two sheep's eyes floating on a plate, in a desert tent, somewhere in Iran. The first is pleasing to my palette, the second rocked my world.

*The Independent* newspaper occasionally aligns with my world view. That's why I read the *Telegraph*.

Sometimes I read the other to get some comfort and feel validated, but it's the views of those who think otherwise that move me forward. I chose Switzerland as potentially so boring as to be riveting.

Lastly, how to get there? I'd hitch-hike. It's the best way to travel. Hands down. At least back then. It's all about the bubble and vulnerability. Sit on a train or bus and maybe you'll speak to the person next to you. But the journey is predictable with starting point, destination and ETA. Nothing unexpected will happen. Now hitch-hike. Plant your feet, raise your arm and extend your thumb and you are signalling to destiny.

Car after car pass, each a gateway to a person and their world. Each a blind date in a tiny moving box, just you and them. No escaping down the aisle or into the pages of a book. Better than a blind date. There is no unpleasantness when parting. No onus to say let's meet again. The separation is so clean. We'll share our lives from Junctions 12 to 27 then go our different ways.

Of course, there are risks involved. A friend was killed that way. She was hitch-hiking from London to Oxford. A very pretty girl, she got in the wrong car on the wrong day. She had survived living with the Bedouin for two years and another with whalers in the Arctic, but never lasted the fifty miles to Oxford. At the trial it all came out. The driver was a psychopath taken over the edge by a coat hanger. He was a middle manager, recently promoted. All the others of his rank had wooden coat hangers, a recognition of their status. The company had run out and he was stuck with wire. He beat my friend to death with a baseball bat.

I had my share of lucky escapes. I was in Turkey travelling west. I was nineteen. A van with three guys picked me up. They were tailors and I sat in the back surrounded by hanging shirts. More of a mobile market stall than a van. At journey's end they demanded money. I'd never hitch-hiked in the third world and didn't know the score, which is to pay a contribution. I showed them my empty wallet. No money. My European skin said otherwise. The tension grew. One drew a knife and drove it into the earth between us. Was I to die as well amidst coat hangers? It seemed so improbable. But knives are knives, and the message was clear. We were to fight and the first to touch the knife was to drive it into the other's flesh. Bad business.

I reached into my little shoulder bag and pulled out a stub of sausage. Maybe they had expected a gun and laughed when only cooked meat appeared. A lad with half a sausage against three Turkish tailors. I mimed the passing of the sun from dawn till dusk and somehow managed to convey that this fragment of food was all I had to last a day. I stood there, my trick spent. The Turk reached for the knife. My body tensed, waiting for the thrust I had to somehow parry. Instead he turned and retrieving bread from the van, cut off a piece for me. Soft curd cheese and olives followed. I shared my sausage and we picnicked.

An untimely death by the roadside and an alfresco meal shared, divided only by an outstretched hand arching across the sky. They drove me all the way to Istanbul. They paid my ticket to see a wrestling match and we partied afterwards with the winner. The following morning, the wrestler brought me chocolates and said he was in love with me. I ran back onto the highway and raised my thumb again. A life lived in fear is a life half-lived.

With Ryanair you travel faster, 30,000 feet above the tailor's vans and soppy wrestlers, your only thrill the scratch card and betting on which of the Brit lager louts will puke first. I would hitch-hike; destination: Switzerland.

I'm an old hand at thumbing a lift. Success is in the detail. First, take your backpack off. Without it your silhouette is human, fragile, not a threat. With it, you loom large and convey menace. But keep it close, compact, ideally against your leg. That way you're less intrusive. Next, the stance. Face the cars square on. Expose yourself, be vulnerable. Smile at each driver and never condemn them for not stopping. Your grace on being rejected will be noted by the following car. Recognise that most won't stop because they feel sorry for you, but rather because they think picking you up will be fun, a plus.

A friend of mine is a strategist for Save the Children. They raise money by making people feel guilty, by appealing to their better natures. I think they would raise far more if the promise given was that the donor would feel great about themselves. The same is true for any request for charity, and hitching a lift is just that. So promise pleasure and not the saving of a down-and-out.

I made good time, travelling from London to south-east of Paris in three days and ending up in Chalon-Sur-Saône, north of Lyon. A bit of a detour, but the last of my rides was with a guy who invited me to eat with his family. Decent bloke and great home cooking. Nothing untoward so far and Switzerland nearly reached. After lunch, a farewell cognac and an exchange of addresses, he drove me back to the main road and wished me luck. What price can we put on these encounters?

As a young man, barely out of school, he had been in La Résistance, and over ragout of beef and local wine enthralled me with stories of the war. He had a son my age and a wife with a beautiful smile. It's not the monuments and museums that define a nation. Those places are the country's Sunday best. But to have some notion of a place and its people, you need to see the work clothes, the daily rituals which, summed over time, make us who we are.

Perhaps an hour of waiting, proposing to and thanking the passing cars, and one pulled up. All the signs of trouble were in evidence. First, it was a mini, a yapping Chihuahua of a car, highly strung, all teeth and bombed-out marble eyes. Then, the way the driver stopped. Not like the resistance fighter, who signalled from a distance and eased into the lay-by. No, this car just swung in, at the last moment, on a whim. Finally, the human content. Three teens strung out on drugs and booming rock.

In fact, they hadn't stopped for me at all. They had been to Ketama in Morocco and bought a brick of hash to sell. The only trouble was that they had smoked the lot on the drive back home. As I watched, they staggered out the car and tossed the motley contents on the ground. Half-eaten sandwiches, an impressive collection of empty spirit bottles, some filthy clothes, a bundle of porn mags and an ornate hubble-bubble pipe, their only souvenir. They were arguing each with all, a triangle of accusations as to who had lost the little remaining hash. Two thousand kilometres of constant puff and they were frantic, their bodies craving more. They even took the seats out and combed the floor for crumbs.

These days I only smoke my spliff when warranted, listening to music at night around the pool or dreaming in the hammock from time to time. But I remember those moments of desperation. The rummaging in drawers and trouser pockets at 3am. The blurry attempts to relive where you last saw your stash. The paranoia that your mate swiped it when he came over for a smoke and chat. The unfounded terror that you accidentally threw it away, leading to you sitting naked in the kitchen, going through the rubbish. Then starting all over, in case you didn't look properly first time round. All that only to realise that you've smoked the lot.

They found slim pickings. Mainly hair and dust, dead skin and ash. I had a little lump in my alternative first aid kit, along with playing cards and my knife – it's surprising what scrapes you can get out of with a magic trick or two.

"*Merde!*"

"*Putain!*"

"*Ca me fait chier!*"

I speak French and understood. "Shit." "Whore." "That pisses me off."

But why should I assume my reader does? It annoys me when writers quote from another language and don't translate. An intellectual arrogance, a mystification, like mass in Latin, to keep the faithful in their place. So I'll pretend they all spoke broken English. Better to slightly distort the truth so all can understand than write in French for the benefit of the few.

I told you there were three of them. Now let me give some detail. One was big, an oaf, whose name I later learnt was Henri. He was blond and seemed to have no bones. Maybe he was a Li-Lo come to life, pig skins replacing plastic sheet, pumped up with marijuana gas in lieu of air? He was the heavy of the three, the kind of boy who'd blown up frogs at school and when it was his turn to give the Indian burn, you'd know he'd go too far, wanting to inflict real pain and smiling all the time.

Philippe. There's always a Philippe. The dupe of the gang. If they'd been proper hoods, he'd be the one found with the body in the boot. Philippe, the hanger-on, neither the brawn nor the brains. The shit in the shit sandwich. They got him to search the car whilst they swigged from a vodka bottle.

The brain, or what was left of it, was Pierre. A wiry type, all nerves and sinew, I disliked him from the start. His kind of Indian burn would leave a Cherokee in ashes. But then he wouldn't light the fire himself, he would get Philippe to do it, in exchange for photos of his mother in the nude. He had bad acne and greasy hair combed down and across.

Some people's expressions invite you in, others suggest they want to learn from you, or offer something. When he looked at me, I knew he was only assessing how I could be of use. When he moved, he struck poses, a series of stills rather than fluid motion. Oh, the self-satisfaction in every gesture, a sneer his answer to the world.

A dodgy lot. Game on.

"'Ey, you," said Pierre, "You 'ave 'ash, shit?"

"I do, as it happens."

I held it out, like the combination to a safe they wanted open. A smile from Henri, slow and dumb, the kind that would grace his face when he heard the frog go pop. Philippe smiled because Henri had. Pierre didn't. Bad for business, to express interest.

"'Ow much you want? We buy your 'ash."

"It's not for sale…"

Pierre looked like Hitler being told that dogs weren't allowed in the bunker. Henri clenched his fist, a habit picked up at birth.

"But you can roll a joint if you like."

They were on their way back to Neuchâtel, a hop across the border into Switzerland, and took me with them. To be fair, it was the hash they took, but as I was attached to it, I went along as well.

Twice I nearly left that fucking Mini. I've had my share of dodgy rides. A stint strapped to milk churns dragged by a rickshaw until the whole contraption overturned. Two hundred miles of terror in Afghanistan with a truckie who kept falling asleep at the wheel. I nudged him in the ribs every time we swerved towards certain death and vomited when he dropped me off. But the fucking Mini beat the lot.

It was like living in the head of a madman. A proper bedlam loony. Four of us, bombed out, stuffed in a Mini going at breakneck speed. French apocalyptic rock screaming out, all the more metallic and nerve-jangling as issuing from a cheap cassette player. The car stank and we travelled in our own microclimate of Ganga fog and condensed sweat. I, of course, sat in the back with Philippe, the brains at the wheel and the brawn beside him.

These guys were fucked. Henri would rock his head back and forth, banging a beat with the empty vodka bottle on the dashboard. Beat isn't the right word. There was no rhythm, just banging accompanied by a constant, "Du du du," from spittle-splattered lips. Pierre, that deluded runt, drove with driving gloves and played the gears as though at the racetrack. He would constantly overtake, only to slow down, to overtake again, rewinding and replaying his misplaced superiority.

Every so often, Henri would shout out some insult at a passing car. Maybe they were driving too slow or he thought the woman in the back too fat. Perhaps it was their choice of colour or the fact they had a roof rack. It didn't matter. Nothing was right. Everyone else a fool, *un stupide*, someone whose mother he would fuck or head he would shit on. Then back to vodka bottle drumming and more spittle on the windscreen.

Philippe would attempt the same. But his choice of victim would never please his bosses. Once the chosen car had a number plate with three sixes, therefore cool, and Philippe a cunt. Another time the car was white, the colour of cocaine and thus exempt.

Pierre was pickier as to when to launch his insults. Even then, they weren't really insults. No expletives, and far more chilling because of it. When we filled up with petrol, the car in front took too long and didn't use the locking catch on the pump handle. The chap was therefore a fool and Pierre told me that, if they had more time, he would follow him home and pour acid in his tank.

Nearing the border we were passed by a Ferrari. The vodka banging stopped, the music turned down. They knew the car. It belonged to the man. The main man. He ran the whores, the drugs and the extortion rackets of Neuchâtel. He was their hero.

"One day I 'ave this car," said Pierre. "But mine will be solid gold. I will 'ave a driver an' fuck in the back."

"Me too," said Henri.

"And me," said Philippe.

"You will never 'ave this car," said Pierre. "This is boss man's car."

I think I'll go all Dagenham and give my little cast of characters nicknames. Pierre shall be Le Ferret, Henri we'll christen Du Du, and Philippe, the Stooge.

The verbal exchanges which went as conversation were really just delusional monologues, shouted above the engine's tortured whine, the rock and bottle drumming. Here's an example:

Le Ferret: "I'll go back to Ketama an' buy ten kilos. I'll make a million francs. New francs. I will go to Rue Chartreuse an' buy a silk suit like Ricard wears. Then I am off to ze casino at Pontarlier. I 'ave a system. All the rich people know it. That's how they made their money. I will cash a million francs of chips. The cashier will tell the manager an' soon everyone will know I am ze big man. They will give me my own table. All the whores will leave ze other men an' stand around me. I will bet one number and make 36 million. I will break ze bank an' give the croupier a thousand francs. The manager will give me his own daughter. People will point at me in ze streets an' say, 'That is Pierre Le Maître, the man who broke the bank at Pontarlier.'."

Du Du: "I will bet five times an' be ze richest man in Neuchâtel."

Stooge: "I will bet a hundred times an' be ze richest man in ze world."

Le Ferret: "Then you are fools. The system only works once."

We arrived in Neuchâtel around ten at night and went to Du Du's flat. His parents were away. Smart middle-class place with lots of antique, heavy furniture and windows to the ground. High ceilings and doors. Lofty, cerebral.

Having done the ransacking of the fridge for munchy foods, found none and bought pizzas, we ended up in Du Du's father's den. French bourgeois dens are the antithesis of the American. Where the latter are an antidote to an otherwise ordered life, the French one's are a distillation, the showcase of their owner's success. A kind of shrine built by an aspiring god to worship himself. Where the American has his battered comfy sofas, basketball net and fridge for beers, the French have fine turned chairs, encyclopaedias and decanters. Trophy fishing photos seem to be ubiquitous. But whereas the Yanks will pose in soft hats, crouching and smiling, the French will stand in rank, aloof, erect, a veritable Maginot Line of alternating fish and men.

Both have projectors and home movies. Video was just emerging and a rarity. Both have some porn. But with the Americans, the porn would be separated out. A shelf would hold the family films, labelled by year or the name of the child whose birthday had been filmed. The porn would be hidden in a locked drawer or in a box, covered with old clothes. Not so the French. Du Du's father had his collection in a dainty cabinet of bevelled glass and colonial wood, *Deuxième Anniversaire d'Henri* (Henri's second birthday) set jowl to cheek with *Les Saloperies Anales* (anal tarts).

When it comes to affairs, the rest of us have 'a bit on the side'. The French have *'mon cinq à sept'* (my five to seven), thus incorporating into the schedule of the day, along with taking the children to school and a stint at the office and lunch, a venal couple of hours with their nominated lover.

Anyway, Du Du passed over his birthday reminiscences for the anal tarts, picking, I suspect, the least interesting of the cakes. I had, however, never seen a porn film and admit to getting a hard-on. The format helped. Super 8. It gave the clichéd formulaic scenes an air of realism, just another home movie, the players caught *in fraganti* by a handheld camera.

Exhausted, stoned, head still ringing from the mini monster ride, I fell asleep on the floor, my lullaby, dubbed moaning; my twinkling mobile, two strung-out teens wanking; my mural, Le Ferret posing in the mirror with Du Du's father's shotgun.

I woke up at noon, several hours before the others. Being young is quite fantastic. That ability to rave all night and still feel capable of kicking the sun over the horizon the next day. Like in cartoons. Tom gets shot from a cannon before being squashed by a building landing on his head. He lies flattened like rolled out pastry. But then he re-inflates, and the game of cat and mouse goes on. With age we just stay there, on the pastry board, waiting for the crimped moulds to make us into petit fours. I went for a walk.

I keep saying French and not Swiss. Neuchâtel is a hybrid, wanting to be Switzerland but never really leaving France, Gallic but with fondue and precision engineering. Well, precision everything, really. They make the watches and then obey the goose step movement of the triumvirate of hands. The place is like a clockwork toy town, crafted out of wood and hobby Paris plaster, hand painted by a man we can guess wore rimless specs and had perfectly manicured nails. I imagine it being wound up at dawn by the dainty key he keeps around his neck. The little shutters open, tiny heads with real hair appear and the church bells ring. Some whirring and pedestrians glide forward, moving on hidden rails, to stop at zebra crossings, timing their advance to the changing of traffic lights with fairy bulbs. Artificial snow adorns the hexagonal towers and the whole model is landscaped with a lake, marina and sailing dinghies. All detailed up, right down to a dog with a bandanna barking from the prow. He's even made a soundtrack of, "Bonjour, Monsieur; Bonjour, Madame."

A master craftsman's work, every detail is perfect. Tiny truffle chocolates, each individually wrapped and set like cannonballs on stands. My God, the patisserie looks good enough to eat and the butcher's meat might well be edible had the cuts not been so neat. But he's just a craftsman, not an artist, and it takes art to bring craft to life. It's all too perfect. As though itself inside a souvenir shop, so touched up that's it's become its own postcard. Neuchâtel, a clockwork town, a *Truman Show* but with everyone unwitting.

On my eleventh birthday I had a party, and all my classmates came. *Fireball XL5* was our TV show of choice. We all knew the theme song and sang it at the party. Anyway, as my father had only left us two years earlier, there was still some money kicking around. A marzipan replica of the spaceship and two crew members appeared, candles lit, and we sang our song. It too was perfect in every detail.

We all gathered round, some fifteen wide-eyed boys, all Olivers wanting more, even before the first slice. I blew out the candles and was given the knife. At first, I didn't want to cut it. It was so perfect and would turn from a gateway to the universe to just a cake with the first incision. But then I did, as wonder turned into shock and scattered boys. The rocket was inhabited. Not by little chocolate coins or Bakelite robots to take home, but by ants. Hordes of them. They raced up the knife and along my arm, spilling onto the table. An alien invasion come to eat up earth. The cake was inedible, rotting from within. So, perhaps Neuchâtel was not a clockwork town, only a monumental masterpiece of marzipan, something apparently edible but, as we will see, eaten from within.

I returned to the flat with a bag of croissants. Du Du and Le Ferret were drinking beer and eating jam straight from the jar. They pounced on the croissants and tore at them like lions do a kill. When down to the last one, I feebly suggested that maybe we should keep it for Stooge? They looked at me as though I was proposing that a stool has rights and shouldn't be sat on.

That croissant caused a bit of a showdown. Du Du and Le Ferret eyed each other, breakfast bun hands twitching. It was, by right of rank, Le Ferret's. He was the leader after all. But Du Du was enormous and Le Ferret skin and bone. For he to have had it would have been an injustice, like a eunuch chosen over Eros to take a girl's virginity. What the fuck, I reached out, snatched it and stuffed it in my gob. You've got to eat up and be counted now and then.

I think the croissant-snatching business raised my status. Either that or I was seen as something of a curiosity, a kind of ethnic souvenir. The hubble-bubble was good, but how much better to bring home a traveller who lived with lesbians and spoke with an accent?

I confess I've done the same myself, favouring those who come from far away. My best catch was a Tibetan refugee. How much more interesting one thinks one becomes when saying, "I have a Tibetan friend staying. A political refugee." Of course, it's all bullshit and the kudos is only a trick with mirrors, mere reflected limelight.

No reason can be discounted, except for human kindness, as to why I ended up a guest in the Le Maître's family's house, but stay I did.

Le Ferret you've unfortunately met. That's three to go. His brother, a down's syndrome boy of fifteen who, for reasons which will become apparent, I will call the Trouser Douser; his mother, fat and crude, *la Grosse Salope*; and Dad, the Dickologist. Of the four of them, the only one I didn't have some form of sex with was Le Ferret.

The house was in fact a hostel and I fully expected to have to pay. Indeed, a sum was mentioned and agreed, but never asked for. All things considered, I paid my way, just not in cash. I stayed for a week and, having nothing better to do, accepted a temporary job helping a friend of the Dickologist lay carpets and lino. He was recently divorced, drank and worked too much, and treated me like toxic scum. Unlike my little 'Z' team, there was no humour or adventure in our work, just a necessary evil to pay bills.

My boss believed that the employee only understands the fist and the wallet, the stick and the carrot. I dance to neither tune. My motivation is my pride, the sense of achievement in a job well done. I worked on the black, of course, and the bastard never paid me. He laughed when I asked for the money. He said I had no rights as I was working illegally and, basically, "Tough shit."

I was going to let it pass, but on my last morning I overheard the Dickologist talking to him on the phone. He was demanding his cut for passing me on, a migrant worker who had been set to work for free. The carpet man had the shoe shop which his wife used to run. He was determined to sell all the stock before the settlement of assets went to court. So we went over there to discount price the shoes. I reckoned he owed me a hundred quid and stole stock to that value.

On my second night Le Ferret's father took me out to a bar. No, not the type that will be springing to your mind. There's no portly owner serving *petites bières* and calling to his wife in the kitchen. There's no guy with moustache and cap reading the sports page and berating the Marseilles goalie. Don't look for blue-clad workers tucking into *duck a l'orange* and table wine, talking with their hands. No, quite another kind of bar, the type not in the tourist guide though ubiquitous to Europe. The kind I hate.

The façade was black and windowless with the name Le Chat Noire (The Black Cat) in neon and a flush metal door with a small round window offering a dim view of the poorly lit interior. We went in. There were no more than half a dozen people inside. There never are. No music, no card games, no groups at tables chatting. Just us, two couples at little, high, round tables and another man and woman at the bar, drinking on their own. All black interior, punctuated by strips and tubes of chrome and all submerged in eternal twilight. Mirrors, of course, behind the bar, and an unholy collection of spirits.

The place was a visualisation of an unimaginative lecher's mind: the basic model without the erotic extra trim; the wet dream of the prematurely impotent. In those days, I longed to get a commission to design a brothel. What fun I would have, recreating the gamut of human desire, searching for the colours of submission and domination, of awoken innocence. What silk pavilions

I would install, what care I would take when overseeing the dungeon's lighting, the chinoiserie of the boudoir, the right fruit for the bath-side bowl, the perfect lattice work for the confession booth. But Le Chat Noire didn't aide the imagination; it crushed it.

There is a wonderful, chilling scene in Tarantino's *True Romance*, one of my top ten films. James Gandolfini has found the suitcase of coke under the bed, "Snow at the end of the rainbow." So all that's left to do is kill Patricia Arquette. He delivers one of Tarantino's classic monologues, so perfectly constructed that his words have shape and taste. He talks about his first kill, admitting he threw up before he became inured, desensitised through repetition, ending with the confession that, "Now I kill just to see their expression change." That's why the regulars of Le Chat Noire came, I think, to drink and fuck: just to see their expressions change. I doubt if they ever did.

The bar was worked by a hard-faced woman. Too much make-up, podgy, stumpy, tough as old thigh-high fuck-me boots. The kind who would wring an orgasm out of you like the life from a chicken. A saucepan used to boil up dead men's clothes, no longer fit for cooking, the peep show mop, the box for dead Jews' teeth. You get the picture.

Le Ferret's father ordered drinks. Whisky for us both. The booze, like the women, was all hard. She set them down for us like the crone at the school canteen would dump a scoop of mash.

The woman sitting on her own along the bar sauntered over. Time to go to work. She placed a hand on his arm.

Christ, what must it be like to have to say the same lines every night, to feign interest in an oaf, your only reward the right to be fucked by an obese, semi-impotent, bourgeois wretch and take home the rent money to square another week?

"So... would you like to buy a lady a drink?"

Now, bottom line, the answer must surely be 'no'. If her request had been subtitled it would read: *You are being offered the opportunity to buy a stranger who has no interest in you some coloured water at exorbitant cost and she's not even thirsty.*

The punter always says 'yes'.

"Of course. What would you like?"

What's really being proposed is that the man demonstrates his wealth by squandering money. That and a vague, clichéd attempt to turn the sordid proceedings into a date.

Next on the menu comes the question of what the man does. Never the other way round. I mean, what's the point?

Punter: "So, what do you do?"

Tart: "I extract semen and cash from lonely losers like yourself."

No, it's always the woman, and always accompanied by the stool being brought a little closer. Hats off to them. Their ability to feign interest is impressive and whatever the man says, from janitor to astronaut, the answer's always the same: "How interesting."

In the case of Le Ferret's father, he presented himself as a penoligist (literally, a Dickologist).

"How interesting," said the whore.

Now, of course, penologist is fantasy. He was in fact a landlord collecting rents on a couple of flats he had acquired via his wife's inheritance. He certainly didn't study cocks and was so fat that I doubted he had even seen his own in years.

If he had been twelve, I might have understood. At that age, boys tend to collect and use words valued as naughty or sophisticated. Often the meaning of the words is lost on them, and the boys use them out of context, merely to shock or impress. I imagine him and two mates at school.

Mate One: "That's total penis."

Mate Two: "Don't be such a mythologist."

Ferret's future dad: "When I grow up, I am going to be a penisologist."

Understandable at twelve, but not at fifty.

Unfazed, the tart moved on.

"And what about your young friend. What does 'e do?"

"'E is my assistant."

Would I be? Hmm.

What normally follows is the tart explains that she is only doing this work to raise money to open a beauty salon, followed by the man explaining that his wife doesn't understand him. Around the second glass of coloured water, the hooker pushes her leg between the thighs of the man and moves her head so close to his that it goes out of focus. Like good sales operators, having asked his name, she uses it continuously. That and other silly tricks like lighting two cigarettes at once and passing the second to the mark. The man by this time has shelled out half a day's pay and has basically made an investment with no return. Should he fold or raise the stakes? This is where man's best friend comes in. Self-delusion.

The facts are there for all too see. A blurred and ugly woman is proposing that a man she despises pay her a large sum, a chunk of which will end up with a pimp, to fake an orgasm and allow him to empty his ball sack into a latex bag held in place by her fanny.

Now let's put all that into the self-delusion shaker, add a splash of alcohol and pour it out again. A mysterious and attractive woman who needs money to open a beauty salon is possessed by lust. She tells a man whom she really understands that she wants to have sex and do 'everything'. Safe sex, of course, because she's a good girl.

Other factors play their part. Good old-fashioned lust – me man, you woman – as well as macho pride. Men are told by other men that they should want to fuck all women. In a chorus of:

"I'd give her one, I'd give her one."
Who's going to go solo and sing,
"I wouldn't give her one"?

In essence, these factors are really the three ages of man:
16-35: Me man, you woman.
36-50: I'd give her one.
51-70: Self-delusion.

Of course, there's a fourth phase: 70+. If you don't get a fuck, you don't give a fuck.

In actual fact, most men don't fuck at all. I've known my share of whores and lived with one for a month. Of ten men that go to a brothel, only an average of two end up taking a room, and of those that do, only about half ever come. So that's one in ten that ever consummates the evening. The rest just talk and fantasise. Even sadder, I think. Somehow more abusive.

The Dickologist, who was a pervert through and through, doubled his bet and added a wager on the side. I was to fuck the hooker and he would, in his capacity as expert in the field, give instructions and advice. To see my reply, consult the chart above.

We retired to a room at the back. In the bigger places, there's a woman who hands out towels and condoms and gets a coin or two. An ageing employee taken out the field and given a desk job, a latter-day Charon, rowing you, if not to Hades, then close. Le Chat Noir was one star, if that, with all the money spent on the front of house: the back rooms an afterthought. So, just a corridor with a naked bulb leading to a room, a sink, a chair and a bed with under-sheet and single pillow. Oh, and the ubiquitous cheap print on the wall.

Maybe if you buy a thousand condoms, one comes free? Or maybe, under Mitterrand, a law was passed that all brothels should have art? Ours was a hunting scene, pastoral and charming, with a bit of death thrown in. I'm tempted to weave an analogy between the shooter and the stag and the hooker and her client. But who's the hunter and who's the prey? Anyway, there are no trophies here worth putting on the wall.

And so to business. The whore, of course, strips, starting with her wristwatch, which is set on the chair. We had twenty minutes. Then a bit of fanny washing in the sink, like rinsing the plate in a burger bar between customers, between servings of meat in buns. Thankfully, the Dickologist didn't strip. The ageing pervert rarely does. Self-delusion works so much better when the competing reality of your cock's decline and fall is kept from view. But she did. My God, uncared-for bodies can turn ugly! I mean that. They turn against their owners. Like a drunk driver being forced to look at photos of the damage he has caused, the lives he has taken, the body is a living album cataloguing multiple offences of neglect viewed in the mirror every day.

I stripped and she sucked my cock whilst the Dickologist gave instructions.

"Good, that's good... now play with your fanny whilst you suck... good. Take him deeper... let's see some tongue. Excellent. Hold 'er 'ead. Push 'er down... good. As it should be... move your 'and, I can't see. Yes. Now grab 'er breasts. That's it. Rub 'arder. She is a pig. She's all excited. Now fuck er a little..."

Sorry, I can't go on. The best and worst of sex are almost indescribable. The best because the emotions felt are too exquisite and ephemeral to pin down and the worst because there are none. All we had that night was something akin to an IKEA storage box, manufactured from mechanically separated meat, with the Dickologist reading the assembly instructions.

The twenty minutes came and went. But I didn't. I couldn't come. So, two faked orgasms. Hers and mine. She knew, of course, and smiled as though to say, "Welcome to my world."

More slaving laying carpets, dreary monologues from my boss slating his ex and walks around the lake. Some beers with students and card tricks, a meaningless drive round town in the Mini with Le Ferret and the gang. Some binge drinking, lino gluing and café food. Two days to go.

She came in the middle of the night. *La Grosse Salope*. Stark naked and decided. I was fast asleep and thought the ceiling had caved in. But it was only Le Ferret's mum on top of me. I was blind drunk and horribly disorientated. I thought it was her face above my head. I thought I was kissing her mouth. You should forgive me for my anatomical confusion. You see, I was running my hands through hair, so understandable. But then, the double take. If this was her mouth on mine, who was sucking on my cock? For one horrible moment I ran down the check-list of possibilities – the Dickologist, Le Ferret, the Trouser Douser… But then I moved my hands and found a hole. Christ, either she had been shot in the head at point blank range and was in fact a zombie or… oh fuck, it was her arse. The lips of course belonged to her pussy and the hair, a kind of built-in cushion on her bum. I was being *soixante-neufed* by an ape.

*La Grosse Salope* then mounted me and banged away. Her weight was off the scales. If she had punched her kilos and height into one of those self-diagnostic websites, the answer coming back would be that she was either dead or twins. With each downward lunge I disappeared into the mattress. I was being dunked into a sea of foam and springs only to emerge, breath in and sink again. She masturbated frantically and when she came, she shat. Not an epic doodle, just a ping-pong ball of turd. She dismounted leaving me looking down at my erection and her parting love gift. She saw it too and, smiling, scooped it up and left.

I suppose we should always look on the bright side, see the positive. She could have, after all, not held out so long…

That leaves the Trouser Douser. Here's how it went down. We were all sitting round the telly. Le Ferret, bolt upright in his chair, doubtless planning how he would poison the other three and take the house, sell it, go to Morocco, buy the hash, the suit… you know how that one ends. Le Dickologist as usual in his armchair, reading the paper and denigrating everything and everyone except a banker who had done a runner with the cash. His wife, *la Grosse Saloppe*, knitting and soaking her feet in a plastic bucket of hot water. I and the Trouser Douser shared the sofa. The TV rumbled on, some undecipherable soap in German with all the women in raincoats and the men seemingly living in saunas. The Trouser Douser was in his pyjamas and smiled throughout.

I don't know what got him going. Was it some fetish for macs, some crossed wires in that jumbled head of his? Was it the men in towels? Christ knows. For whatever reason, he started to hump my leg.

Now, to my knowledge, no one has ever written the appropriate protocol for when a DS child masturbates on your leg. With dogs, I know the score. A brisk shake, a slightly embarrassed smile and an, "I see the poodle's got his lipstick out," will usually do. But what to do when the humper is a boy, and you are a guest in his parent's house? Pin him to the floor? Gently ease him onto another leg? Which to choose? His mother would seem the obvious choice. At least the sex would be heterosexual. But somehow that makes it even grosser, adding more credibility to the deed, drawing it deeper into the fold of more accepted sexual practice. His brother? Sure! A fine welcome he'd get there. That left the father. Keep it as something between dad and son, like showing a lump on your dick which gives concern.

In the end, paralysed by the surrealism of it all, I didn't pass the bucking. I just sat there immobilised, searching for places to put my hands, until he came on my trousers and rolled off, spent and satisfied. *La Grosse Salope* looked up from her knitting just long enough to say, "Leave your trousers out tonight. I'll put them in the wash."

Then back to making mittens.

Le Dickologist didn't even notice and carried on reading passages out loud which met with his disapproval. As for Le Ferret, he just smiled, relishing my discomfort. I left the following morning, my busman's holiday complete.

Now, you don't get that with Ryanair.

# Blue Eyes

It was good to get home. You know that life's OK when it pleases you to come home. How awful it must be to return to where you live and wish you weren't there. Test it for yourself. The reaction must be immediate, not intellectualised. Open the door, turn on the light, put down your luggage and look around. Are you smiling or frowning? It's that simple. The same is true, I think, of love. The phone rings; it's the one. Do you smile or not? The rest is superfluous.

Nina greeted me and, having asked about the trip, wondered if I had returned with chocolates. No, I hadn't.

I checked the answerphone. Have I told you we had one? A monster of a machine, salvaged from a skip. Reel-to-reel magnetic tape and the size of a suitcase. You could have fitted a dwarf inside it to answer the calls. There were eleven messages: four invites to parties, three offers of work, two calls from a girl I was trying to avoid, and one from Alistair, who had been reading a book on orchids and wanted to tell me about it. He was a fanatical horticulturist with an encyclopaedic knowledge of plants. The last message was from Peter: "Call me."

First, a proper kip. I slept for a day. As I fell asleep, I realised that I had had sex, of a kind, three times in Neuchâtel but hadn't come once. That's it, the experience in a nutshell: nothing seminal. I woke up refreshed and laughing.

"Hi, Peter, it's me, Laurence, back from holidays. What's up?"

"First things first. Did you enjoy yourself?"

"Not exactly, but it was, as you would say, rewarding."

I proceeded to give Peter the gory details. As always, he listened patiently, rarely interrupting. His take on the Le Maître family shamed me though. He worried for Le Ferret, rightly pointing out that he probably felt a little abandoned with his parents' care lopsided all in favour of his brother. The mum and dad he saw as sad, lonely people who must have been desperate to seek such bankrupt human contact. As to the poo, he was dismissive: "Just some stuff that comes out of us," he said.

That was his strength, but also his moral Achilles heel. He forgave and, in forgiving, sanctioned everything. His stance was not to take one, to see us all for what we are, silly boys and girls, trying to make out, to find solace. Is that copping out or in? It's an important question, really crucial, and one I need to answer, at least to my own satisfaction. Bottom line, I think it's both.

My gym teacher touched me up at prep school. He touched us all up. He told us wearing underpants for gym was unhygienic. When in mid-flight, vaulting over the horse, he would grab and part our legs to take a peek. He would also line us up, strip down our shorts and spank us for imaginary misbehaviour. His name was Mr Nichols.

Now, let's be clear. I didn't like being an object of his lust. I was twelve. Not fair. So what would Peter have said? Probably that he just wanted a little thrill and that we all have our needs. Sure, he's right. I don't suppose Mr Nichols made a conscious decision early on in life to be a paedophile. He just turned out that way and couldn't help himself. Didn't Mr Nichols also have the right to be happy? But where does that leave me? What about my right to be a child, to be protected by those I trusted to be my educators? In a perfect world, one where compassion and pragmatism walked hand in hand, sentencing would be replaced by arbitration. The judge, representing society and thus the good of the collective, would assess the needs of both parties. He might sum up my case as follows.

"Both parties have their needs. Mr Nichols needs to see and touch little boys' genitals to be happy. Laurence here needs to feel protected as a child and reared in safety until he's of an age to freely select his sexual partners. The fulfilment of their needs is mutually exclusive. For one to be happy, the other must be sad. On balance, Laurence's pain outweighs Mr Nichols's pleasure, as Laurence's right to choose, his liberty, was taken away. So it is that I judge Mr Nichols should be imprisoned, not so he sees the error of his ways, which he won't, but to ensure that future boys can pursue their path to happiness unobstructed."

Universal compassion, even empathy, does not imply an inability to act, to take a stance. What it strips away is only the moral approbation, the turning of arbitration into the sentencing of evil.

On my first night in India, staying in a hostel dorm, I had my wallet stolen. What a start! The doors were locked at night, so the thief was someone in the room. I barred the door and demanded that each in turn went into the bathroom. Whoever had my wallet, was to leave it there. If anyone went in and saw that someone before him had left it, he was not to tell me. I didn't want revenge, just the return of what was mine.

Miraculously, they all agreed and when the last returned, I visited the bathroom. Against all odds, the wallet was there. That was that for me, but one of them broke down, actually knelt in front of me and cried. A confession followed. He was a German junkie; he couldn't help himself. He was addicted and couldn't stop the nicking. I felt sorry for him and even offered to take him for breakfast. He declined. Then I went to the station and tried to buy a ticket. The bastard had returned the wallet but kept the cash!

Six months later, in a market in Madras, I saw him begging from the tourists. I punched him in the face and broke his nose. As he went down, I said, "Nothing personal. Good luck."

I've never achieved that balance before or since. The synthesis of punishment and compassion. I hit him to say that he had taken something from me, like Mr Nichols had, and reduced my chances of being happy. But I wished him luck. After all, he was just trying to make out, to find solace.

That inability of Peter to take a stance was why I ended the sex for cash. That and Ella.

"So, Peter, what have you got lined up for me? Anything would be an improvement on Neuchâtel."

"Well, there is something…"

By now I was a true paid-up member of the community. The people in the shops knew my name and I theirs. I looked out for an elderly Jewish couple, fixing leaks, easing a lock, being the son they never had. I would order coffee and a smoked salmon and cream cheese bagel from Evering Road bakery for breakfast. Then two extra coffees to take away in Styrofoam cups: one for me and one for Chris, the mechanic round the corner. He'd lay down his buffing cloths, turn the compressor off, and we'd just stand there, making conversation. Nothing deep, just routine stuff, the beauty of the predictable. Predictable as my endless reiterations of 'walking round the garden, like a teddy bear' for my son. He knows two steps will follow and a tickle. He laughs each time, not from the surprise, but from the delight of having constancy in his life, something to rely on, like his Duplo blocks that always fit together.

Sue had moved out and her place was taken by Leslie Dyke. You can guess her sexual preferences! Does your name have an impact on how you turn out? Was she destined to be a lesbian from the day of her christening? I think so. Not in some mumbo-jumbo written-in-the-stars way. No, more down to earth. A sort of constant whispering, reminding you not of who you are, but who you could be. A predisposing rather than a destiny.

Incidentally, the dentist in my local town is called Dr Marfil (Dr Ivory.) I imagine some person of influence in his life remarking, "With a name like that you ought to be a dentist." Must have got her thinking, at the very least.

Not all parents seem to get it right. The manager of the local council estate had christened their son Richard, Richard Head, Dick for short. Misplaced expectation at the very least.

Lesley was on holiday and Nina had moved on. I guess we were all just partying in the transit lounge, waiting for our flights to be called. I had the flat just to myself. Small incremental steps from quasi-commune to nuclear family.

Alistair was madly in love with an extraordinary girl called Caroline. Beautiful and wild, opulent, she once rode her horse from England to southern Spain and later joined a circus. She must have rocked that gentle academic's world. He went off-radar, secluding himself on a sofa made for two in his parents' country house at Cray. She was the most exotic of blooms, irresistible to a horticulturist.

This year I've planted out a vegetable garden. Tomatoes, cucumbers, lettuces… the lot. I watch over them, stopping my writing several times a day to check on them, to water, count the flowers, pick off dead leaves. So it must have been with Alistair, watching over his Carolina Opulencia at night. Keeping her warm in his seeding bed. I worried for him. When such a man as he commits, they do so to the marrow of their bones. What if the flower of love that they had germinated died? I also felt a little envy.

I had my lion's share of sex and fun, but he had love, the most dangerous adventure of them all.

Peter had been clear. I was to go to Junction 6 on the M1 and wait at the petrol station, by the exit. A dark green Rover would pull up and ask if I wanted a lift. I was to say yes, get in and… what? Peter hadn't been specific, saying something about 'listening to the tape of his wife' and if I didn't get out the car, 'to take it from there'. OK, so more hitch-hiking and maybe some amateur singing. Couldn't be worse that the Mini. Surely?

I thumbed a lift to the junction. It got me in the mood, into character. It was bloody cold and raining hard. Rain in the countryside is bliss, the promise of life. But on a service station forecourt, the promises fall on deaf ears, washed into drains along with petrol spills. What a dismal setting. Alone and cold, standing with the rubbish thrown from cars on the M1. A flayed strip of the earth's skin, gone black, with teeming metal creatures running up and down the sore. Wet darkness, and the only thing on offer, Colonel Sanders' tubs of chicken legs. It's all right when you're in a car. The motorway is your habitat. But take the car away and you become abandoned on another planet which cannot support your life form.

Then I saw the Rover. It had been parked up all along, some twenty yards away. Who knows how long the man inside had been watching me. Now, I've been watched by lecherous men whilst having sex with their wives. But this was different, an altogether more intrusive vigil. I was wet, alone and vulnerable. Was this all intentional? Had I been beaten like a pheasant until flushed out and exposed, all the better to bring down?

Back to that shoe-shine boy from Cockenomics. The capo had killed his dad and he had sworn revenge. He suffered cleaning shoes to get closer to his mark, to gather information. He shops the capo to the police, but the cops are in the pocket of the Mafia. They say he needs to wear a wire and set up a meeting with the capo. They promise to be there and bring the killer down. The rendezvous is classic. An isolated parking lot. There, too, it's dark and raining. The boy waits. Why haven't the police arrived? Then a car pulls up, stops, the engine killed. He can hear the beating of his heart, that and the tap, tapping of the rain. The headlights snap on, full beam. He shields his eyes. And then he realises there are no cops, just him, a rabbit running scared, caught in the hunter's headlights.

The Rover eased across the forecourt, holding me steady in its gaze. The seeing and the seen. It stopped beside me, and the window opened. We said our lines:

"Need a lift?"

"Yes."

"Get in… no, not the front, in the back."

The seats had nylon covers and a compass, an outside temperature gauge and a second digital clock were fixed to the dash. The woman beside me was wearing a mac, had her hair tied back and never looked at me. A vein in the driver's neck bulged in the light of passing cars. No one spoke. I should have figured it out. The clues were there. Trouble.

We drove in silence, heading north, until he pulled off at the third exit and rejoined the traffic returning the way we had come. The steady nagging of the rain, the low whir of the car's heater, the metronomic waving of the wipers, the hypnotic pulsing of headlights, the almost inaudible squeaking of the husband's driving gloves on the worn rubber covering of the wheel punctuating the otherwise black and airless silence began to lull me, to dull my senses, to anaesthetise my will.

Then he pressed play on the car's cassette recorder.

Three hours have passed since I wrote that last line. Time and time again I have set my fingers to the keyboard only to withdraw them and slump back in my chair. I can't do it. I simply cannot tell this story.

At first, I thought it was the shame and the knowledge that the telling would dimmish me in the reader's eyes that was holding me back. Like the time I accidentally ran over my wife's favourite cat right here on our drive. I buried her under an almond tree and said she must have wandered off. For months I woke up telling myself that on this day I would confess, only to take my secret back to bed with me.

But no, it's not just the shame that's paralysing my mind, it's something else, the almost dreamlike nature of events so dehumanised that they have never truly attached themselves to me, never became part of the fabric of memory leaving my task today one of trying to recount a hallucination, experienced by my alter-ego, fragmented and peppered with non sequiturs.

So no, I cannot tell you this story and in lieu will share with you only the building blocks of one: sounds, gestures, images, disparate moments rising out of an unfathomable darkness.

Then he pressed play on the car's cassette recorder.

"*Errrhn. Harder now! Errrhn, aaah! In her mouth... deeeper... deeeper... ewerwerwer... ewerwerwer...*"

The rain was easing up now and the wipers squealed a little on the glass.

"*Eeeh, wok, wok, wok, eeeh...*"

Another ten minutes. The three of us sat in silence. Ten minutes, six hundred seconds of gasps and groans and squealing.

"*Aah... aaah...*"

Filling the cabin and reverberating off the doors.

"*Eeeh, wok, ahh... errrhn... ahh...*"

Seeping into the carpets, the seats.

"*Wok, wok, eeeh... harder... aaah...*"

Crawling into my ears, my nose, my mouth.

"*Fuck her harder... eeeh, errrhh, aaah, wok, wok...*"

Synchronising with the pounding of my blood.

"*In her mouth... ewerwerwer... ewerwerwer... wok, wok, wok...*"

I tried to roll a cigarette, break the tension with something familiar, but my hands were shaking.

"No smoking in my car."

"*Aaah. Fuck her harder. Eeeh, errrhh, aaah, wok, wok, harder, wok, eeeh, ewerwerwerwer...*"

"You like the tape?"

"I…"

"I said, do you like the tape?"

"I… yes."

"You know who it is?"

"I think so."

"*Iiii, aiii, aiii…*"

"The woman in the back. Undo her mac… Is the mac undone?"

"Yes."

"Now touch her cunt."

Her breasts had been bound with ropes. The nipples were pierced with rings, like the noses of bulls. She had a leather collar round her neck.

"I said touch her cunt… What have you found there?"

"A dildo."

"Push it into her… now pull it out. In… out… in…"

"*Eeeh, wok, wok, wok, eeeh…*"

My mouth, my hands, my brain were voided of the past, oblivious of the future: not mine.

"Show her your cock."

I unzipped my fly.

"Tell him you like his cock."

"I like your cock."

"Louder."

"I like your cock."

"*Ahhh, eeeh, wok, ahh, wok, wok, eeeh…*"

"Louder."

"I like your cock."

"Is his cock hard?"

"Yes."

"Louder!"
"Yes."
"*Aaaagggh... eeeh, wok, eeeehhh, wok, aaaghh, eeeh...*"
"Is his cock big?"
"Yes."
"Say, his cock is big."
"His cock is big."
"Louder!"
"His cock is big."
"*Aaaagggh, aaaagggh, aaaagggh... wok, wok...*"
"You want to fuck her?"
"I..."
"Well?"
"*Eeeehhh, wok, aaaghh...*"
"I do."
"What did you say?"
"I want to fuck her."
The car pulled up in the driveway of a detached house.
"In there."

A front room. The curtains were drawn. Bright halogen lights. The sofa and armchair had covers over them. More nylon.

"Sit there."

He was muscular with a thick neck. He had a T-shirt on and heavy woollen trousers. His belt was fat, pulled tight. His arms were tattooed with symbols. No names.

"Strip."

She stood in front of me, eyes lowered.

"Open your mouth... wider."

He peered into it.

"Hands behind your back."

There were no pictures, photos or books in the room.

He slapped her breasts. Over and over again.

"You too. Strip."

The clock on the wall marked 8:15pm.

He brought his head close to hers, breathing on her, making a low growling sound in the back of his throat.

"Turn. Bend. Pull your arse cheeks open."

He removed his belt and threaded it through the ring on her collar.

"Down! On your knees. Spread your cheeks."

He put two fingers in her anus, pressed down, removed and wiped them on her hair.

"Fuck her throat. Heeerr... deeper... heeerr... deeper... heeerr... out... suck his balls... suuuck hiiiis baaalls... slap her face... harder... back in her mouth... deeeper... deeeper... ewerwerwer... ewerwerwer..."

I can't remember the colour of her eyes.

"Hold her nose."

"Ewerwerwer... ewerwerwer..."

"Faster."

"Ewerwerwerewerwerwerewerwerwer..."

He retrieved a rope from under the sofa and tied her hands.

"Look at him. Look at his face."

Maybe her eyes were green, no, brown. I can't remember.

Spit.

"Smack her face with your cock. Harder. Again. Keep loooking at hiiim I said. Harder. Now back in her mouth."

"Ewerwerwer... ewerwerwer..."

The vein in his neck really stood out.

"Now fuck her. Fuck her hard."

"Aaah... aaah... aayiiii..."

He inserted the dildo in her mouth.

"Pull her hair."

He kept his car keys on a chain attached to a belt loop on his trousers. The chain was thick.

"Aaah... aaah... aayiiii..."

He squeezed his crotch from time to time.

"Put your finger up her arse."

"Aaay... aaah... ahr..."

His black boots were perfectly tied with double knotted bows.

"Three fingers."

"Ahr, ahr, ahr..."

"Work them in. Deeeper."

He took off his shirt and pulled on his nipples, downwards.

"Aaah... ahr... aaah... ahr... aayiiii..."

"Now put your cock in her."

"Aaaaah... ahr... ahr..."

Again.

Again.

Again.

The clock on the wall marked 9:45pm.

"On the chair... legs up... up, I said."

More rope.

"Hrrr, hrrr, hrrr."

"Back in her mouth... deeper... faster..."

"Ewerwerwerewerwerwerewerwerwer…"

My grandfather used the same type of rope to pull my sledge.

"In her arse. Right up. Balls deep."

Firm knots.

"I said, baalls deep!"

"I have to go."

"You'll go when you're finished!"

"No, I have to go now… I have to go… my clothes… I must go… sorry… take the money…"

I couldn't go on. I had to leave. Enough! Enough! I dressed, clumsily, hastily. The woman was still supine on the chair. The man, hard-faced and angry, cold-eyed, casually untied her. No one spoke. The clock on the wall marked three minutes to ten.

When we got to the car, I realised I had left my scarf inside.

"Hurry up."

I went back and knocked on the door. She had it in her hands. Her eyes were blue.

We drove in silence, and he dropped me off at the same service station.

I cannot describe how I felt. Chaos cannot be described. But I can try and recreate that night when madness found me lost and alone and walked with me.

10:31pm: *The takeaway is still open. How much money have I got? Loads, I drew out fifty quid yesterday. Am I hungry? Fuck. Fuck. Fuck. Fuck. Fuck. Fuck. Fuck. Fuck. Fuck…*

10:42pm: *Maybe I should sit down? Come on…*

*concentrate. Con-cen-trate! Herrr, Herrr. Focus. Don't just stand here…*

11:14pm: *Walking. That's better. If I angle my head forward, I can stop the rain getting in my jacket. Fuck it! Shit! Maybe she enjoyed it… You're being paranoid. Fuck. Fuck. Fuck. Fuck it! Got to look up. Ten steps down, then look up. One, two, three, four, five, six, seven, eight, nine, ten, look up, one…*

12:17am: *Concentrate. Three miles. How long have I been walking? Say an hour? Did she like it? So if I walked eight hours a day, I could do… twenty-four, say twenty-five, miles each day. Maybe she did. So in a week I could do a hundred and seventy-five miles. No. I would need Sundays off…*

2:26am: *Thirty-eight, thirty-nine, a new record for not looking up… That bastard Peter. I fucking bet he knew. Maybe not. I wonder if I can go a hundred steps… shut up, you wanker. Concentrate. Was it rape? No, at least not that… surely not… surely?*

3:14am: *And he's down to his last throw. This is it. If I hit the tree, then she enjoyed it… Smack in the middle! What the fuck are you doing? Stop fucking about!*

4:42am: *Fifteen miles. Stop. Have a rest, I think. Oh God… what have I done? Stop the bullshit. OK, so she didn't like it. Accept that. Say it. Shout it. She didn't like it… I need to sleep…*

5:06am: *She fucking hated it, OK. But she didn't struggle or say no… so I didn't rape her. But she hated it. Six miles to go to town… I wonder when the first train is?*

*6:17am: I enjoyed it. No. Yes. Fucking brambles. Fuck, fuck, fuck! Calm yourself. One bramble at a time. Ouch! Slowly. OK. Take a rest. So I enjoyed it at first. It wasn't wrong? Or was it? She could leave? Who are you kidding? What did I buy yesterday? Fruit. That was before I drew out the money. Ahh, the pub. Two quid there. So, forty-eight quid, about right...*

*7:03am: Smells like shit... oh God, it is shit... Find a leaf... cardboard... soaking wet... Who cares, no, come on, clean it off. Handkerchief... stick... use a stick... bloody cold. Stop! Stand still. Come on, I've got to come to a conclusion...*

*7:42am: I could take the train. Cheaper. No. I don't want people. Take a taxi. Forty-eight quid. Plenty. No, a minicab. Cheaper and... better.*

*8:07am: If I don't say anything, the driver won't talk. I'll pretend to be asleep. Maybe I'll sleep... Shut my eyes now... think better after a sleep.*

*8:14am: You fucking used her! I fucking used her! Think of something else. Come on. No. Don't. Accept what you did. Deal with it now. Christ, so many people get up early. Shitty day. Peter must have known. That's it, finished... but where does that leave me... No one will know... How sick... This isn't about you... Christ, what kind of a person am I? Maybe everyone's the same. Maybe most men would have done the same... Does that matter? Yes. No. Yes... I don't know... must sleep.*

I arrived home and immediately showered. I scrubbed myself manically. Between my toes, behind my ears. I cleaned my teeth twice. I put my clothes in the dirty linen basket in the bedroom, went downstairs, went back, got the clothes, went out and threw them away. I made a cup of tea and went up onto the roof. I lost my balance climbing out the window and cut my arm. I went back inside, rinsed the cut and stuck on a plaster. I started to climb the stairs again, stopped halfway, walked back down and rang Peter.

"Hello."

"What the fuck did you think you were doing? The—"

"Is that you, Laurence?"

"Yes, it's fucking me. The guy was a control freak. A fucking control freak. That woman he's got there is like a fucking slave. You fucking knew, didn't you?"

"Steady on, Laurence. You seem all upset. Are you—"

"Of course I'm bloody upset."

"So you didn't do the job. That's not a—"

"That's just it, I did do the job, as you fucking call it, at least to begin with."

"So you must have enjoyed it, then?"

"Yes. No. Fucking hell. I couldn't control myself. Not at first. I lost it. I stopped after a while. I couldn't go on. I did wrong, Peter. I broke my only rule. You sent me into trouble. Bad, bad, bad."

"Just calm down now, Laurence, everything's going to be fine."

"Tell me her name. No, don't tell me, I don't—"

"I don't know her name. I don't know his name either."

"What do you mean you don't know their names? Of course you do."

"Laurence. Laurence. It's Peter you're talking to. Your mate. I—"

"You're not my mate."

"Now, that's hurtful, that is. What's bothering you?"

"I've told you and I'll tell you again, but first, how come you don't know their names? He must have given a name?"

"Oh, he gave a name. Mr Dott. But that isn't his real name. He said at the beginning to call him Mr Dott."

"How do you know it's not his real name?"

"I told you, he said to call him that. People don't say 'call me something' if it's their real name. They say I am and then they say their name. I don't like to see you all upset. What happened?"

"Do you know where they live? I know it's Abbots Langley, but not the street."

"No, I don't. Sorry, Laurence, I'm not being very helpful, am I? He always arranged to meet at the petrol station."

"Am I the first of your boys you've sent to see him? Answer me that."

"No, not the first."

"How many? How many before me?"

"Oh, I don't know."

"Think."

"Well, let me see, I suppose… four, no, five."

"Five times."

"No, boys."

"And times?"

"Maybe seven. A couple went twice."

"And what did they say?"

"Who?"

"The guys who went."

"Oh, you know."

"No, I don't know."

"Well…"

"Well, what?"

"Said he was a bit rough. Stuff like that."

"A bit rough!"

"Yes, a bit rough. But they all seemed to have enjoyed themselves. Had a bit of fun, like."

"I know, spread the love, eh?"

"Yes, that's it, Laurence. Now that's more like it!"

"There was no *love* to spread, Peter. *No love*. I hurt her."

"Oh dear. But she's a bit of a looker, isn't she?"

"Yeah, a looker who cried. Not much love in crying, you know."

"Oh, dear. That must have been upsetting. I had a cry myself yesterday—"

"I don't want to hear about your crying, Peter."

"Well, I don't know what to say. You've right upset me, you have."

"Good."

I slammed the phone down. I never spoke to Peter again.

I made a cup of tea. Everything was falling apart. The phone rang. I let the answerphone pick up the call.

"Hello. Hello. Oh, this is one of those answering things. It's Peter, I just—"

I unplugged the phone and erased the message. I lay down on the bed. What I needed was sleep. After twenty minutes lying there, I got up and climbed back onto the roof. Better. Better up there. Calmer. After an hour, crouched on the tiles, I had come to some conclusions. Well, that's not true. Not conclusions, more like containment. Yes, that's it. I reached a point where I could contain what happened. Put it in a box. What doctors call an 'effective cure'. The illness is still there but dormant.

That's what I managed to do. Ring-fence it. At first with a temporary stockade, then fortified over the years. Upgraded until secure. It hasn't gone away. It's there, behind the fence. I've just learnt to live around it and not stray over the wall. Not until today, writing this.

It's been hard going back inside. I've had to stop a dozen times. Go for little walks. Cuddle the dogs. I even watched a Mexican soap this afternoon. Anything to get away, back to the present, back to walls that know nothing of that night. Yesterday I scrubbed the kitchen floor.

I don't write the chapters in order, you know. I pick the one to work on most suited to my mood. This is the last one to write. I've waited until my wife and son are away. They've gone to the beach. I didn't want them in the house whilst writing this.

Anyway, I would have been unbearable. I've been living in my lungi from India and an old pyjama top. They make me feel safe. I haven't shaven or eaten much besides biscuits. When I want to go to the toilet, I use the one downstairs. To take more time. To delay returning to that night, to behind the fence.

I repeatedly click on the word count. Someone told me first novels should ideally be 80,000 words. Sounds nuts to me. But then, I'm new to the game. I have this crazy notion that if I can get past this magic number, I will reach the promised land.

So now, all these decades later, have I come to a conclusion, what others, I suppose, call closure? I tried and actually wrote a list. I even numbered it. One to nine. It got my word count up. How pathetic, this notion that if we make a list we can somehow control and make sense out of chaos. I deleted the lot and wrote another list. I did this three times. Then I realised, however many editions, the list would always be different. No list.

So what am I left with?

I had done wrong. I hadn't understood my beast. I saw him as the better part of me, the pure and noble. The one who jumps from the waterfall. My beast and the other part of me, my conscience, I suppose, are each other's familiars. They each need each, are an indivisible whole. Ignore the beast, starve him, and you'll walk the earth incomplete, only half-alive.

But give the beast free reign and life's a lottery. He'll take you to heaven, sure, but also to hell, not knowing the difference. You must listen to the beast when he tells you you're not going far enough and must return the care, curtailing his excesses. That's what I learnt. The challenge of being alive is to hold nature and nurture in balance, in equilibrium. I'd gone too far one way; I'd slipped and fallen. I'd done wrong.

That was it. No more assignments. I couldn't trust my

grip on the beast's lead. Maybe I had to go too far to find the limit. Like Spike Milligan's recipe for perfect toast: cook until burnt, then fifteen seconds less. I guess I had been lucky, just charred along one edge, retrievable.

Odd thing. I didn't cry once. Worries me at times, that I ended with a bang but no whimper.

# Ella

I don't know how long I slept for. I didn't keep track of time. I only left the flat to buy bread and canned food. But as the hours and days went by, the shame of that night began to fade or, rather, was put in perspective. On the whole, my 'entrances' had been a hoot, exciting, mind-expanding and rewarding to me and perhaps others. OK, they had ended badly, but all in all were worth it, at least to me. Anyway, ending badly was inevitable. I had been free-climbing, scaling heights without a rope. Free-climbers climb ever harder, higher faces, until the inevitable fall. Perhaps I was lucky to only have been wounded.

I even felt that maybe I had been too hard on Peter, blaming him when the blame was mine. I wouldn't go back to how it was, but decided I would ring him at some point. After all, as he said, you've got to take the rough with the smooth.

I couldn't stop feeling sorry for that woman, though. If there was something I could do…

I hitched back up to Junction 6 on the M1. Good ride. One car all the way. Friendly family, the car full of laughter and empty crisps bags. Then another lift to get me to Abbots Langley. Then on foot, criss-crossing the town, looking for familiar landmarks. I remembered a park of sorts and a manor house. Two hours of hoofing it, and I found the place. Breakspeare Road. The curtains of the house were drawn, no sign of life. I waited a couple of hours and was about to leave, feeling foolish and uncomfortable, when the door opened.

She looked so normal. A little woollen suit and a headscarf. I had come this far but had no clear plan. Now that she was there, calling distance away, I didn't know what to do. I felt uneasy and put off the confrontation. So when she walked away, all I did was follow.

She went into a greengrocers. I saw her picking and inspecting apples. Such an ordinary thing to do. But then, what was I expecting? We all eat. Apart from the shopkeeper, who was reading the newspaper, she was alone. I went in and confronted her. The meeting was brief.

She froze when she saw me. Just stood there, cradling a cauliflower. I took a step towards her, and she turned away. Another and she put the cauliflower back and went to pay. I felt an idiot and the grocer was giving me odd looks. I followed her outside and said, "I'm sorry. I just wanted to say sorry."

She carried on walking but then stopped. She didn't turn. Just stood still, as though to say 'I'm listening'. I caught her up.

"I'm sorry for what I did. Doesn't make it right, though. Can I help?"

"Leave me alone."

"Whatever you want."

"I think you should go."

"I just want to help."

She looked up. Those blue eyes looked straight at me.

"It's what I've got. It's my life." And with that she turned and went. I didn't follow.

I don't know what I was expecting. Probably something more spectacular, more conclusive. I came looking for forgiveness, I guess, and a chance to put things right. How naive! It took me six hours to get home, and what, if anything, had been accomplished? But I felt better; I had tried. I like to think that she did too, knowing that someone cared, albeit it was I, the aggressor, giving comfort. I like to think I sowed a seed in her mind. Planted a possibility that might grow into something certain, an imperative for change. But then, who knows?

It was like that with my granny. She had an abusive husband, noticed by the lodger. He nudged her, sowed a seed, said something about, "That man of yours is no good." Apparently, she didn't even reply, just smiled and put the kettle on. But a year later, on one day like any other, she wrote a note which said: *Your dinner's in the oven and I'm off.*

Incidentally, she ended up marrying the lodger, who became my granddad.

When I got back to the flat, there was a message waiting from Paul, Sue's sister's boyfriend. He had just come back from Russia, had vodka and a proposal. Would I like to house-sit in the country with him? A proper break. Perfect.

The house was wonderful, classic Oxford charm and comfort. All duck-down sofas and a walk-in larder. The kind of place you know the marmalade will be chunky and homemade. The doors had latches, little wooden see-saws and no locks. The third tread from the living room creaked. I imagined that was the step the owner stopped on when turning to say, a second time, "Night-night, dear," to his wife.

It was a big rambling place that smelt of wax and flowers. Huge bathrooms with books and children's drawings, nooks and crannies with no function other than the pleasure of discovery, places to break your journey between more purpose-filled rooms.

The garden was quietly overgrown, just enough to let nature have her way, but not enough to impose on the croquet. The tennis court was a little ragged and thus all the more inviting to amateurs like us. Of course, the house came with a Labrador and, of course, she was fat, but up for chasing balls. The English country idyll. Heaven on toast.

I found Paul in the study, a little drunk, reading *Moby Dick*. We swigged from the vodka bottle and talked. We weren't close friends but got on well. He was a published writer and I a little in awe of him. I mean, the guy had a steady girlfriend who had a car! He'd written a play I'd gone and seen. A proper member of the 'others'.

You know what it's like with friends. Each evokes a different you. Some you keep for jokes and beers, smutty comments and takeaways. Another may be prized as perfect for walks and long train rides in silence. Some you'd lend money to, others not. One or two are close enough to share intimacies with, even confessions. Others you never let too close but enjoy them all the more because of that: the relationship is light, non-committal. That was Paul. Someone to hang out and relax with.

We chatted, joked and drank. He told me that, in fact, we were sitting half the house. The owners had split it in two. I can't remember who had the other half. Anyway, they had gone on holiday as well, so had a sitter too. Her name was Ella, and I knew her.

Looking back, it was a set-up, like my boxed-up notes: my bait to bed girls. The whole thing, the invite, was just to get me in the house with Ella. They'd planned it between them. She fancied me. Fair play.

I had met Ella two weeks earlier at the premiere of Paul's production. She had done the sets and costumes. I hadn't liked her work and told her so. I was very forthright with my criticisms in those days. Probably too insecure, irrationally fearing that if I praised another person's work, I would somehow be diminished. But sparks had flown; a little fire between us had been lit.

It's curious but true that an early confrontation, even an argument, can often turn in the blink of an eye to friendship, even love. People instinctively think that love and hate are poles apart. They're not. The end-stops of a relationship are immersive interest and total indifference. Hate implies interest. Whilst you're fighting, you're involved. No, it's when you can't be bothered to fight, when the other person is of such little importance to you that he or she doesn't evoke a reaction, that you know that whatever was between you is gone for good. I guess that's the big dividing line. With most people, we don't care enough to risk a confrontation. We don't want to needle them and, in so doing, open them up, revealing what's inside. We're simply not interested enough. So maybe I was keen on Ella from the start and my criticisms just a way of attracting her attention. I don't know.

She rolled up around midnight, tall and grinning, bearing cheese. She had style. She did things well. The cheeses were from Harrods, nine small wedges, all beautifully wrapped. She was church-mouse poor but had bought the best of cheese. That was very Ella. I tell you, I was transported. I felt like someone who had been left for dead and wakes up in bed, propped up on feather pillows, with sunlight streaming through the windows.

Incidentally, precisely that happened to me once. I got ill in Afghanistan. Really sick. I spent most of the train journey back to London in the toilet. I had amoebic dysentery, though I didn't know it at the time. I somehow dragged myself from Victoria Station into the nearest hospital and promptly fainted. When I surfaced, I was tucked up in bed, safe between starched sheets and a pretty nurse was smiling at me. What a great moment that was!

That night in Oxford was a kind of rebirth too. Just cast your mind back. I'd been crushed, shat on and sprayed with semen in Neuchâtel. I'd sunk so low as to collaborate in the abuse of a woman, or if not, almost as bad, in having sex without any certainty that she wanted me to. After all, it's our motivation that counts and mine had not been good. I'd walked all night, fell out with a friend and eaten baked beans for a week. I was, shall we say, pretty low.

But more than low, I felt I'd blown it, lost my way for good. Yet here I was, cradled in the bucolic bosom of Oxford, surrounded by books, a chap I would play lawn tennis with and a lovely girl bringing cheeses from around the world. Put that way, I think my analogy of the hospital falls short.

But there was more than that. There was the sense of being welcomed back, of not having been steeped in filth so far that there was no return.

I remember going with a lover to see her parents. She was a prostitute and ex-junkie and hadn't seen them for over three years. She was terrified that they would reject her and needed my support. We went shopping for a dress for her, something that showed a little less skin than her work clothes. For half an hour she wouldn't leave the car and twice backed down inches from the door. Eventually, one hand in mine and the other clutching flowers, we knocked. Her mother, on opening the door, saw the flowers and said, "How nice, tulips. They'll look lovely in your room."

That was it. Everything said. The road back had not been blocked. Her room was still there for her.

Back to Oxford.

The three of us chatted, passing round the vodka and then some port we found. We laughed and with each passing minute I became more attracted to Ella. Not in the way I had been attracted to Lady Trocknell, Shiaza or Marilyn. Not a blood-pounding, blinding rocket of attraction, the kind that takes you out of your atmosphere but then is jettisoned to fall to earth as scrap. No, something steady and accumulating, each increment so tiny as to virtually go unnoticed.

Her gangly legs that she swung, her own see-saw. The way she cut the cheese, keeping its triangular shape to the last slice. Her bum, of course, as cheeky as they come. The way she pushed my shoulder and said, "Don't be silly," when I was. Her boisterous manner, almost the tomboy, but laced with gentle sweetness, glimpses of a coy and tender girl.

Remember I suggested that when women decide to do something, they just get on with it? Well, Ella certainly did. It was getting seriously late, and we had drunk too much. She asked me if I wanted to see the other half of the house and I agreed. Step two, I suppose: the easing out of the chaperone.

It's very exciting, walking round a house at night with someone you're attracted to. Particularly one that belongs to neither of you. Neutral ground, so a good start. Then there's the fact that there's nothing to do. You're not eating, driving or sitting in a cinema. You just walk into the room and stand there, close together. You feel almost the onus to touch each other.

Let's also not forget that houses have their share of bedrooms. Two people, mutually attracted, standing in a bedroom, is quite electrifying. Double beds are big; they fill the room. A monster statement, they almost say, "I am an empty double bed, waiting for two people to lie on me and share their dreams and bodies. You are two young people and it's late at night. Come to me."

In fact, we ended up in a single bed and almost didn't have sex.

We had reached the top floor. The light on the landing was out and she couldn't find the switch. Even more intense. The two of us in semi-darkness, just shadow puppets, each waiting for the other to pull the strings.

And then she kissed me. Now, during my paid entries, I'd had in my mouth knickers, cunts, tongues and spit. But never had a kiss. Not a real lover's kiss. Not done. Too intimate. All sex workers are the same. They don't kiss. Well, they'll kiss your arse and even your mouth. But a true lover's kiss is too exploratory, a genuine duet. No one's on top or taken from behind. There isn't a doer and a done. Just lips and tongues knowing each other. A mutuality.

First, the tentative approach, a brushing of skin on skin. Then, one gently parts the other's lips, inviting themselves in, a statement of interest in learning more. You risk a little tongue. No, not true. You act on instinct. Again, not quite right. No, I let the waves take me, I floated out to sea. I let go, rocked by the ebb and swell, lulled by booze and bonhomie. It was a dance of a kiss. The 'shall we?', then the nervous smile, hands that reach out, miss, then connect. Fingers folding into fingers. Mismatched steps, the lightest of giggles and then the ever-growing synthesis of movement as two bodies answer to a single tune. You grow in confidence, throwing in a double step, a turn. The other reciprocates, a clash of tooth on tooth, the waltz transforming into tango. You converge, the space marked out as no man's land reclaimed as common, the borders of your sovereign selves approaching and uniting. The kiss, once just a liquid question, becomes a declaration shouted loud, full on, frank and open. You pause, come up for air, to sink back down, a history of trust and mutual longing already being written.

The emotions of that kiss were so complex that even to begin to recreate them now, I'll have to be a precious stonecutter and see them from multiple perspectives. So let's turn that ruby jewel and begin again.

A cat's cradle, a loop of string. At first, the bond is negligible, the chord not even held, just draped across fingers. Then the weaving begins, the steady incremental binding of you into two. Where once a single strand connected you, a complex web is formed, eating up the space between you until your hands are so close that to carry on, they must work as one. You end up marvelling at your creation, amazed that a simple piece of string could be so beautiful. But it's not the string, of course. The same string could have been used to tie the hands of that blue-eyed woman. No, bonds can separate or join. That kiss with Ella was a uniting.

Still joined, now at mouth, at shoulder, hip and knee, we staggered through a door and into bed.

I couldn't get it up. I'm glad of that. I muttered something about coming out of a bad relationship. I lied. The reality was more a shovel used to gather rubble no longer fit and decent to turn her fertile soil. But she was patient and laughed it off. We sank into each other's arms and sleep.

I had a nightmare. I was trying to run along a road but sinking into the tarmac. When I woke, gasping like a drowning man breaking through the water, she comforted me.

By the dawn's early light we made love.

I have no intention of detailing our week-long frolics in that bed. I have neither the right, nor the inclination. Too private and irrelevant. I say irrelevant, not because the sex wasn't fine and dandy, intimate and passionate, but because what really mattered, what really tells its story, is how it lifted and enhanced everything else we did.

Scientists tell us that a mighty meteorite once fell to earth. It's gone and, anyway, of little interest. What is of note is what it caused: the extinction of the dinosaurs, a change of global climate and the rise of mammals. Our lovemaking was my meteorite. I cannot describe this rock that crashed into my world, but I can the effect it had. We cannot look straight at the sun, but we can marvel at the plants that grow under its golden gaze. So, welcome to the garden grown from our love.

To visit, you have to change your sense of time, slow it down. Real time isn't measured in minutes and hours but in what happens. Some days last an hour, others a week. If nothing changes, nothing captures your attention, time stops still. This is metaphor but also fact. It's said the universe will fizzle out, dismember itself into ever smaller pieces till approximating to zero. There will be no more change. Time will stop. The first second of the big bang must have lasted an eternity. The same is true for kids. Remember that summer when you were twelve, the one that never seemed to end? Now spring was only yesterday and tomorrow the leaves will fall.

In our lovers' garden, time expanded. We zoomed in, the smallest detail filled a page, each nibble a megabyte. We seemed to have lain in bed playing until noon, but when our tummies rumbled and we went down in search of breakfast, the clock said nine.

That afternoon, did we really tell our life stories before the tea got cold?

The way you touched my arm and looked at me, all-knowing, could it have happened whilst the Labrador retrieved a ball?

Next, breathe in. Again. Intoxicating, isn't it? The unpolluted air of lovers. Like Asterix's potion, it makes us superhuman. My low-res world upgraded to Full HD. My God, those cheeses tasted good! But more than milk and handed down secrets went into their making. The magic ingredient was our love.

We listened to Elgar's cello concerto, just a cheap cassette, whilst we sat on the lawn. Years later I forked out 5000 euros for a music system, but Jacqueline du Pré never performed again as she had that day. The quality of sound is not determined by the electronics of the stereo but by the sensitivity of the ear that hears it. It's the same with everything. Ten men can bite an apple. Five may be indifferent, one pleased; three may declare it yummy, but only one, the one who ate Eve's apple, will really taste it.

Let's wander down the path, stopping here and there to appreciate the blooms.

"If you two are going to kiss between every point, we'll never finish the set."

"Sorry, Paul, my serve, I think."

"Love fifteen… love thirty… love Ella."

"Oh God, I don't think I can take this lovey-dovey stuff."

"Sorry, Paul," in unison.

She sat on the window seat, drawing. I watched her from the bed. I don't think I've ever felt so comfortable. I didn't want to move a muscle. I just focussed on how good I felt. Like after a Turkish bath and massage. They leave you there, literally drooling, arms slack at your sides, holding for as long as possible that exquisite, delicious feeling of ease. But this was better. The ease was doubled. Hers and mine, both enjoyed by both. Her pencils were strewn around her, the beautiful tools of her trade. She frowned as she worked, her tongue slightly protruding. She was wearing my shirt. She must have felt my gaze and turned to say, "Hello, my lovely man."

"Up a bit… up… there. Scratch there."

"You've got a lot of freckles on your back."

"Hmmm… mmm."

"I'm going to join them up. See if you can tell me what I'm drawing."

"Mmmn? Mhh. OK… a man with a hat smoking a cigar?"

"No, silly, it's a cigarette."

"Of course. Silk Cut?"

"No! It's actually an elephant."

"I knew, of course. Mmmm."

"Liar."

"Common mistake. Now me. Lie on your back… comfy?"

"Very."

"You've got strong shoulders. Do you swim?"

"I love the water… that tickles!"

"OK, serious stuff. Tell me what I'm spelling."

"I… L, and I think I do too."

"What, you knew I loved pickled onions?"

"Oh."

"Only joking. I hate them."

"Me too. Mmm… that's really nice."

"So are you."

"And you."

"I said it first."

"But maybe I thought it first."

"OK, sit up. God, I love your smile."

"Why, thank you, kind sir."


"So. Let's have the conversation. When did you first decide you fancied me?"

"That's a girl's secret."

"I'll tickle you!"

"Ahh… ha ha. OK. OK."

"So?"

"When you were sitting with Paul watching the play. You sat there so involved. So alive, like at any moment you would get up on the stage and join in."

"You mean, I don't know how to mind my own business?"

"No, I mean you… I don't know… just alive."

"Kiss me!"

"Wait. Fair's fair, when did you decide you fancied me?"

"Oh, that's easy. When you put the cheeses in the cupboard and not in the fridge."

"That's not very romantic or sexy."

"It was from where I was standing. Kiss me!"

"What do you mean? Tell me what you mean first."

"When you bent down. I got a great view of your bum… Ow!"

When I finished cleaning my teeth, I went to put the toothbrush away and saw hers in a cup by the basin. I put mine in there too. There they were, two skinny brushes, hers with a mop of hair and elegant pink handle and mine a little squished and battered. I arranged them so they faced each other. Later on that night, when returning from the loo, she brought the brushes with her. We performed a play, there under the sheets, with a torch for stage lighting, starring Miss Colgate and Sid the Signal Man.

"OK. I think we should only buy food that starts with an E."

"Or an L."

"Or Z."

"Nothing starts with a Z."

"Zebra burgers. Z-bone steak. A twenty-sixth of Alphabetti Spaghetti. In fact, I can't think of any food that doesn't."

"You're mad."

"No, just in zove."

"Mmm, your lips taste of ice cream."

"What flavour?"

"Ella flavour."

"So, what shall we buy?"

"Whatever you want."

"No, you decide."

"Let's decide together."

"OK, but don't forget I'm a lactose intolerant Jewish-Muslim vegan."

"So, how about milk-raised pork chops in cider?"

"Sounds great. Kiss me."

My love affair with Ella lasted over a year. In the early months I kept thinking, *Hmm, I must ring Peter.* I once even sat down to call but couldn't find his number. I promised, *I'll look for it tomorrow.* But the next day brought new thrills and I never did. Then as time went by, I stopped remembering. I never rang.

Ella and I ended badly. I was too selfish, too immature. I wanted everything, everyone, not realising that if you do so, you end up with nothing and no one.

Halfway through our loving, we drove to Italy in her 2CV. We had the roof down, the music up, enjoying each other and the sun. We went into a tunnel which seemed to last forever. The darkness and the echoing rumble of the traffic made me grumpy. We argued and I even got out of the car, saying I would go home.

Looking back, I realise that was a metaphor for what we had, for maybe all relationships. They all start in the sun, roof down, driving at speed, your love a magic wand which turns everything into joy. But sooner or later you enter a tunnel. A dark place with walls so thick that the wands can't breach them. Fools like me get out, disenchanted with the gloom.

Now I know that if you stay the course, keep driving, the tunnel will end. On the other side you won't find the same landscape. The sugar-coated trees, the champagne lake, the chocolate mountains have all gone. But something equally amazing takes their place. Less showy, more real, harder at first to appreciate. But if you make the effort the magic's there, hidden all around you. The magic of the everyday. Sustainable and sustaining. Sorry, Ella, I wasn't ready to dump the wand and use my eyes.

Ella and Blue Eyes, for very different reasons, brought to an end my sex-for-sale days and precipitated my search for enduring love, a journey which ended twenty-three years ago when I met the woman whose arms I hope one day to die in. Thank you, Ella, for pointing me in the right direction.

# PILLOW TALK

Over thirty years have passed since my days of sex for sale. Three decades, twelve thousand breakfasts, a hundred miles of loo roll, a million words spoken and received, a bucket of toenail cuttings and another full of love letters. But also just a blip. A single exhalation of the universe.

So where are they now, those pioneers? And what came of the growing rumbles, the ideas, the shapes of things to come? It's the people in this book that I most value, so I'll leave them till last.

Cockenomics has, of course, gone on to rule the world, offering happy hour 24/7. Own-brand champagne in tetra packs for all. But then the wake-up call, the seven-year morning after. Crash went the economy, bang went demand, and wallop went the line of credit. That autobahn to hell was never finished. Someone nicked the EU subsidy and stupidly we, all in new cars, foot down, talking hands-free drivel through blue teeth, drove off the cliff.

By 2012, twenty per cent of the adult population in Britain was diagnosed with depression or anxiety, with half a million added in just three years. Our politicians beat the dispatch box, promising economic growth, a return to the good old days. But people with depression and anxiety don't have good days. OK, so they'll be able to wipe their eyes with a silk hanky and not loo roll. No real difference, just stuff.

Down in the bottom of the drain there's not much light. So maybe it's hard to see the simple truth that all that matters is to be happy, to be content, to say, at the end of the day, "It was worth the ride." Money, sometimes a means to get there, has become the end of ends, Judgement Day. Whilst the USA pressed third world countries to burn their coca crops, the lending institutions became the new drug dealers, offering credit to addicts who couldn't say no.

As to the rest of the bankers, what can I say that you don't already know? They squandered their money and then stole ours.

The meritocracy delivered on its promise. We all have the equal right to be humiliated on TV. Two twins can now be famous for their haircuts and stupid expressions. You can be an obnoxious loud-mouth with big tits, and five million people will cheer you when you're the last one left in the house. Anyone who can answer correctly when asked their name can be a millionaire. The fact that they'll lose all their friends and values is a plus. We'll get the double whammy and do a documentary on their fall. The fattest man in Britain, the shortest, the ugliest, the angriest, the thinnest, the one with the most tattoos, the largest testicles, these are the ones who steal the limelight. I thought my band of brothers laid claim to 'excess spelt success'. We were fucking amateurs.

"Community" is now old English, along with 'thee' and 'thou'. We don't keep an eye on each other. Why bother? That's what the CCTV cameras are for. Anyway, the city centres have been cleared of unloved youth, expelled by ASBO orders, flown away by Ryanair to Magaluf for a final leap from the hotel balcony, a walk off-role in another prime time documentary.

The pubs have shut, leaving only wine bars with signs advising, *No dogs or children*. Note that 'dog' comes first. The average white British couple have 1.63 children and 2.47 dogs. You could argue that children live longer, but do they? The average life span of a dog in Britain is fourteen years. My daughter by fourteen was no longer a child. Dogs keep their innocence, that's their appeal. But how could she, when the world around her has none?

Cockenomics tells us that more is better. So five-stars are now for losers. The real players only stay at hotels with seven. They're building one down the road from me near Almuñécar. Every suite will have an 'unparalleled view of the sea and its own swimming pool'. There you have it. The sea is charming, so you can have it as your background for the required selfie. But you swim alone in your pool. Now you can go to a hotel and meet no one! All the toys, but you have to play alone.

Oh yes, the individual now holds centre stage. A group of academics from Boston University set out recently to get to the bottom of the Facebook phenomenon. Anything with billions of followers is worth studying. They were looking for the essence. Social network implies community. Maybe I'm being a Luddite. I hope so. After all, community is good, even a virtual one. But you know what they found, what underpins Facebook? The possibility of writing and posting pictures about yourself to lots of people without them interrupting.

Everything has been monetised, all actions and interactions optimised to increase productivity. I used to make my own Christmas cards and hope to do so again. But it's faster to buy one. No, better still, pick one from Moonpig and get them to send it. Wait, there's a new, improved, enhanced service. They'll pick one for you. Add the purchase of a thousand friends from internet sites which stock them and you're ready. You can now send a thousand people you've never met a Christmas card you've never seen. Beat that for productivity!

Immigration is a tough one. The trickle in the '60s became a stream by the '80s, and by 2066, studies suggest the white British will be an ethnic minority.

The UK has, of course, opted out of the EU in a futile attempt to turn back the clock and rekindle some mythological bucolic green and pleasant land with milkmen, friendly bobbies and pubs with Cornish pasties. Of course, the reality is a crumbling economy and no one to do the tough jobs previously done by EU migrant workers, leading to an actual increase in migrants from countries less culturally and ethnically aligned with the UK. Meanwhile, immigration has become the top electoral issue with our current prime minister promising to dump the migrants on Rwanda and in floating prisons posing as hotels.

Now, frankly, writing from my mountain refuge in southern Spain, an immigrant myself, I don't care. It does seem odd though. You know, to have fought two world wars to retain sovereignty only to give your country away. Of course, there's been some integration, the blending of colour in all senses, to create novel and exciting shades. But for every new hue there are a dozen cries from a divided Britain. This isn't racism, irrational prejudice based on colour or ethnicity. This is the rational fear, voiced by an indigenous population, of being marginalised in their own country. There will be trouble and I keep watch for the rise of a populist 'Trumpesque' politico in the UK. Please may I be wrong, but with close to a billion new births predicted for the African continent in the next decade, where global warming is due to leave much of its land mass uninhabitable, I'm not holding my breath.

Anyway, to my mind, all for the best. White Brits haven't the time nor the inclination to reproduce enough to keep them going. Wait long enough and white Britain will be deserted, repossessed by the global land bank. Better someone else lives there than see it go to waste.

I'm an optimist. I see green shoots growing out of the rubble. All isms have their day, but where's, say, feudalism or communism now? Churned back and recycled. For the first time in forty years, there is net migration from the cities in Spain as people look for community.

Bankers and politicians are no longer untouchable and are now in court. Families are eating together at home. OK, they've been driven back, unable to afford eating out, but it's a start. "Buy local," first a whisper, is now shouted loud, and a stand at my local market only sells local-grown produce. They've even credited the grower, so now I can enjoy 'Miguel's tomatoes', adding humanity to something otherwise industrially produced in a plastic greenhouse. Basic, enduring values seem to be making a comeback. Let's wait and see.

Now for the people, my motley crew. Where are they now?

Alistair Townley died in 2009. He had been playing squash with a friend, then went for a beer and a chat in the local pub. A taxi driver, parked up and bored, noticed a man get out of his car, leaving the engine running and door open. After fifteen minutes and no sign of the driver, he went over. He found him by the bottle bank, dead of a heart attack, doing his duty, caring for all of us till the end. What an exemplary death! A little sport to warm the blood, some camaraderie and beer, then off to do his bit, before going home to resume his duties and his pleasures as a husband and a dad. That night he didn't make it and we're all the worse for that. He knew, you know, that his heart was a little dickey and would at some point stop. But he never told us. Why would such a man? It was his cross to bear and he carried it in silence, so we could travel so much the lighter.

I couldn't go to the funeral. I didn't have the money to get there. But I did have time, so I wrote a poem which Big Dave read out, as our friend lay there in the ground.

## Busy Being Born

"Achillea Millefolium. The bastard of Artemis," he announced.
A crossword clue solved? A canny Greek taxi driver?
No. A tiny flower, yellow and white, held out for inspection.
"Good for insomnia, likes poor soil. Never grew at Cray.
"One of Mongolia's biggest exports. Picked by children for Boots.
"Something for the newsletter, for Jane and the girls."

There you have it. A man's passions in the palm of his hand:
Family, the Classics, the fruits and plagues of earth,
Arcane facts stored away, like string or nails,
For uses as yet unknown.

That was his gift, the way he wove his life, thread on thread,
To form a mantle that was more than his, was him.

We walked. Another leg of the journey began as boys,
Such misfits that they fitted. A walk down sixth form angst
Reading Kafka and snickering over the National Geographic.
On through hallowed cloisters with books Newton might have held.
Walking in the streets and parks of Stokey, to the squat of some girl
Thought to kiss for England. Walking into Screens on Greens
To leave them crying, to pubs to laugh, to parties to get off,
To the hope of Marley's songs, the debris of Thatcher's '80s.

We fought, we rivalled, we forgave and forgot. We lost our way,
Trod paths untrod, always to return to markers left along the trail,
A private joke, a shared regret, old times burnished by their telling.

On we walked, he to dig the soil, I to build on it.
We walked to love, to children,
The gambolling of kids becoming the strides of men,
The measured steps of fathers.

Now one of us has stopped. My friend is dead. I cannot sleep.
I sip my Achillea and plan the weekend hike.
We'll go higher than before,
He'll like the cold clear air.

The Spaniards say that no one really dies as long as someone's left to remember him. That's why I've included the poem. So you all, even if just for a moment, can remember him and in so doing, keep him woven into the fabric.

As to Big Dave himself, he became a kindergarten teacher! A giant amongst toddlers, they adored him. He joined a choir, married the soloist and emigrated to Australia. I went and visited him in the Blue Mountains, and we talked about old times. I was tempted to take croquettes but took olive oil instead. Extra virgin. First cold press, of course.

The 'Z' team was eventually disbanded, the circus packed up and driven off. Sparkie Dave finally took off his dressing gown, laid down his tea and, putting on a suit, now runs a business, installing high-voltage power lines.

Pepe the Knife is, I imagine, saving up to have *FUCK YOU* tattooed on his dick. Colin remains in no hurry and Liz misses the fact that no blokes look at her tits anymore.

Young Mick is doubtless in a rest home telling the old biddies, "If I were still a young man I'd have you on the Zimmer frame."

Ed Walls? Who knows? But if an ageing Irish plumber fits your boiler, check for wires and an alarm clock round the back. 'Z' team, RIP.

Nina is living in Nova Scotia and runs a garden centre. In the end, all women germinate. Sue is in Australia, I believe. Martin Stone has gone to ground, thinking somewhere. The rest of the Glading Terrace mob I can't track down. Well, all except for Buster Blood Vessel, who's "Hangin' Loud." If anything, his tongue looks bigger.

Terry Gilliam, Michael Palin and Julie Christie continue to enrich our lives.

If you're a man in a shop being told by a woman that the chèvre is moist, you know what to expect. If Neuchâtel hasn't been eaten and you're there when a gold Ferrari stops, don't get in.

Sarah is married, has three children and lives in a triple-decker. If you go over to her place, take a bottle of chianti and don't mention dipping woodwork. Marilyn is now a finished and perfect painting living in the States, maybe running anger management classes.

As to the Barbican boys and girls, we can bet good money they are in prison or in Government. All except Roland, who eventually divorced and lives in Dorset where doubtless he tinkers with hydraulics.

Maria I never saw again, but we can safely assume she married José Manuel, with whom she dances the paso doble till her rose falls loose.

Mick died in 1981. Trish made crab sandwiches for the wake and afterwards Ben took her home in his cab. Who knows what happened to the Turk, though after what he saw of England, I wouldn't be surprised if he's an Islamic fundamentalist.

Jeanie Morrison-Lowe, the scourge of the Hasidic bus-taking community, now lives in New Zealand. Sales of soap up Stanford Hill are doubtless down.

General Building Supplies shut last year after seven decades trading. The brothers, when interviewed by the press, said they were going to have a holiday, the first in twenty years. Hey, Michael, take *Brave New World* with you, and David, don't forget the sausages on sticks.

Bethnal Green baths and steam rooms closed. In its place, a chain has opened York Hall Spa. Beans on toast and tea have been replaced with a low-fat wrap and carrot juice, and the intimacy of species with individual cubicles where only mud and hot stones serve as company.

Luigi has packed his pepper grinder and bowl of parmigiana, and his son has set up round the corner in Church Street. Try the minestrone.

Shangri-La remains off the list of Ryanair destinations, though there is talk of reconstructing it in Florida.

Ella Huhne went on to design for Sadler's Wells and the Royal Ballet. In 2007, she set up Landance: it's a wonderful project, performing with children in the countryside, in real landscape, nothing sugar-coated.

Sam, of course, is dead, one Special Brew too many.

So is Peter.

He died in 1986 of AIDS. Ben told me.

"P-P-Peter's d-d-dead. AIDS. I'm going round the h-h-house. Clear up his r-room. Things in there his m-m-mum and dad shouldn't see."

They were all there to see him off, including the Dagenham boys and dear Sue, who married Take the Mick. Also a horde of people I didn't know, from all walks of life, but mainly 'the broken, the down and out, migrant workers, cripples, the damaged and the damned'. Also Peter's sister. I never knew he had one. Big John said I should say some words, what with my being 'all educated, like'. I couldn't. I felt too confused about my feelings. In the end, the farewell speeches were left to Half Bob and Peter's mum.

Half Bob's speech:

"We all knew Dazzer. 'E 'ad his funny ways but then who ain't. He was a good mate, 'e was. Looked out for his own, 'e did. Never 'ad a bad word for anyone. Always paid when it was 'is round. Once when I was in the hospital, 'e went round and checked up on the missus an' the kids. Brought 'em presents. 'E would give 'em rides on his back. Never asked for nothin' in return. Said that's what mates were for." (Bob cries.) "Sorry, lads. I've gone all soppy. Peter wouldn't like that. He'd say, life's too short for tears. 'Is life was too short. Ain't fair, is it? All the cunts who stay alive, an' 'im gone. Pardon my French. I mean, Pete, well, that's what 'e tried to do. Play fair. But life like didn't play fair wiv 'im. Better luck next time, mate. Good friend to all of us, you were. We'll miss you, son."

Peter's mum's speech:

She signed, her hands moving silently, spelling out a mother's grief. Somehow more appropriate than talking.

If the dead listen, then surely it's to hands, not words? I was standing next to Peter's sister and asked her what the little dance of fingers meant.

"Did we tell you we loved you? Maybe not enough. We did, you know. Were you happy, Peter? Some of the things you did, you know, in your room. Did they make you happy? As you would say, got to have the love. Sets you up like a cooked breakfast. Did we set you up? We're going to stay with your sister now. Have I already told you that? We never knew you had so many friends. Dark horse, you were. Anyway, we'll chat again tomorrow. Goodbye, son, stay warm. Mrs Jenkins says the winter's going to be a cold one. Ta-ta, son. We love you."

Why hadn't I called him back, said sorry? It wasn't him I should have been angry with, only myself. All he had done, ever done, was hold the door open. I was the one who walked through.

I went and sat under a tree. I needed to think, to reach some kind of closure. The dead have it easy, the ultimate closure, the coffin lid. I couldn't think straight. Just images, fragments emerging and submerging in my brain. That's how we remember people. There is no magnum opus, no alpha and omega, just scattered glimpses, occasional words, a phrase or two.

"I like my teaspoon to stand up."

"Must rush, Mum's signing me."

"Still friends, I hope?"

Yes, Peter, still friends.

I didn't recognise the man who came over. A guy about my age; he approached with uncertainty.

"Are you Laurence?"

"Yes."

"Oh, good, Peter said you might turn up. He gave me a note to give you, just in case you came."

He handed me a folded paper serviette.

"Sorry, there wasn't paper in the hospice."

"That's OK."

He turned to go.

"Wait! How did you know Peter?" I asked.

He paused, deciding whether to reply or not.

"I did stuff for him. Like you. I spread the love, as he would say."

We both laughed at that and chatted in an easy, meandering way, about Peter.

"I'd best be off now. Got to pick the little one up from play school."

"One more thing," I said. "Did he take a cut from you, some of the money the clients paid?"

"No, never."

"I thought not, thanks."

I sat holding the serviette. I was frightened to unfold it, read perhaps recrimination from a man beyond the reach of my apology. I put it in my pocket to read later and set off for home. On the way out, near the gates, a Bentley passed, stopped and, reversing, caught me up. The window opened and a familiar head appeared.

"I trust you are staying firm, young man?"

"Always, Madam."

"Good. Now go and do something useful with your life."

As the window closed, I heard a man inside say, "Trockers, who on earth was that?" And I caught Lady Trocknell's reply: "Silence, Henry, save your questions for the courts."

Well, that's about it. Just me left. What can I say? It's taken until now to cover six months back in 1980. We'll be here forever if I detail thirty years. Bottom line? A single phrase to cover three decades?

"It's been worth the ride."

I guess I owe you one more explanation. I made a promise to reveal why I'm writing this book now. It's simple; it's a homecoming.

I strayed, you see, and bought into cockenomics sometime in the '90s. I was hooked, I learnt the lines and I sunk. I warned you early on. I said I was no Odysseus, I said I heeded the siren's call. I built a modest empire, collecting businesses like once I did books. I fell from grace. I caged my beast and pawned my conscience as too expensive to maintain. I became someone whom I despised.

But recently, something wonderful has happened. I climbed too high, too fast, and lost the lot. Well, almost everything: enough to still the cascade of cash and in the ensuing silence to be forced to listen to myself. I could go back and make it all again. The thing is, I don't want to.

Mind you, it wasn't easy, that fall from financial grace, and when I look back to those days, I see a suitcase full of everything I owned. One by one, keeping rhythm with the letters from creditors, the contents are removed, saluted and sold off. At first you fight, maintaining a tug of war you're bound to lose. Then there's a period of adjustment, of living without the thing, and the slow realisation that you're no worse off. Anyway, you've got the rest. But then another possession goes under the hammer and the fight and adjustment begins all over. And so it goes on, as the suitcase empties.

Each time, you recalibrate your life, lower your expectations or find new ones you never knew you had. Finally the case is empty, and you go to throw it away. But as you shut it, something catches your eye. Maybe a love letter or a drawing your child did, maybe an old belt that takes you back to better days. We all have our memento mori. Mine was a serviette.

I found it in the attic, in a box with teddy bears and the blanket from my cot: Peter's parting note. I'd gone looking to see what I had left to sell. I made a coffee, rolled a fag and went and sat in the garden on my own. I remember my wife waving from the window. That helped.

It was worn, hardly legible; wobbly letters written by a dying hand. Four words. More than enough.

*You're all right Laurence.*

I sat there for hours thinking about those days when I was busy being born. One of the dogs came and rested his head on my lap and I ate a peach, leaving the stone and a little flesh for the ants to have for supper.

*Am I all right?* I wondered. Could all that I had done be validated as being merely the inevitable consequence of having 'a fascination for life'? Probably not. No, definitely not. A lot of ego and self-indulgence in the mix. But as the hours went by and the sun dipped below the craggy escarpments of the sierras, I realised that we all fuck up, that the journey of becoming a good human being must take us through failure, that to reach redemption we have to accept and embrace our shame.

It was a beginning, a corner-stone to build on. I started writing that very day and haven't stopped. I knew what I needed to do. Give the past a proper burial and shout out loud it's heartfelt epitaph: this book. Only then can I build again. Nothing fancy, less spills and thrills this time. Something strong, handmade with love and care, both for myself and others.

I'll groom and feed my beast but keep him in the garden, out of mischief's way. I'll get my conscience out of hock, dust it down and listen to its warnings. I'll be all right.